Cinderella's Sister

Also published by Poolbeg

The Pineapple Tart

Kissing the Frog

The Dolly Holiday

A Soft Touch

Anne Dunlop

Cinderella's Sister

POOLBEG

Published 2007
by Poolbeg Press Ltd
123 Grange Hill, Baldoyle
Dublin 13, Ireland
E-mail: poolbeg@poolbeg.com
www.poolbeg.com

13 5 7 9 10 8 6 4 2

A catalogue record for this book is available from the British Library.

ISBN 978-1-84223-307-8

Typeset by Patricia Hope in Caslon 10.75/15.5

Printed by
Litografia Rosés, S.A., Spain

Note on the Author

Anne Dunlop has lived in the Middle East, where she flew long haul and taught English as a foreign language.

She has also lived in Africa with her husband Nick, four children and an army of maids and nannies.

Anne currently divides her time between a housing estate in County Kildare and a farm in County Derry.

Anne enjoys ironing, driving in traffic and shopping in Oxfam.

Acknowledgements

Special thanks to Bess Scott for her excellent help with the African part of the story.

For Nick

Chapter One

All our lives Camilla and I have been so physically identical – with our dark-red hair and hazel eyes and smooth peachy skin that tans such an envied, unfreckled, golden colour on the slightest exposure to the sun – that even our mother has never been able to tell us apart.

It started the moment we were removed from the faultless hospital nursery and our name-tags were taken off.

Mummy was presented with one sleeping cherub dressed head to toe in pink; Daddy was presented with the other.

The brisk, meticulous midwife announced, "Now, Mrs Reverend Simms, this is Francesca. Reverend Simms, you have Camilla."

Mummy was doubtful. "Are you sure this one is Francesca?"

The midwife had already met my mother. The day we were born she'd asked, "Mrs Reverend Simms, how are you going to feed your babies?"

Mummy, confused, had said, "How? Don't you mean who is going to feed them?"

So this time the midwife tried to be helpful.

"Mrs Reverend Simms, it might be easier for you if you didn't dress them identically. Not at the start anyway."

But Mummy wouldn't listen. In Mummy's mind there was only one advantage in having identical twin daughters and that was to make them look as alike as possible. So we wore identical Babygros, slept in identical cots and played with identical dolls.

"But I thought that was Camilla." Daddy did his best but he was never singing from the same hymn sheet as my mother. "I thought you said Camilla did all the screaming."

"Why do you do it, Madeline?" Aunt Grace scolded. "Most people look for bargains in life. Two daughters for the price of one. What you are creating is one daughter for the price of two."

Mummy was unrepentant.

"I'm the first to admit that it's perfectly possible that the one who answers to Francesca could actually have been baptised Camilla. But I can't see that it'll make much difference in the long run. Mixing them up. I've always thought individuality overrated."

Mummy's best efforts were in vain because even with identical haircuts, anoraks, shoes and parents, Camilla was always the brighter variation on the theme. In school

2

uniform or pyjamas she sparkled and I always had my nose stuck in a book.

"I cannot believe they came out of the same womb," said Aunt Grace. "Are you quite sure they have the same father?"

My father is the minister of a small country congregation of farmers. 1st Derryrose is a modest, unadorned and enormously practical church with acres of shiny black tarmac for parking and no trees, not even a traditional yew or laburnum to weep over the tidy formations of headstones. Derryrose Manse sits beside the church. Our garden was the graveyard and our closest neighbours were the dead.

Camilla and I grew up in a surreal type of isolated splendour. Suitable friends were invited for tea, but under my mother's critical gaze they were always on their best behaviour, and they were always afraid of the graveyard.

Sometimes we got invited back again but Mummy insisted she come too, just in case we said things that weren't suitable for a minister's daughters to say.

"Yes, Mummy, no Mummy, three bags full, Mummy," said Camilla.

Before long Mummy had frightened off our school friends and we had one approved playmate – Sam Dawson, whose father was an anaesthetist in the South Derry and whose mother was Mummy's only friend. While Sam played hide and seek with us in the graveyard, Mrs Reverend Simms and Mrs Doctor Dawson impressed each other with their childrearing theories. Children should be seen and not heard. Spare the rod and spoil the child. Give me the child till he's five, and I'll show you the man . . .

"Do you think we'll both have to marry Sam when we're older?" Camilla mused.

"Both at the same time," I asked, "or can we take turns with him?"

Camilla had charm, charisma and confidence. She laughed loudly when she was happy, screamed loudly when she was angry and wept bitter tears when she didn't get her own way. She was careless, affectionate and flirtatious. She was the life and soul of the party. People always asked, "Where's Camilla?"

"She's utterly without hidden depth," said Mummy in bemused exasperation. "And so loud and chatty and amusing Francesca never gets a chance, poor little mouse."

Aunt Grace shook her head sadly. "Poor Camilla, destined to a life of attention-seeking antics. Hardly any surprise really, when you look at the other one."

I was perfectly content to be known as 'the other one'. I knew my place. And more than anyone I missed Camilla's infectious good humour and high spirits when she wasn't around. We had such fun; Camilla's favourite game was 'Confusion' when she changed into me.

"Let's play Confusion," she'd whisper and her mischievous eyes would become suddenly solemn, her expressive face serene. The bounce left her step, rebelliousness left her mouth, her cracking fizzing energy was perfectly distilled into an innocent otherworldliness. She became an enigma, an angel, a girl from a fairytale.

"Do I really look like that?"

"Let's ask Mummy."

Mummy never suspected a thing. I watched from a safe distance, fascinated.

"Where's Camilla?" asked Mummy.

Before bed every night, when I was saying my prayers, I fervently prayed that I would die first because I could never imagine the loneliness of life without her.

Aunt Grace was disgusted. "You're making those little girls into freaks, Madeline."

She had stiff words with my father and, with the kind-hearted ambition of exposing us to a more gregarious, 'normal' childhood, Camilla and I were removed periodically from the ordered and aseptic calm of the Manse and introduced to the warm, noisy, untidy world of Lisglasson Lodge, where Aunt Grace lived with her rough, tough sons Frank and Philip, her darling, petted daughter Naomi and her chain-smoking, hard-drinking husband, Uncle Denis.

"From the sublime to the ridiculous," sniffed Mummy.

Lisglasson Lodge had once been the dower house on the Lisglasson estate. Designed by an imaginative Edwardian, it was as impractical as it was lovely. It had fourteen-foot-high ceilings, cast-iron fireplaces in every room and huge windows in the drawing room.

Upstairs the main bedroom looked over a wild-flower meadow and a thousand acres of Lisglasson parkland.

At Lisglasson Lodge, while Aunt Grace sat with her feet up reading a book, Camilla learned to ride Ginger the pony – she was a risk-taking natural – and Naomi and I played hunt the thimble with Mrs Murphy the house-keeper. Mrs Murphy was a big, strong countrywoman with several grown-up children of her own. She cooked for us with a cigarette balanced between her lips; when ash sometimes fell into the food she said: "Tastier than salt." If we were feeling unwell, or had a temperature she gave us extra-big spoonfuls of medicine with bread and jam to kill the taste. She never wasted good weather – the first blink of sun we were put into our wellies and sent outside to pull blackberries for jam, or hunt for hens' eggs in the yard, or to pull bunches of flowers in the wild-flower meadow.

It was from Mrs Murphy that we learnt that Santa Claus (she called him 'Santy') leaves only a bag of coal for naughty children, and she wasn't afraid to wash out Naomi's mouth with soap and water when she started swearing ("Thou shalt not take the Lord's name in vain, Naomi Walsh!") or put Frank and Philip over her knee and spank them when they were 'bold'. Camilla and I tried to copy her soft accent. "It's grand," we'd say to each other, and "That's right, so".

Mummy strongly disapproved of our visits to Lisglasson Lodge. She strongly disapproved of Aunt Grace taking us to see Darby O'Gill and the Little People at the cinema. She strongly disapproved of Aunt Grace taking us to the seaside on Sunday instead of church. She strongly disapproved of Aunt Grace buying us sweets. She strongly disapproved of Aunt Grace inviting us for sleepovers and letting us choose our own bedtime.

"I wish you would remember your Bible, Grace. 'A man reaps what he sows . . .'."

Aunt Grace was unrepentant. "I promise we'll put 'She

knew the price of everything and the value of nothing' on your headstone when you die, Madeline."

When we were teenagers Camilla loved boys ("the more the merrier, so many boys, so little time") and boys loved Camilla and not just because she loosened her school tie and opened the buttons on her school shirt to expose the plump ripe peachy swollenness of her pubescent breasts. And not just because she rolled up her school skirt to reveal subtle flashes of tanned, toned thighs. Camilla was fast but she was never cheap. And she loved to keep them guessing, sitting quietly beside me at the front of the school bus, with her knees pressed demurely together, pretending to read one of my books – one of the shorter ones. With pictures.

"I can't see the point of books. Why read about Lucy Glitters when I can live her?"

"I've been hearing Chinese Whispers," said Mummy anxiously, "in church on Sunday. When we walk together up to the front to our pew. I hear the word 'slapper'. What's a slapper?"

But then of course Camilla went too far. Not satisfied with the admiration of every other boy in South Derry she wanted Alex Flood too. Alex Flood's parents had recently bought Lisglasson, he was Aunt Grace's neighbour and his mother, Lady Millicent, was Mummy's new best friend.

Officially Alex Flood wasn't my boyfriend – we didn't 'shift' – but we spent every spare minute together. I know I bored Camilla to sobs talking about him in bed at night.

"And then Alex said . . ."

"And then I said . . ."

"And then Alex said . . ."

Derryrose Manse had many bedrooms but Camilla and I always shared a room, hugging in a double bed to keep warm.

After months of 'And then Alex said . . .', 'And then I said . . .', Camilla finally said, "Is all you ever do talk?"

"Yes," I said, suddenly embarrassed. "What else would we be doing?"

"That nastiness."

"You mean sex?" I shook my head. "No. Of course not."

"Wouldn't you like to?"

I hesitated. Fatally. My identical twin leapt for the kill. "Don't you think Alex might like to? I mean, what seventeen-year-old boy doesn't want to have sex?"

"But he's never even kissed me!"

"Have you asked him to?"

I felt myself blush in the dark. Of course, I hadn't. I really was not that sort of girl.

Camilla called me Francesca the Puritan.

"It's one of three things then," Camilla announced authoritatively. "He's frigid, he's gay, or he doesn't fancy you."

"I'm nearly sure he fancies me," I said firmly for sometimes when we were out riding together I felt the heat of his eyes on me, and my legs would melt to jelly. And when we were in his car together, with the windows steamed up, sharing a packet of crisps, our fingers would

8

sometimes touch. And linger. "Intimacy has nothing to do with how naked you are . . ."

"Well, I think he's frigid," Camilla insisted. "Would you like me to find out for you?"

What was I supposed to say? No, no, no? But that just wasn't me. I never chased men or buses . . . and I trusted Camilla.

"I think Alex's feelings might be hurt, if he thought I was sharing him with you."

"But he doesn't have to know. Of course, I can be you!" Camilla boasted.

Even when we were seventeen it still took very few physical adjustments for Camilla to cause confusion. We swapped clothes. She combed her hair off her face and secured it back with my Alice band. She washed her face free of make-up. She cut her fingernails.

She stooped a little when she stood and toed in a little when she walked. It was Francesca standing in front of me.

Mummy said, "Francesca darling, why don't you wear some lipstick this evening when you go out with Alex? Brainy girls are allowed to look pretty too, you know."

And wicked Camilla smiled my hesitant, innocent smile and said, "Perhaps I will, if Camilla will lend me some."

It was the end of Alex of course. The next time he didn't even come into my house.

From the doorstep he said, "I'm sorry, Francesca. I can't see you any more." And he turned on his heel and walked away.

"What did you do to him, Camilla?"

Camilla shrugged. "There's definitely something wrong with that boy. He wouldn't even kiss me. And as for anything else . . ."

"So he is frigid."

"Or gay . . ."

I know I should have gone after him. And said I was sorry. And said I just didn't know what had got into me. And said that I still respected him. I could even have blamed Camilla and said she'd put me up to it. But I never did.

I was the silly, proud girl who never chased men or buses.

And I had 'A' Levels looming. And it was so much easier to agree with my sister. Maybe he was frigid, or gay, or maybe he just didn't fancy me.

Mummy said, "Cheer up, Francesca. You're a lovely girl. You'll meet somebody else."

Aunt Grace was furious. She was very fond of Alex Flood, and she'd harboured high hopes of a proper romance blossoming between us.

Soon afterwards she and Mummy joined forces to consult with a matchmaker "before Camilla goes to university and really gets into trouble".

I was curious. "How does the matchmaker do it? How does he match people? Does he use a computer? Or a crystal ball?"

"Mr Moss is not a fortune-teller, he's a matchmaker! He started off as schoolmaster, he taught me when I was girl, and he taught your father. He told me that once you've taught a lot of young people in their formative years you realise that there are very few truly unique people in the world. The majority of us shake down into certain stereotypes and we're easily matched with each other. How do you think I found your dashing Uncle Denis?"

"Really? But I thought you married for love!"

"Oh, Francesca, you're such a romantic! Just like your father – and look at the botched job he made when he married Madeline. She's not suited to the role of a minister's wife, poor woman. She's far too obsessed with keeping up appearances. If only Roger had listened to me and asked Mr Moss to find him a wife instead of going to a prayer meeting and falling in love with the youngest woman there. Love at first sight is so unreliable . . ."

"But what does Mr Moss actually do? Do you have to fill in a questionnaire? Does he have a book with photographs and you pick somebody you like the look of? Does he play psychological games with you to reveal your innermost thoughts?"

So I went too. Mummy, Aunt Grace, Camilla and me squashed into Aunt Grace's sports car, hurtling through wet country lanes under cover of darkness because Mummy could hear Chinese Whispers again, "Bad reputation. They'll never get a nice boy to take her . . ."

Camilla was sulky and a bit frightened. "You can't force me to marry somebody I don't like."

"Where is your sense of adventure, my dear?" Aunt Grace asked her impatiently. "We're not forcing you to do anything. We're merely taking you to meet Mr Moss, who will interview you and suggest a young man he thinks might suit you. Whether or not you decide to marry the young man has absolutely nothing to do with Mr Moss."

Mr Moss said, "I have the perfect man for her. Adam Robinson. He's a young minister, recently ordained, lives in a lovely big old Manse with stables. Nice young fellow but very quiet. He needs a confident girl to help him win over the congregation."

Camilla cheered up a bit. "Better the devil you know, I suppose."

Mummy and Aunt Grace were thrilled. "How amazing!"

"Not really," said the matchmaker modestly. "She's a very commonplace girl. And the pretty, flighty ones are always the easiest to match. Men never refuse them." He pointed to me. "I'm so glad it wasn't this girl you needed matched. I've nothing to suit her. Never in forty years of matchmaking have I been able to match this type of girl."

Mummy immediately took offence. "What's wrong with Francesca?"

"She's already matched. I can see it in her eyes."

Aunt Grace never stopped hoping that Alex Flood and I might kiss and make up.

"Alex rode by about half an hour ago. He's gone to look for foxes in the little wood at the end of the avenue. Why don't you walk down and talk to him?"

"What would I say?"

Aunt Grace sighed. She was a tough old boot who didn't invite pity but Life had been unkind to her. Darling, petted Naomi, 'my one and only', had died young and she'd adopted me as her protégée – my lost romance with Alex Flood was an affront to her sensibilities.

"I'm sure you'll think of something. You never stopped talking about him before Camilla ruined your chances! Time heals almost everything, Francesca, even wounded pride . . ."

"Camilla says there are plenty more fish in the sea."

"Only if you're a herring or a mackerel! If you're not a herring or a mackerel there really aren't that many fish in the sea. It makes my blood boil when I think of the way you allowed her to manipulate you. What was it she said? She was doing you a favour, finding out if he was frigid or gay! Some favour!"

"I won't make the same mistake again."

Will Dallas was well briefed about Camilla before he came to Ireland for our wedding.

"Not the tattoo thing again," said Will. "If I hear once more about Camilla's tattoo . . ."

Chapter Two

Before Will and I became 'we', when we were still individuals, I was a pilot and Will was an expatriate Zimbabwean builder and we met in Oman when I had a stopover. I'd fly into Seeb International airport, bug-eyed with exhaustion and eyeliner, stinking of airline food and Duty Free perfume and he'd meet me, any time of the day or night, wearing short shorts and a wide smile – the *Weekly Telegraph* under his arm.

Will's father's family had been in Africa for over a hundred years. His great-great-grandfather was a contemporary of the famous white colonial, Cecil Rhodes. His mother had emigrated to Zimbabwe as a teacher after the Second World War.

Will said that was the first thing he noticed about me. My accent. It was the same as his mother's.

We had a sunshine courtship, a holiday romance: drinking coffee together in the airport coffee shop, dining on hummus and tabbouleh in the Crew Hotel, chatting under the chill-out hum of an air-conditioner. I was out of touch with reality when I was with him and I liked it.

Then one day the Sultan's palace was built, his contract was finished, and he was leaving Oman.

"I'm going to Botswana to build a hospital," he said and my eyes, under a ton of eyeliner and mascara, brimmed with sudden tears. We'd been together for six months. 'Minimum rest' often, twenty-four hours sometimes, a whole weekend never. We didn't amount to much, just a holiday romance, a brief encounter. Over and over again. We'd never even talked of love. There never was the time.

"Botswana," I said brightly, ignoring the stupid tears, "in Africa?"

"You don't fly to Africa, do you?"

I'd been a pilot for twelve years. I was used to things changing. The stupid tears would dry up in a second, before the eyeliner and mascara began to weep down my face.

"Will you miss me?" he asked.

"I don't know," I said.

My decision to leave Ex-Pat Air, get married, and go to Botswana with Will was greeted with disbelief by my crew.

"I don't believe you!" said Marian, the chief stewardess.

I could hardly believe it myself. After Will proposed and I accepted, I repeated, "I'm marrying Will. I'm marrying

Will," over and over a thousand times in my heart during the long night flight to London, then over and over again during the long day flight back to the Middle East. When we landed I went straight into Debriefing to announce my intention and the words still sounded foreign and unformed in my mouth.

"I'll work my notice," I told them. "I'm still up for the trip to Singapore on Monday."

"Very good, Captain."

There really wasn't anything else to say. Marriage is so commonplace. Most women manage it at least once and, like everything in life, some are better at it than others. For years Camilla, currently married to husband number three, had tried her best to give me a leg up onto the marriage ladder with an unflagging succession of increasingly awful and unsuitable introductions.

"This is Fred. Fred is four inches shorter than you and forty years older, but he still has all his own teeth."

"This is Marcus. Marcus is a bit gay, but he's such a laugh and he loves a woman in uniform."

Marian, my chief stewardess, quite fancied herself as a matchmaker. "Excuse me, Captain, there's a millionaire in 1 Alpha who'd like to see the flight deck . . ."

I'd always stoically resisted their best intentions and one day, quite by chance, woke up to realise I was a woman of a certain age and women of a certain age don't get married.

There's a rule somewhere that says single women of thirty-seven at the peak of sterling careers have chosen to sacrifice their romantic opportunities. We've missed our chance. The fresher less desperate girls, ten years younger, will always be a better catch.

Only Aunt Grace wasn't surprised.

"I knew he wasn't a herring or a mackerel the minute I laid eyes on him."

(She'd been flying round the world with me, in First Class, as my 'designated spouse' since I'd made captain. We'd been to the Taj Mahal together, and the Empire State Building, and the Eiffel Tower. We'd gone international shopping, in every street market from Bangkok to Casablanca. We were in Mutrah Suq in Oman haggling over the price of a decorative Omani hat when she'd spotted Will. "Look at him, Francesca! He's not a herring or a mackerel!" Then she'd pretended to faint almost on top of him.)

"Aunt Grace, with the greatest respect, I think you have a fish obsession."

When Mummy saw a photograph of Will she said, "Well, *I* think you're making a terrible mistake."

"Yes," I said patiently, "I know you do. I know you think a middle-aged Zimbabwean builder isn't good enough for me. I know you think he dyes his hair. I know you think I shouldn't have resigned from Ex-Pat Air when I've only just made captain in the past year. I know you think I'm mad to bolt to Botswana with him –" I paused to take a breath. "Is there any thing else you want to add to the list, Mummy?"

Mummy sniffed. "I know you think I'm just boring old Mummy, with my twinset and support tights, unable to see beyond the boundaries of my own little world. But, Francesca, we know nothing about this man. *You* know nothing about this man. By your own admission you've had a holiday romance. Holiday romances don't make for happy and successful marriages . . ."

When Camilla saw the photograph of Will she said, "He's tall, dark *and* handsome! Where did you find him?"

"I went to the ends of the earth. The only pity is it took thirty-seven years."

"Worth waiting for," said Camilla. "And I should know since I've kissed a lot of frogs. I've even married a couple. Or three. And not one of them has ever been tall, dark *and* handsome." She winked. "If you ever get tired of him, would you be kind enough to send him packing my direction, and we'll swap husbands? You don't even have to tell him. He'll never know the difference. I promise."

"Naughty Camilla! Your current husband would know there was something amiss immediately. And I don't just mean the tattoo."

Camilla had met James Snotter, her current husband, when she was very vulnerable and lacking confidence following her second divorce. James was a sensible, stolid man who ate potatoes every day for his dinner and played golf. He was exactly the sort of man flighty women are advised to look for; for he was sober, steady and older than Camilla. But he was also ugly, he used the adverb 'basically' in every sentence and he was so pompous I thought it was a joke when she started going out with him.

"Haven't you tried dull and sensible before? How long did your marriage to Adam Robinson last?"

"You're right. It wasn't a success then and it won't be a success now," but then she discovered she was pregnant, and before anyone could say 'shotgun' Camilla and James Snotter were married.

"Just Camilla's little joke," said Mummy loyally when Camilla insisted on marrying in white and insisted James vow to obey her.

"Are you quite sure she's not taking the joke a bit too far?"

"Shameless girl," said Aunt Grace severely. "Attention-seeking as usual. I blame you, Madeline. You've always spoiled her."

It was the week before my wedding. I was home from the Middle East. My hands were painted with henna in the traditional Arabic way for marriage celebrations; my wedding dress was folded up in my hanging wardrobe; I had no engagement ring so my crew had clubbed together and bought me a fake Cartier Love Bangle in the Gold Suq in Bahrain. There'd been a raucous presentation on the aircraft on my last-ever flight – a Muscat Turnaround. Muscat rugby team were on board and most of them managed to get into the flight deck to make provocative jokes about the Mile High Club during the hour we were at cruising altitude.

"Wishful thinking," said Marian, my chief stewardess.

Mummy had been in an evil mood since I'd landed.

She didn't like the henna on my hands ('dirty looking').

She didn't like my wedding dress ('unsuitable'). And she especially didn't like the lack of pomp and ceremony surrounding the wedding arrangements.

Will was flying in from Oman on an Ex-Pat Air flight with Marian the morning of the wedding. They'd hire a car at the airport. If there were no delays they'd be at the church at two o'clock. There'd be time for a cup of tea after the service. Then Will, Marian and I would take the hire car back to the airport and we'd catch the shuttle to London Heathrow at six o'clock. Marian would rejoin her crew, Will and I would fly on to Botswana.

"This man is *touching down* to marry you," said Mummy in a dangerous voice, "and what about the rest of it – the guest list, the reception, the honeymoon –"

"Optional extras."

"Francesca, what's the point of having a daughter if we can't marry you off properly? This DIY effort by yourself and Will Dallas – people will think you have something to be ashamed of. He hasn't even invited his mother."

I laughed. "Have you been hearing Chinese Whispers again? Are they saying that the minister's daughter is pregnant and has to get married in a hurry? We should be so lucky! Unfortunately, Oman isn't the place for a torrid romance!"

Mummy stuck her fingers in her ears. She looked close to tears.

"I'm not listening to you, Francesca. You might be thirty-seven and have flown round the world twice but you're still our daughter and we'd like you to get married properly." ('Properly' meant Will proposing to me on bended knee and asking my father for permission to marry me. It meant special wedding shoes, a hundred guests, and a row with Mummy about my taste in wedding hymns – Mummy says 'Fight the Good Fight' is not suitable for a wedding.)

"I know you have no pride, Francesca. I know you don't care what people think of you. I know you can't hear Chinese Whispers. But it's cruel of you to make a mockery of the sacred institution of marriage and leave me behind to pick up the pieces afterwards."

I was gracious in defeat.

"All right, Mummy. I'll put some bells and whistles on the wedding! I'll ask Mrs Murphy to bake me her best cake. I'll ask Will to fly in a day or two early so you can have a little chat with him and ask him if his intentions are honourable. And if there's anybody you'd especially like me to invite . . ."

"Mrs Doctor Dawson and Lady Millicent Flood. Thank you, darling."

Mrs Doctor Dawson and Lady Millicent Flood, Mummy's two best friends, also happened to be the mothers of my two old boyfriends – Sam Dawson and Alex Flood. Mummy had always hoped I'd marry either Sam or Alex. She'd never made any secret of it. She was more surprised than anyone when Camilla married Sam (her second husband), and utterly devastated when it ended.

"Just one thing, Mummy. Camilla and I are not going to wear the same dress on my wedding day."

This was not a tease. At Camilla's first two weddings

22

Mummy had persuaded us to wear identical outfits. The first time, when we were twenty, we wore simple white with long sleeves and our hair was loose and curly round our faces. The next time, when we were twenty-five, it was a sophisticated cream suit each and our hair pulled back in identical chignons. The photographs are amazing, of course, but, as Camilla says herself, the marriages might have had more of a chance if the photographs had been of the bride and her husband looking amazing. So she took no chances when she married James Snotter.

"Third time lucky," she said, and if Mummy hadn't been there, insisting that I join in the photographs, no one would have recognised us as sisters at all. It's quite shocking how a hair cut, and a couple of stone either way changes you.

Will accepted the embellished wedding arrangements with a minimum of fuss.

"Prolonging my agony," he said cheerfully when I asked him to come to Ireland a couple of days early. He even agreed to attend a specially scheduled pre-marriage class with me the night before the wedding.

"What a wonderful idea," he said solemnly when, at lunch, Mummy announced that she'd managed to persuade the church's marriage guidance expert to give us a condensed version of his ten-week pre-marriage guidance course. "Will there be an exam at the end? Will I still be allowed to marry Francesca if I fail it? "

Camilla sniggered. "You know he's going to tell you that the husband is the head of the household, don't you?

And that a woman's place is in the home. And that it's a wife's duty to obey her husband and have the dinner spotless and the house cooked and soft music burning and subtle candles playing when he comes home from work in the evening? And if he'd rather watch football on the television than have sex with you, you're not to argue with him . . ."

Camilla blew a kiss across the table to James Snotter, her current husband, who was silently blushing into his glass of tap water.

"Maybe I've got it a bit mixed up," she said softly. "I've heard it so many times."

In the tiny painful silence that followed I concentrated on my boiled ham salad and was careful not to notice Mummy's dismayed expression. Mummy thinks Camilla's failed marriages are noisy, embarrassing family skeletons and, much as I love my sister, I have to agree with Mummy that they are nothing to boast about and should never be invited to lunch.

"More beetroot, Will?" asked Daddy.

Will caught my eye and suddenly started to laugh. We all stared at him in alarm. Was he having hysterics? Was he choking? James Snotter, who's a doctor, began to look medical and concerned.

"Are you all right, Will?" I asked anxiously.

Will immediately stopped laughing and said loudly and firmly, "I'm going to have to assume that Camilla is pulling my leg about the content of the pre-marriage classes. Because I will absolutely refuse to marry Francesca if she changes into the wife Camilla has just described."

Then there really was a painful silence. James Snotter stopped chewing, set his knife and fork carefully on his plate, wiped his mouth fastidiously with his napkin and looked as if he was now ready to go into cardiac arrest. Mummy's mouth, which had opened during some part of Will's speech, had forgotten to close again.

But Will wasn't finished. He rounded on my modest and unassuming father who was furtively trying to pick a piece of boiled ham from between his teeth.

"Are you the head of this household, Reverend Simms?" he challenged Daddy.

"Only when Madeline allows me to be," said Daddy.

The pre-marriage class was abandoned. After lunch I noticed Mummy hastening up the stairs to the manse office, followed by Daddy and a box of Kleenex, and I knew they'd gone to phone the marriage expert and explain that his services weren't going to be required after all. I followed at a discreet distance, in time to overhear Mummy sobbing into a hanky and Daddy saying, "I really think you should give him a chance. Francesca hasn't let us down yet."

"You frightened them."

Will shrugged. "Perhaps. But it's hardly any wonder your sister's first two marriages failed when her husbands had such unnatural expectations of marriage."

"Will, you don't know the half of it. The marriage expert – his name is Adam Robinson – he's actually Camilla's first husband."

"How sick is that?" asked Will.

"Adam Robinson was besotted with her. If Camilla said

'Jump', Adam asked 'How high?'. Everyone thought it was going to be a marriage made in heaven. Adam giving, giving, giving. Camilla taking, taking, taking. But, of course, she made his life miserable and in the end she left him. That's when he became a marriage expert. He's been magnanimously advising young husbands how not to make the same mistakes as he did ever since."

"How sick is that?" Will repeated.

Our wedding was a surprising success.

Sir Bobby Flood, Lady Millicent's husband, offered us the use of Lisglasson's picturesque and charming private chapel down by the lough. The ancient graveyard was a carpet of snowdrops, and our guests were free to throw confetti (1st Derryrose church committee had banned confetti after Camilla's first wedding – 'So messy and unnecessary.')

"What an unusual dress," said Mr Doctor Dawson when she saw my wedding dress. "It suits you!"

"What a handsome fellow," said Lady Millicent when she saw Will. "I rather fancy him myself."

Aunt Grace insisted that she host our DIY wedding reception at Lisglasson Lodge ('Derryrose Manse is so unfriendly.')

Mummy had been uncharacteristically generous about this arrangement. "She has no daughter of her own any more, and I've been Mother of the Bride three times already thanks to Camilla."

There was a fire lit in every room, and buckets of Bollinger, courtesy of Lady Millicent and Sir Bobby ('I told you inviting them was a good idea . . .'). My cousin Philip took the photographs – he was a photographer in the RAF – and when Marian wasn't flirting with him she played the piano in the drawing room – Ex-Pat Air had a grand piano in their First Class lounge area – all chief stewardesses were trained pianists.

"Which would you prefer, Captain, '*Salut D'Amour*' or 'Fight the Good Fight'?"

Once Philip had taken the official wedding photograph (of Will in his borrowed morning suit and me in my unsuitable wedding dress and both of us flashing the plain gold rings Marian had flown in from Bahrain Gold Suq), Mummy spent the rest of the reception sneaking up on Camilla and myself and photographing us with her digital camera when we weren't looking.

Only Aunt Grace wasn't her usual fun self. This should have been Aunt Grace's greatest moment. Her protégée was marrying the man she'd handpicked and she'd had a magnificent and very unsuitable outfit made in Fantasy Tailoring in Bahrain for the wedding, but instead she wore black and announced during the speeches, "Francesca's life is going to change utterly the Christmas she's forty. Mark my words, Francesca, the Christmas you're forty . . ."

Everyone laughed. "She shouldn't be allowed anything stronger than cooking sherry," they said but I noticed Mummy, bleached white and looking very sad, grabbing my aunt in a sort of half-nelson wrestling hold and frogmarching her gently out of the drawing room.

"What's wrong with your aunt?" asked Will.

"I don't know. Do you think I should go after her and ask her?"

But at that moment Marian announced, "Forty minutes to departure. Captain, have you all the paperwork signed and the luggage on board?"

So Will and I were reluctantly driven back to the Manse to get organised for Botswana.

Mummy came with us.

"Is Aunt Grace all right?" I asked for she'd seemed very shaken and old when I'd kissed her goodbye.

"Today is Naomi's birthday. She'd have been forty today."

When we got to the Manse, Mummy marched Will and me up to the office and spent half an hour playing back all her digital photographs again on the computer.

"We've got to go," I said anxiously, for I hadn't even changed out of my unsuitable wedding dress. "The shuttle to London leaves in an hour. They won't let us on board if we're not at the gate in forty minutes . . ."

Will had begun stripping down out of his borrowed suit and was edging for the office door.

"Just a minute, Will Dallas!"

His brand new mother-in-law snapped her fingers at him.

Triumphantly she'd finally found the photograph she was looking for. Of two redheads bent together in conversation. It was the way it was taken of course. A head and shoulders shot of Camilla and me, with no obviously incriminating clothing on view. It was the camera angle, the light, and the way our heads were tilted. Even I couldn't tell which one was me and which was Camilla.

"Well, Will Dallas, can you tell them apart?"

Will's eyes scanned the photograph with confidence.

"Francesca is the one wearing my wedding ring," he said.

Chapter Three

Our first few months in Botswana as newlyweds, Will and I had no friends. We lived out of town in the dusty bush and we shared a bakkie so when Will went to work in the morning I was out of touch with reality and time seemed to freewheel. Morning and afternoon passed without my noticing until he came home again. Every evening we made love under the mosquito netting, our bodies and the sheets sticking in the heat.

"Hurry up, Will," I urged as my husband's tongue lingered in sensual softness behind my ear and delicious shivers skipped up and down my spine.

"Why hurry? When I married you I vowed to sleep with you, and to wake up with you, forever and ever, until death do us part . . ."

"I don't remember that part of the wedding vows . . ."

We'd never spent a night together before we married;

I'd never seen him naked; we'd rarely even kissed. Our very old-fashioned courtship had taken place in Seeb International airport, and the very public restaurant of the Crew Hotel. Oman is an ultra-conservative country. Will had to wear long trousers when he ate with me in the Crew Hotel and our passion was restricted to holding hands under the tablecloth. Besides, I hadn't known him well enough to instigate anything else, or to agree to anything else.

He, of course, on occasion tried to move things a step forward.

("Pretend to be sick and stay with me!"

"But I'm not sick!"

"Can't you pretend?"

"No! Who will fly the aircraft if I go sick? The crew will be grounded too.")

Now we were making up for lost time.

Will ran his fingers along the accordion pleats of my ribcage, rubbed himself along my stomach, kissed my lips until they were bruised. The same repetitive rigmarole every evening. And every time it was just perfect. I loved the smell of his skin, the roughness of his hands and the violent history of his life mapped out for me on his naked body. Penknife scars on his arms. The big chunk taken out of his leg by an angry warthog. Bullet scars in his back. The African tan. There was never an evening I didn't want to get naked with Will.

"Why the penknife scars?"

"I was only three when Dad died. Mum had to go back to work because our farm couldn't support us. My sister

Kate was already at boarding school and I didn't have a nanny to keep me out of trouble. I had a little Ndebele boy to be my companion. I spent most of my time in the compound with him. Ate his food, spoke his language, we kept moles, mongooses, tortoise, and bush babies for pets. We were blood brothers – that's where the penknife scars come from . . ."

"It sounds idyllic."

Now he was running his tongue along the inside of my thigh. I could feel the scratch of his stubble. I was beginning to ache.

"It was the ruination of me. I ran wild. Mum says she couldn't get me to wear underpants when I started school, and I wouldn't wear shoes. I was expelled for smoking dagga when I was fourteen – I got it from the locals in Plumtree."

"You still don't wear pants."

"Old habits. I can't bear the feel of them round me." He cupped my breasts in his hands. "Perfect. I never dared hope they'd be this beautiful shape . . . so pert . . ." He began to suck.

My mouth went dry, my head grew hot, I handed him a condom. "Please let's stop making conversation, Will –"

"I don't like condoms. They're against the teaching of the Catholic Church."

"I didn't realise you were Catholic!"

He grinned. "I'm not, but after I was expelled from the Boys' School in Plumtree I was sent to the Jesuits. I'm not a Catholic but I had a very thorough Catholic education."

"It's my understanding that men who say they don't

31

like condoms can't maintain an erection putting them on."

Afterwards we fell asleep with the fan blowing hot air over us.

In the morning, once Will had gone to work, I boiled water in a saucepan and made myself a cup of tea. This was a novel experience for me who had lived for twelve years in hotel bedrooms, and had phoned Room Service when I wanted a cup of tea, or a three-course meal, or a bottle of water, any time of the day or night, depending on the destination and my jet lag.

My cargo, containing twelve years of international shopping, was coming by ship from the Middle East. Until it arrived Will and I were making do. We were camping. We had no telephone, no kettle, no television, no washing machine, no vacuum cleaner and no clean clothes. We had a bottled-gas cooker and the gas kept blowing out and had to be watched all the time.

Will couldn't see what all the fuss was about.

"This is Africa. People live outdoors in Africa. No-one stands cooking in a hot kitchen. We'll have a *braai* when I get home from work."

"*Braai?*"

"African for barbeque. And we don't drink tea, sweet-heart. We drink beer."

"Show off! Just because you were brought up in the bush in a farmhouse that didn't have doors or windows!"

Violet presented herself at my gate. She was a tidy woman

in her early thirties with clean clothes and a little girl – Gloria – in tow.

"I think you need a maid, *Mma*," she said politely.

Violet was not the first lady to turn up at my gate offering her services. Word had spread through Tlokweng about the white couple with no maid and I'd been inundated with offers of help.

"No, thank you, *Mma*. I don't need a maid."

Will was perplexed. "That woman is looking for a job. She has a child to feed. I'm not saying you have a *duty* to provide employment, but don't you want someone to help you? You had servants in the Middle East, didn't you?"

I had Suma and Janet, quiet and deferential, armed with feather dusters and pretty aprons, treading softly through my international shopping while I reclined, face-packed and hair in hot rollers, slices of cucumber on my eyes, inhaling lavender to help me relax before a long night flight . . .

"I'm no longer a pilot, Will. What will I do all day if I don't do my own housework? I can't sit idle while that woman cleans up after me. Mummy instilled a work ethic – when the Church Committee offered to buy the manse a dishwasher Mummy said, 'Thank you so much, but we don't need another dishwasher. We have two dishwashers already' – Camilla and me!"

Will shrugged. "I promise I won't say 'I told you so' when you change your mind."

It took a whole week for me to change my mind. The thin red African dust blew in and over everything, day and night. As soon as one tiled floor was mopped and wiped down, the red dust settled again – and we had no mop bucket so I had to wring out the mop with my bare hands. By the end of the week I'd broken all my nails and my hands were destroyed with blisters.

And since I hadn't done any laundry for twelve years – why bother when Charming Laundry was just down the road in Bahrain and my clothes were washed, dried, ironed and returned on metal coat hangers the following day? – I'd conveniently under-estimated the effort involved in rinsing out (Mummy said they should always be rinsed in three changes of water) when we didn't even have running water.

By the end of the first week I was ready to welcome the next willing helper with open arms.

Will didn't say "I told you so", he didn't even smirk. Instead he said: "I've got Violet's cellphone number. Do you want it?"

Violet arrived at seven sharp the following morning. Within two hours she had the dust subdued, and the tiled floors shining. At lunchtime I offered to make her a sandwich – I was hoping for a chat – but she politely said she'd prefer to rest in the servants' quarters at the bottom of the garden.

The servants' quarters was a simple one-roomed building with a toilet – I'd ignorantly mistaken it for a fancy garden shed when we first moved in. I watched, amazed, as Violet and Gloria stretched out and slept deeply on the tiled floor.

("Why does that impress you?" Will asked. "I've seen you fast asleep standing upright."

"Only during Ramadan when there were extra Haj flights to Mecca, and we were supposed to cheerfully fly with two broken legs and chicken pox!")

In the afternoon Violet tackled the washing in our bath while Gloria stood to attention watching the gas stove, poised to raise the alarm the minute it blew out. By the end of the first day I didn't care how much she cost or what perks she demanded – I had to have her.

"She's coming to live in the servants' quarters at the bottom of the garden," I excitedly informed Will that evening, "and she says she'd like a bag of mealie-mealie and a deodorant every month as well as her wages."

"Before we married, you were a captain in command of an aircraft, a crew and two hundred passengers. Now you're in a flap about a servant."

"Violet is not a servant, Violet is a housemaid. And she's such a nice lady! She actually ironed out the creases in the bed sheets when she was making our bed. I can't remember even Suma and Janet doing that! And she wants something called Cobra to polish the porch, and she wants a big tin bath to do the clothes-washing, and she wants a bunch of twigs to sweep the yard. And she wants me to buy her a housemaid's uniform."

"Does she also want frilly curtains for the windows in the servants' quarters and a frilly holder for her toilet roll?"

I refused to be teased.

"I've already told her I have curtains coming in my cargo from the Middle East – and she's welcome to them. I might even have a frilly toilet-roll holder, I think I bought one in the Philippines once . . ."

Now I was no longer wrestling with the housework, I became obsessed with finding Violet a suitable uniform.

Game was the big warehouse in town where it was possible to buy almost everything – including maids' uniforms – but if you didn't buy the very second you spied, if you hesitated for even the briefest reflection, when you went back it was gone and you went without until the next time the supply lorry came through from South Africa.

I became Game's most faithful Sunday shopper as I watched and waited for the lorry to bring a suitable uniform for Violet. There were a variety of uniforms sent every week, but they were all ghastly and I believed it to be quite beneath Violet's dignity to wear them. Every week I hoped for a consignment of tasteful flowered patterns, maybe even a pretty check, and every week I was disappointed.

Will began to worry that the heat and dust and lack of air-conditioning were making me bush crazy. An obsession with the maid's uniform was only the start of it. Before long I would be swimming naked in the crocodile-infested dam, walking barefoot in the snake-infested bush, and drinking Chibuku Shake Shake with the locals.

"Botswana has its own airline," he told me in desperation. "Air Botswana. They fly all over the country. Why don't you send them your CV? A pilot with your experience, I'm sure they'd be thrilled to have you."

The honeymoon ended – abruptly – four months into the marriage when I discovered I was pregnant.

"No," said Will that evening. "No, Francesca. No way and don't ask again."

"But I don't feel any different!"

"Well, I feel different and the answer is no."

"But you did it last night, and the night before, and I was pregnant then . . ."

"I didn't know you were pregnant or I wouldn't have touched you."

"But what did you expect to happen when you won't use a condom?"

Will was intransigent. "I will not be touching you again until the baby's born."

Was that normal? I didn't think it was normal. I didn't think *he* was normal. But who was I going to ask? Should I make another appointment and wait another fortnight to see the crusty old doctor with the whiskey breath who had confirmed the pregnancy? Should I go into Will's work with him in the bakkie some morning and use the site telephone to phone Camilla in Ireland and ask her?

"Read a book," said Will. "Take your mind off it."

Violet noticed I was down in the dumps and kindly asked if she could help.

"I wish you could," I told her sadly, "but I don't have the words."

Violet rolled her eyes. "I was married once. My husband was a bad man who beat me."

Then they divorced and she had a boyfriend who fathered Gloria but refused to marry her. Now she had another boyfriend who was already married but his wife couldn't have children and he wanted Violet to have his baby . . .

I was not a hardboiled wife and in the quiet moments of my freewheeling day it made me snivel to remember that my husband and I had joined the Mile High Club in the First Class loo en route to Botswana on our wedding night. Then I was so pleased with myself I'd had a T-shirt printed. *Francesca & Will MHC*. Now I wore the T-shirt in bed.

For the first time since my romantic, impulsive bolt to Botswana I began to dream of packing a flight bag and flying off into the wide blue yonder – India today, South East Asia tomorrow, Australia the day after. I began to miss the Middle East with its great shopping and cosmopolitan street life. I began to miss living in a swanky block of flats full of young single female air stewardesses – we had a gym, squash courts, tennis courts and a swimming-pool – there was always someone to play tennis with, to visit Delicious Beauty Parlour with, who'd just had a new party dress made at Fantasy Tailoring, who'd just had her heart broken by a sailor.

Since I'd made captain I'd flown with the same crew and I began to miss them too. At first they'd been afraid of me – and unsure whether they could really trust me when they were used to my former captain Andrew Cunningham, an ex-RAF boy-racer with years of experience – but after one very scary flight, when the landing gear got stuck on the take-off out of Trivandrum in South India and we'd had to fly, together, for four and a half hours back to the Middle East, with the very real prospect of a crash-landing ahead of us, we became a team.

And when they realised I would always turn a blind eye when they were trying to sneak cane conservatory furniture into the hold of the aircraft on the flight out of Dhaka, or wrought-iron chandeliers when we were flying out of the

Philippines, a bond of camaraderie developed between us. (I also had cane conservatory furniture and wrought-iron chandeliers in the hold.)

Even now Marian, my chief stewardess, sent me postcards – from London, where we'd once spotted Camilla Parker Bowles at an airport taxi rank, from Indonesia where her bleached-blonde hair had caused a riot, from Cairo where we'd cantered camels at the pyramids, and from New York – last summer we'd spent so much time in New York I'd sometimes stayed in bed all weekend, ordering Room Service. What a bore!

Will noticed the faraway look in my eyes.

"Are you sorry you came with me?"

I shook my head. When Aunt Grace had fainted on top of him in Mutrah Suq and Will's eyes met mine above my aunt's jaunty grey perm, something warm, familiar and comforting had flooded into my nipples and groin and the pit of my stomach. And it wasn't just because he was tall, dark and handsome and had a kind face and eyes that could get a girl into trouble.

"A job can't love you back again."

Chapter Four

On Sunday morning, as always, I got ready to go to Game to inspect maids' uniforms.

Will was decidedly sulky.

"If I had my own car I could go during the week when you're at work, Will."

"Please stop fussing about Violet's uniform," he suddenly pleaded. "Now you're pregnant you should be spending Sunday morning in bed. Listening to relaxing music. Knitting baby cardigans. Doing the crossword in the *Weekly Telegraph*. Eating for two. Go back to bed and let me scramble you some eggs."

"Oh, do shut up, darling. Pregnancy isn't an illness."

I leapt into his bakkie and drove away from him in a shower of red dust towards Game.

I didn't want to admit it, even to myself, but Will's outrageous decision to stop sleeping with me during the pregnancy was causing a pronounced plummet in my self-esteem and short of begging I'd tried as many conventional seduction techniques as I could think of. To encourage him to change his mind. I'd taken off my combat trousers, Hi-Tec boots and big knickers and *braai-ed* for him, naked. I offered to soap his back in the bath. I asked him to soap my back in the bath. Subdued lighting in the bedroom, the hypnotic click of the table fan, the deafening noise of the African night beyond the thatched roof and French windows of our bungalow . . .

"Thank you, darling, that was lovely." He kissed me chastely and tucked me into bed. "Can I make you a cup of Horlicks to help you sleep?"

"It's not Horlicks I want!" I screamed after him while he retreated, sanctimonious and serene, to the camping mattress in the spare room at the far end of the hall.

Sunday morning is a special time in Botswana. Bouncing down the road in the bakkie, I saw a dozen little church groups meeting in the bush. The group who wear white and stand in a circle were singing and swaying, the group with the badge who dress in green were marching in formation. African winter mornings are sharp and bright and infinite across flat parched landscape. I waved to housewives who spend Sunday morning drawing water and washing clothes.

Game was packed. It was the pay weekend and everyone had money; there were endless queues of families with their trolleys piled high, and lines of modest young men buying a bar of soap and a tube of toothpaste to last them a month.

I headed straight for the 'Uniforms', but was temporarily distracted by the sight of myself in a full-length mirror. What was wrong with Will? I looked exactly the same as I always had – a tall, thin redhead wearing too much eye make-up. Not beautiful, but striking, and definitely good enough to sleep with. Especially if you'd only just married me.

Then Dorothy tapped me on the arm and said in a familiar accent, "God spoke to me this morning. He told me there were pink gingham maids' uniforms beside the outsize underwear. I've just bought one for my maid. Better hurry, there are just a couple left."

I'd never seen her in my life before. She was probably older than me, but not by much.

And she wore a great deal less make-up. A tall, rather plain woman in shapeless safari clothes and well-worn boots.

"You're expecting."

I felt myself blush. The first time in twenty-five years. "Is it noticeable?"

"Only to me. I'm a doctor at the Mission Hospital."

She smiled, and the smile transformed her face and I never thought of her as plain again.

Out they erupted in the middle of Game beside the rail of maids' uniforms, the suppressed words I hadn't been able to utter.

"In that case, can you tell me please – is it normal for a husband to refuse to sleep with his wife when she's pregnant?"

I became Dorothy's patient at the Mission Hospital.

"Isn't the world very small!" I told Will. "Dorothy tells

me she studied medicine at Queen's in Belfast. She was four years ahead of Camilla. That's why she approached me in Game – she thought she recognised me . . ."

"What's she doing in Botswana?"

"She came on a work placement when she was a student doctor, and never left. We had a coffee together at the Italian Deli and she invited me to join her Book Club. We're meeting on Sunday at Mokolodi Game Reserve . . . I wonder why she's not married?"

Will frowned. "What's the name of that book you were reading, the one about the spinster who couldn't catch a husband and all her friends were married and she had a name for them – what did she call them? Smug Marrieds. Don't be a Smug Married, Francesca. It doesn't suit you."

"So you don't think I should ask her?"

"I think you should first ask yourself why you didn't get married until you were thirty-seven. And then decide whether you want to open a can of worms which might be better left unopened."

I took his advice.

"Your husband is suffering from a Madonna-Whore Complex," explained Dorothy. "Don't look so worried! It's not terminal! If it only started when he found out you were pregnant, everything will return to normal when the baby's born."

"I don't understand. Madonna? Whore? Perhaps he just doesn't fancy me any more."

"I doubt that! You can blame Freud; he says that men who are rejected by their mothers in infancy seek a mother figure in a wife. When the man finds his perfect woman he idolises her but refuses to have sex with her . . . You're pregnant and Will has put you on a pedestal to idolise. It's flattering in a way . . ."

"It's only flattering if he doesn't go looking for sex somewhere else."

"I'm sure you won't let that happen," said Dorothy, and I thought she sounded distinctly wistful.

The gloves came off our marriage.

On Sunday morning I got ready to go to the Book Club.

"We might go for a game drive after lunch. One of the Book Clubbers is a game ranger."

Will scowled. "Why can't you stay at home with me when it's the only day in the week I have off?"

"I'll stay at home with you if we can have sex."

No sex. I went to the Book Club.

Barbara was a small plump woman with frizzy blond hair, wearing a pretty sundress and a pair of high-heeled sandals.

"I wasn't always a game ranger," she told me with a laugh. "I used to be dentist. I worked in Harare, I had a nice successful practice, a very nice house, and a long-term boyfriend, but one day I woke up and decided that I never wanted to look into another human mouth again, so I came to Botswana and did a game rangers' course."

Margaret was a diplomat with the British High Commission. She'd worked in China and the Middle East before being posted to Botswana. Her long shorts had tidy creases down the front, there were no chips in her red nail varnish, and I could tell, from years of Duty Free window-shopping, that the understated scarf round her neat neck was a Hermes. She was rather intimidating until she threw her novel on the table and loudly asked, in her posh English voice, "Can someone please tell me what a 'Brazilian' is?"

Attractive, professional, forty-something women. They were me if I hadn't married Will.

We decided to meet every week and discuss what we were reading. Until I became unmanageably pregnant we agreed to buddy up and play tennis together at the Sun Hotel. Every Sunday I would meet them at church for a sing a long with God.

It wasn't better than sex with my husband but it was better than nothing.

Thanks to Dorothy, Margaret and Barbara, I snapped out of my freewheeling timelessness and bought an ancient Range Rover that Mokolodi were trading in. Once I had my own car I visited various plant nurseries with Violet's boyfriend, Charles, who advised me what to buy and planted it out for me in my dirt yard.

"Bougainvillea thorns are better than an electric fence. Electric fences cannot work when there is no electricity. The thief can break in easily to rob you when you have no lights to see him and no gun to shoot him."

Before long I'd bought myself a gardening book and when Will came home from work he found me with the book up, absorbed in the mating habits of pumpkins and sweet potatoes.

"Put the book down, Francesca. I'm home."

"I'll put the book down if we can have sex."

No sex. I continued reading.

"Margaret took me to the most fantastic warehouse this afternoon – it's simply full of Rhodesian teak furniture! I've ordered a ten-seater dining table – and ten chairs, of course!"

"Francesca, you've a ton of cargo coming from the Middle East!"

"Sex would be cheaper, Will."

Still no offer of sex. I was going to have to raise the bar.

"Barbara wants to take me to the Rhino Sanctuary in Serowe. She says it's soft camping, to get me broken in. We're going to stay in a chalet and there's an ablutions block and we don't even have to bring firewood, because they provide it. We're going rhino-tracking with a guide. Did you know it's very difficult to tell the difference between white rhino and black rhino because they're all grey and they're all as big as motor cars? But, apparently, the young of white rhino run ahead of them, the way white children are pushed ahead of the mother in a pushchair and the young of black rhino follow behind, the way Africans carry their babies on their backs."

"What are the young of a rhino called?" Will asked nastily.

I didn't know.

"I'll stay at home if we can have sex."

Still no offer of sex. I went to Serowe with Barbara.

"What is that smelly stuff you've got on your hair?"

"It's a special conditioner to treat nervous anthrepsis – a stress-related hair problem – I suffer from it when my husband won't sleep with me."

"Francesca, we're living in the African bush. Nobody notices stressed-out hair."

And nobody noticed a stressed-out wife either. For no particular reason I suddenly reached the end of my tether and my bravado deserted me; I turned on my heel and walked away from him, out to the pumpkin beds. There was a huge lump in my throat and I wanted to be sick. Maybe Mummy was right. Maybe holiday romances didn't make happy and successful marriages. Maybe I shouldn't have impulsively bolted to Botswana with a middle-aged Zimbabwean builder. There was a song, wasn't there, about a desperate woman of thirty-seven?

Will brought me a cup of tea.

"Before you ask, I boiled the water. I put two tea bags in the teapot. I boiled the arse out of the teapot on the top of the gas stove. And I used fresh milk."

I took a sip to please him. "It tastes horrible."

I'd never done kiss and make-up with a man before.

Will said, "It's not like you to lose your nerve. You're the pilot who flew from South India with your landing gear stuck – four and half hours you were up there, preparing to crash- land when you got to the Middle East . . ."

"And you're the man who was waiting for me in Seeb airport, and when you found out we'd been diverted to Abu Dhabi to crash you got into a car and drove the whole night through the desert to Abu Dhabi. To be there for me."

"I thought you were dead. I never thought you'd be able to land that 767. I kept expecting to hear breaking news on the car radio: *Pilot, crew, two hundred passengers killed* . . ."

"But you still came."

The months passed. I gradually became resigned to the crisis of a sex-free pregnancy. By November my cargo had arrived and, thanks to string-pulling and Margaret's High Commission contacts, we had a telephone, a washing machine, a better quality gas supply and a ceiling fan in our bedroom.

But still no sex.

Chapter Five

It was November. The sun beat down on us relentlessly, there wasn't a cloud in the sky, and the mosquitoes ate us through our clothes at night. My right arm was sunburnt from resting it on the open window of the Range Rover when I was driving. My left arm was still pale.

I was now so enormously pregnant that only one sundress fitted, and so hot I never wore underwear under it.

Will said, "Lead us not into temptation," when he discovered me leaving for church with a bare bum.

"Mind your own business. Since you stopped sleeping with me you're not my husband any more. You're just the man I'm married to."

Church was in town, in a most unlikely location, between a supermarket and a shebeen called Morning Glory. It was very handy, of course, if you wanted to run into the supermarket for sweets before the service, or nip into

Morning Glory for a bottle of beer afterwards but rather undignified too since occasionally a drunk man rolled in when he heard rock'n'roll gospel on the church piano and Pastor Bruce invariably marched him out again and made a small joke about him being full of more than the Holy Spirit.

Pastor Bruce de Villiers was a sex-symbol clergyman. He was broad at the shoulder and slim at the hip, he wore a checked shirt with enough buttons open for everyone to see his blond hairy chest. He played rugby for Botswana. Church was always standing room only.

Every week at the end of the service Pastor Bruce's congregation – male and female – crowded round him.

"What a *lekker* sermon, Pastor!"

"You must come for a *braai*, Pastor!"

"Let me touch the hem of your cloak, Pastor!"

Estelle de Villiers, his sparkly immaculate wife, stood quietly by herself at the front of the church waiting for him. Her baby was also due in November yet her tiny designer bump fitted neatly into white leggings and a frilly cotton smock. She wore a striking diamante headband to keep her big hair off her face and she carried a pretty fan which she fluttered provocatively in her husband's direction.

Estelle could not have been a more perfect pastor's wife if she'd been ordered from Mr Moss, the matchmaker. She ran a weight-loss programme and a playgroup, she visited the sick, she made soup for the poor, she organised craft mornings and knitting groups, and the patchwork, placemats, tea cosies, oven gloves and rag dolls that she made were sold at church fêtes – which she organised – to raise funds for the church. She was so fragrant she farted only rose petals.

Every morning, once Will left for work, I visited the British Consul swimming-pool, which was thoughtfully covered with a shade net in summer. Weightless and whale-like I swam up and down and down and up, out of touch with reality, my mind in freewheel. When he wasn't busy, Margaret the diplomat's gardener counted my lengths.

"Three hundred and thirty-one, and no, the baby didn't fall out when I was doing a tumble turn. I checked when I got out."

"What size is the pool?"

"Normal size. Twenty-five metres."

Will, man-like, did the calculations. "You swam nearly five miles?" He was incredulous.

I felt defensive. "What else am I going to do all day? There's no air-conditioning in the house, and no air-conditioning in the Range Rover. Tempting though it is, I can't stand in the chill cabinet in the bottle shop from dawn till dusk. People have started to talk about me!"

"You better go and lie down. Your legs are swollen up like bananas."

"Do shut up, darling. Pregnancy isn't an illness."

Camilla phoned.

"Is it born yet?"

"Nobody yet."

"Oh, what a bore! I thought it might have come before we boarded. I'm going to have to switch off my cellphone and I don't know if it'll work in the Maldives. I'm going to be away for a week. You almost drowned in the Maldives, didn't you?"

She began to laugh manically. Camilla was always manic when she was leaving on a jet plane.

"Does she know the facts of life?" Will asked when Camilla had hung up. "Does she know that babies don't always fit in with her holidays? Or does she think that every woman has an elective Caesarean section six weeks early so she can go on holiday?"

"That was hardly a commonplace holiday. It was a trip to Tonga to welcome in the new millennium. If Camilla had missed that she'd have had to wait a thousand years for another one. I don't know what the fuss was all about. Kathryn is perfectly healthy. Camilla *is* a doctor – she knew what she was doing."

"I don't know where she gets the time to be a doctor," said Will irritably. "Or James Snotter either. Every time we hear from her they're just about to leave to go on holiday or they're just back from holiday, or we're getting a postcard to say they're having a lovely holiday. Wish you were here." He plucked a postcard wedged between the burglar bars on the kitchen window and read: "'*We're in a tarted-up colonial villa on a sugar-cane plantation with a private path down to the beach and a permanent staff of four. What am I going to do? There's no pool!*' That one came only yesterday, from Jamaica."

"She didn't go to Jamaica with James Snotter. She never goes anywhere with James Snotter. James Snotter stays at home with Kathryn and she goes with the gang. I think they've done every island in the Caribbean now. "

"A gang? Instead of her husband?"

"Oh, yes. She's gone on holiday with the gang since she was at university. There are five of them. Men and women. They went backpacking and inter-railing through mainland Europe when they were students but it's all a deal more sophisticated now. They visit very exotic destinations – I don't think there's a paradise island left on the planet that they haven't been to."

"But why doesn't she take her husband?"

"You can't get potatoes on a paradise island and James won't eat anything else. Before she married James she was married to one of the gang. Sam. Samuel. He was lovely. I'd have married him myself . . ."

Next morning I woke up in a very, very bad mood. Everyone was picking on me.

"This is the worst cup of tea I've ever had in my life. Did you boil the water, Will? Did you use fresh milk? Did you use Broken Orange Pekoe or local tea bags? Don't tell me! I can guess."

Once Will left for the site I picked on Violet who was washing last night's dinner dishes in bleach.

"Are you trying to poison me, Violet?"

"The washing liquid is finished, madam," said the imperturbable Violet.

"Why didn't you tell me? I'm not a mind-reader. Why does everyone expect me to be a mind-reader?"

Sighing theatrically, I said I'd drive to Village Spar and get her some. If I'd been a bit less self-obsessed I might have noticed the knowing smile on Violet's face. If I'd huffed and puffed a little less, I might have overheard her whisper to Gloria – "Madam's baby will come today . . ."

I stepped outside. The air was so hot I felt I was being blasted with a hairdryer on 'hot'. The steering wheel of the Range Rover was so hot it burnt my hands. Even the weather was picking on me.

I drove to Village Spar. A bright little beggar boy asked me for money.

"*Impshee!*" I said. "Bugger off!" though I was usually kind to him and allowed him to stand guard at the Range Rover when I was shopping because the driver's window was broken and wouldn't wind up.

In Village Spar a perfectly innocent African man was pushing his trolley along the fruit and vegetable aisle.

I shouted, "Get out of my way! I'm not moving for you!"

At the till the checkout girl was ignoring me.

"Are you going to serve me or will I go somewhere else?"

When she charged me twice for the washing-up liquid I said: "I saw that, you wicked girl! You've charged me twice."

"I didn't see."

"Well, *I* saw!"

When I got back out to the carpark the key wouldn't go into the ignition of the Range Rover. Sweat was lashing off me as repeatedly it got stuck.

A gang of young beggars, wearing black sunglasses, approached.

"Give me a cigarette!"

"I don't smoke."

"Give me seventy thebe to buy a packet of cigarettes!"

"*Impshee*, the lot of you!"

Finally the key went into the ignition and the Range Rover started with a roar.

"Get out of my way," I shouted at them as they flocked around the car, "or I'll drive over you!"

When I got back home again I snapped at Violet, "You've left the clothes on the washing line for so long they're crispy."

Suddenly, my waters broke. I think the only person who was surprised was me.

Finally my sex-free pregnancy was over. Hurrah! Within an hour the stomach cramps had become unbearable – it was time for medical intervention. Will raced home from work and sat revving in his bakkie, shouting and honking on the horn, "Hurry up, Francesca!" while I carried my own bag.

In the Mission Hospital a woman was screaming and the language she was using was disgraceful.

"Who *is* that?" I asked Dorothy when she came to examine me.

"Estelle de Villiers. From church."

"You're joking!"

"Estelle has been labouring since early this morning. She's lonely, frightened and fed up. Pastor Bruce dropped her off when her waters broke. He told us he was going to a

Prayer Breakfast and he promised he'd be back when it finished. But he must have gone on to the Bull and Bush to watch the rugby international on their big screen. I asked her if she wanted me to phone him, and tell him to get a move on, and she said, 'Poor Bruce, he works so hard. I hardly ever see him any more.'"

"Is it her first baby?"

Dorothy shook her head. "This is Estelle's sixth baby. Or is it her seventh? I can't remember to be honest. I think there was a set of twins at the start – they were born in Zimbabwe. Then there was a child born in South Africa, and one born in Namibia. And there was definitely one born in Bloemfontein, South Africa again, before the family moved to Botswana . . ."

Estelle started wailing and cursing again. I was suddenly panic-stricken. With your sixth baby, or was it your seventh, did you not simply sneeze and it popped out?

"Am I going to sound like that later?"

Dorothy grinned. "English isn't Estelle's first language. I don't think she understands what most of those words mean."

"Well, whatever you've just injected, Dorothy, give me more of it."

The drugs were administered and I began thrashing about on the high narrow bed, trying to get comfortable.

"These drugs are not working. I can still feel pain."

"Francesca, if you get any more drugs, you'll fall off the bed and break your neck."

Next door Estelle's screams were becoming increasingly

frantic and Dorothy had abandoned her bedside manner and was barking, "Stop screaming, Estelle! Sit up, hold your ankles and push. *Push*, Estelle!"

I rather felt like screaming myself except Will kept whispering, "Shh, Francesca, somebody will hear you . . ."

Afterwards Estelle came into my delivery room to admire Ella.

Pastor Bruce had not yet come but Estelle had made herself pretty for him – she was a surreal vision in a baby-doll nightdress, high-heeled fluffy mules, fake eyelashes and monotonous small talk.

("I asked her," said Dorothy, "if she wanted a mirror to see what was happening when the baby's head was crowning. 'Yes, please,' she said, 'I need to reapply my lipstick.'")

"A baby girl! To dress with pink ribbons!"

That would probably have been my first and last conversation with Estelle de Villiers and I'd have dismissed her, as everyone else did, as the perfect wife and baby-making machine except she stopped by my bed and picked up the novel lying on the cover.

"Have you reached the part where Emma gives birth to Berthe?"

I shook my head.

Estelle expertly riffled through the pages, found what she was looking for and read: *"She hoped for a son . . . A man at least is free; he may travel over passions and over countries . . . But a woman is always hampered . . . Her will, like the veil of her bonnet, held by a string, flutters in every wind; there is always some desire that draws her, some conventionality that restrains.*" She handed the book back to me. "It sounds even better in French."

"You speak French?"

"I learnt at school. There was a choice: French, Latin or Afrikaans. I chose Afrikaans and French, and then after two years I had to drop one, so I dropped the Afrikaans. Dad was furious. He said 'What's the point of learning French when you're going to marry a nice boy from Plumtree?' And I said 'Dad, I have ambition. I dream of flying away!' I *so* wanted to be an air stewardess. I had a pretty cousin in Pretoria – Doret – she flew for South African Airways. She brought me magazines and brochures from overseas. At Christmas time and family weddings she'd tell me about her travels. Today Paris, tomorrow New York!"

Her enthusiasm was infectious but old habits are hard to break.

"That's not possible. The flight from Jo'burg to Paris takes about eleven hours. The crew would legally have to take at least minimum rest – that's thirteen hours – before they could go on to New York. I've never flown it, but I'm guessing Paris to New York is at least seven or eight hours. Faster coming back with the tail winds. And with the time difference your cousin Doret wouldn't have been landing into New York until the day *after* tomorrow."

Estelle gazed at me in wonder. She said in a hushed, reverential voice, "*You* were an air stewardess . . ."

"Not quite. I was a pilot. I flew Boeing aircraft long haul out of the Middle East. To London, Colombo, Singapore, Dhaka, New York . . ."

"Why a pilot? Why not an air stewardess?"

"I took the easy job! Why did you not become an air stewardess?"

"I'm a country girl! I rode horses, I drove a tractor! I helped my mother make biltong and boerewors – Ma's boerewors was the best in Plumtree – we won every competition – the mix of spices we use is a closely guarded secret. But always I dreamed of packing a small bag, shaking the red dust from my shoes and flying away. Then I married Bruce and we lived happily ever after. I have sons. *They* will fly away . . ."

Estelle became my intimate friend.

"I really know nothing about babies," I explained. "It's amazing, isn't it? I have a university education. I've flown round the world twice . . ."

So she taught me how to breastfeed the baby, how to wind her ("The most satisfactory sound in the world, the burp!"), how to bath her, swaddle her and support her little heavy head.

And I told Estelle about Ex-Pat Air, and the passengers we carried and the destinations we visited.

"Aladdin's Cave," she said when she saw my international shopping. We sat on the cane conservatory furniture in the porch. "Where's this from?"

"Dhaka, capital city of Bangladesh. It's very damp there – you can smell things growing in the ground."

We drank tea from Noritake teacups. "Where are they from?"

"Colombo, capital city of Sri Lanka. We carried

housemaids in and out of the Middle East. They were like flocks of brightly coloured birds in their saris."

I even told Estelle the reason why I'd got on an aircraft and flown halfway across the world to become a pilot at the age of twenty-four. It was a complicated embarrassing story, funny but not 'funny ha ha'. It was a story I could never share with my attractive, professional, forty-something friends.

"This boy at home, I made a fool of myself with him. I spent months afterwards trying to die of shame. Finally I pulled myself together, packed a bag and flew away."

"I have a book," said Estelle, "about a man who falls in love but refuses to touch the girl he loves because he's afraid that the magic of what he feels with her will disappear when it becomes the reality of a relationship."

"Is it a fairytale? Does it have a happy ending?"

Chapter Six

Mummy and Camilla came to visit us in February. They hadn't come immediately after Ella's birth – Camilla was just home from the Maldives and then there was Christmas and then the January Sales . . .

"How nice for you, madam," said Violet. "In Africa, when a woman has a baby, the grandmother always takes care of the baby and the new mother. The new mother must only rest and eat and make milk for the baby."

"I'd better warn you, Violet, that doesn't sound like my mother."

Ella was ten weeks old. Her cries didn't sound like a cat any more. When I picked her up she was no longer a scrawny bag of bones. Her hands were not enormous in relation to the rest of her body any more and I didn't break sweat before I bathed her. She was bright-eyed and content and she lived in a very old, big bouncy Silver Cross pram which Margaret had found in a shed at the back of the British High Commissioner's residence.

"I can only assume this pram came from England during the last days of Empire, when Botswana was known as Bechuanaland and Africa was where they sent second sons and dropouts. It must have sailed here, on a Union-Castle mail ship from Southampton, docking in Capetown a fortnight later . . ."

When Ella cried in the middle of the night I lifted her out of the pram and onto the camping mattress on the floor beside our bed. Then I lay down beside her and fed her. I quickly learned to doze off leaning on my elbow and Will never heard us.

When she'd finished feeding I'd slither back into bed, wrap myself around my husband and fall asleep with my face buried in the black inky hair at the back of his head.

Mummy and Camilla's visit started well. I'd made a few phone calls and called in a few airline favours and Mummy was treated like a VIP from the moment she left Northern Ireland until she landed in Botswana. It was hard to believe this was Mummy's first long-haul flight – before, she'd never travelled any further than London for a honeymoon weekend.

"Your father told me there was no need to travel to find sinners."

Ex-Pat Air's First Class is decorated in beige, taupe and biscuit, the seat covers are leather, pillow cases are linen, the complimentary blankets are cashmere and nobody stops you if you try to steal one off the aircraft.

The flight to Jo'burg was the last word in tranquillity and

comfort – by special request Marian was the chief stewardess and she was famous for her organised aircraft. Every air stewardess was smiling, every arm-rest was polished and every call-bell was answered. There were no air stewardess in-jokes when Marian was in charge, the galley was never closed for 'stocktaking', no air stewardess serving dinner ever said, "Of course there's a choice, sir: you can take it or leave it!" We used to joke that should our aircraft ever explode, Marian's head would be recovered without a hair out of place.

Also by special request, the pilot was Commander Andrew Cunningham, the charming ex-RAF boy racer who had been my former captain. He ate dinner with Mummy at the back of First Class, then invited her into his flight deck – "Come into my flight deck, madam, and I'll show you a sight you'll never forget."

First Class went to Mummy's head. Camilla said it was quite endearing the way she remarked, "Did Francesca really give up all this for a builder?"

The morning of their arrival Will watched, amused, while I rubbed fake tan into my left arm.

"Where did you get this stuff?"

"My cargo! It's to balance up my colour! You know the first thing Mummy is going to say when she sees me – 'Darling, why is one arm white and one arm brown?'"

Instead of sneering Will said, "Turn around and I'll do your shoulder blades, you don't want to be streaky when you meet your mother."

Mummy cleared Customs, stood Camilla and me to attention

side by side for an inspection, and bursting with pride announced, "Even now, even just after you've had a baby, Francesca, if it wasn't for the orange fake tan on your arm, and your ghastly clothes, I don't think I could tell you apart!"

Once she was satisfied with seeing double Mummy quickly became bored with Botswana and very bored with Ella who took an instant dislike to her and squealed hysterically when she approached. (Ella's gentle rhythms were all muddled up. Instead of a relaxing doze on my breast in front of a video of *Friends* – we'd reached the stage where Carol was giving birth to Ben – she was now carefully bathed every morning, powdered and stuffed into a silly pink Babygro.)

"That baby is hungry," said Mummy. "That baby needs solids and a bottle of formula. Your breast milk has no quality, Francesca. It's as thin as water and full of perfumed soap and deodorants. Whatever you're eating is filling her with wind and making her screech. I don't remember you screeching when you were a baby. Of course, you were bottle-fed from the very first day. I crushed rusks into your bottle when you were that baby's age and you slept all night."

Will was indignant. "Why do you allow your mother to talk to you like that? You and the baby managed perfectly well for ten weeks before she swept in on her broomstick!"

Against my better judgement I allowed Mummy to bully me into Village Spar to buy milk bottles, formula milk and little jars of puréed fruit for Ella. The staff took her from me and passed her round when I was shopping.

"Kids!" said the man selling bread. "I love them. They're so innocent."

"I am holding a white child!" said the boy selling meat.

"Are you quite sure . . ." Mummy whispered.

"Yes, I'm quite sure they're not going to steal her."

"This baby is too young for bottles," said the lady on the checkout.

"Put a woollen hat on your baby," said the woman selling cigarettes.

"This baby is too small to be outdoors," said the lady selling plastic bowls in the carpark.

"How very bossy!" said Mummy.

Takes one to know one.

Fortunately, Ella liked eating. Mummy gave her what I considered to be an excessive amount of puréed carrots and she ate them gallantly and didn't spit and then chugged comfortably on my breast for fifteen minutes afterwards.

"I suppose breast milk is useful for quenching thirst," Mummy admitted.

Within a couple of days, under Mummy's watchful eye, Ella had a routine – she took a bottle of formula for breakfast, ate fruit for lunch (washed down with breast milk), had another bottle of formula at 7 p.m. and the rest of the time she was supplemented with breast milk.

"That baby needs a dummy," said Mummy. "If she was chugging on a dummy you wouldn't need to waste so much time breastfeeding her. You could get a life, Francesca."

But this was my life.

Camilla had taken up residence on the sun-lounger in the garden. (Camilla thought life in Africa was an excuse to sunbathe in a skimpy bikini every day.)

"It's a pity you've no pool. I suppose I can always run a bath when I need to cool off."

Violet was mystified. "What is she doing?"

"She wants darker skin."

"But I use Vanishing Cream to make my skin whiter!"

"There's no justice in the world!"

It soon became clear that I was going to have to arrange a hectic schedule to keep Mummy entertained. Already she'd been on a game drive with Barbara, and eaten a dinner of venison ragout in the Mokolodi restaurant. Already she'd been to an Embassy party with Margaret and had been introduced to Princess Anne. Already she'd been to a Bible Study breakfast with Dorothy.

"Lovely," said Mummy after everything. Then the dreaded words, "What's next, darling?"

"I don't know. I don't know what's next. There's nothing next."

"But what do you *do* all day?"

(Mummy thought life in Africa was a glamorous movie – like *Out of Africa* or *White Mischief*.)

"What would you like to do, Mummy?"

"Well, actually, darling I was rather hoping to see some snakes. Is it absolutely necessary that you put diesel the whole way round your garden to stop them getting in?"

Mummy was so bored she turned to Violet for entertainment.

"Where is your village, dear?" Mummy produced an enormous map of Botswana and a spiral-bound notebook full of numbered questions. The same two dozen questions that Charles, the gardener, had been asked the day before.

"How do you travel there? How long does it take? How much does it cost? Does Francesca pay for your travel arrangements? How often do you go home? Is your mother still alive? What age is she? Do you have any brothers and sisters? How much does Francesca pay you?"

"I think you're exploiting your domestic staff," Mummy announced at dinner.

"I beg your pardon?"

Ella started to wail from her pram down the hall in our bedroom. I'd just force-fed her the 7 o'clock bottle of formula and, glaze-eyed with the exhaustion of drinking it, she'd gone down without a murmur and by my calculation had been asleep for exactly seventeen minutes.

"It's a classic example of exploitation of the underclass. I've interviewed Violet and done the sums. You don't even pay her the minimum wage and she cooks, cleans, irons and picks up after you from seven in the morning until six at night. I watched you this morning. You ate your breakfast, that baby started to cry and you jumped up and dashed off without so much as an 'If you please, Violet, if it wouldn't be too much bother, Violet, I would be sincerely grateful, Violet, if you'd clear my teacup away'. That's not the way you were reared, Francesca. We had no servants when you were a child but you were always encouraged to be kind to those less fortunate than yourself."

"Housemaid. Violet is a housemaid, not a servant."

The wailing from the bedroom was now deafening. If Ella screeched any more she was going to burst a blood vessel.

"I'm sorry. I've got to go to Ella. If she screeches any more she'll vomit up her bottle."

"That baby needs Infacol," said Camilla. "It's great for babies with colic. You squirt it into her mouth before you feed her – it lines her stomach. Same theory as drinking a pint of milk before going out for a feed of drink."

Mummy shouted after me down the hall, "Frankly, I'm very disappointed. The Presbyterian Women's Association have asked me to guest star next month with a talk about my travels in Africa. What shall I tell Mrs Doctor Dawson or Lady Millicent Flood if they ask me how much you pay your maid? I can hardly lie to them."

"Stop right there, Mrs Reverend Simms," said Will. Until now there'd been an uneasy truce between Will and my mother but I could tell, as I paced up and down the hall with Ella screeching, that they were about to engage in open warfare. Will has a particular sarcastic impatience with evangelical tourists who, with their bags full of malaria tablets, sunscreen, bottled water and condoms, visit Africa for a fortnight and afterwards preach exhaustively about the evils of colonialism, world debt, racism and apartheid. "What minimum wage are you referring to?"

"The UK minimum wage, William."

"But we don't live in the UK. We live in Africa. And Violet is paid four times the Botswana minimum wage – she earns more than the secretaries on my site. *And* she gets a free house at the bottom of the garden which has free electricity and free running water. She lives there with her daughter and her boyfriend and she rents out the floor space to anyone else she can squeeze in. Sometimes there are more

Africans living in Violet's house than lived on the compound of our farm in Zimbabwe."

Ella was constipated. After much squealing and pressing, her head went bright red with exertion and she produced a solid ball of poo that I could pick up between my finger and thumb. The poo was a gentle orange, the colour of puréed carrots mixed with formula milk.

Mummy had locked horns with Will so I had peace to put my daughter back on the breast and, after a comforting chug, she drifted easily over to sleep. I was slipping her gently back into her pram when I became aware of the uneasy silence at the dining table.

Then Camilla piped up, "Isn't that marvellous, Mummy? You'll be able to tell Mrs Doctor Dawson and Lady Millicent that Francesca is actually running a charity here in Africa."

There was a wicked little pause. I resumed my seat, smothering a secret smile because I knew what naughty Camilla was going to say next.

"Any particular reason for mentioning Mrs Doctor Dawson and Lady Millicent, Mummy?"

I started to laugh, Camilla started to laugh and Mummy, though she tried not to, started to laugh too and the tedious episode was over for another evening.

Only Will didn't get the joke. The next morning he went to a travel agency in town and returned with reservations for an all-inclusive, all-expenses-paid-trip to Madikwe Safari Lodge. Two days and two nights, leaving at lunchtime, and he'd drive Mummy and Camilla there himself.

"But Madikwe Safari Lodge costs an arm and a leg. It's

one of the most exclusive lodges in South Africa. *We've* never been there."

"The alternative," said Will ominously, "is to drive your mother to Khutse Game Reserve on the edge of the Kalahari and leave her there."

"But there's a pride of loco lions terrorising the campsite at Khutse. Barbara says some British Council teachers were there last weekend, and one lion was so close they could feel its breath through the tent material."

"Exactly! And if your bossy mother had stuck her head out of the tent that lion would have taken her in its mouth and eaten her."

Once they'd gone to Madikwe Safari Lodge the glass jars of puréed fruit and plastic bottles of formula milk were put away and Ella and I reverted to our simple, baby-centred rhythms again. Resting, eating, sleeping, watching *Friends* videos.

"This baby is African," said Violet with approval because Ella snuggled up and went to sleep the minute she was safely tied onto Violet's broad warm back.

Chapter Seven

I first noticed the pimple the morning Isobel was baptised.

Isobel, our third child, was six months old and the mists of early motherhood had begun to clear and I was finally normal enough again to realise that my face was unwashed, my hair was uncombed and, yuck, there was the pimple clinging like a small Rice Krispie, precipitous and unwanted, to the side of my nose. Horrified, I began to attack it with furious and self-conscious aggression – squeezing it till it bled, poking it with antibiotic cream, patting it with cotton wool, burying it beneath a dollop of spot-concealer while Isobel screamed to be nursed, Ella screamed for the potty and Hugh screamed because his sisters were screaming and he didn't want to feel left out.

"Will," I screamed at my husband, "take these buggers away till I get my face fixed!"

Will was unmoved by my sudden, desperate narcissism.

He was dressed as he always dressed – in short shorts, long socks and boots. Even though he was going to church to his new daughter's baptism. Even though it was winter and Botswana is bitter on winter mornings.

Will said, "God won't notice a pimple on your nose."

"It's not God I'm trying to impress. It's everybody else. I don't want the Mummy Gang shaking their perfect hairdos and murmuring 'Poor Francesca. She's had three children in three years. It's too much for anyone. Who can blame her for letting herself go?"

Will laughed. "Nobody is going to be looking at your face today."

Blushing, I rearranged my cleavage which was bulging out of a dress designed for a flat-chested woman. I looked like a hooker but if Isobel needed to be fed at the front of the church I'd be able to discreetly undo a couple of buttons without exposing acres of breast tissue.

"It's a pity, isn't it, that should Pastor Bruce succeed in undressing me with his eyes, all he'll find are two large mammary glands leaking milk."

"Is she ever coming off the breast?"

"Some men like big breasts."

"Some men don't. *I've* always thought anything bigger than a mouthful is a waste."

Ella, Hugh and Isobel were presented for inspection.

Ella, now two and a half, was wearing a pretty Laura Ashley sundress, her red curls were squashed under a sunhat made out of woven plastic bags and she had brand-new takkies, with flashing lights, on her feet.

Hugh was one and a half. His red head was shaven, he

74

was wearing a green and yellow Springboks tracksuit, he was barefoot and he was carrying a sink plunger which he insisted was a hammer.

Isobel's bald head was covered with a woollen hat, she wore an exquisite, smocked, hand-stitched white cotton Christening Robe and what smelled like last night's nappy.

"You've done a great job dressing them," I congratulated my husband. "Full marks for 'eclectic'."

The Dallas family circus climbed into the Range Rover and left for church.

By the time we'd parked up at church Isobel was screaming again to be nursed, Ella was screaming again for the potty and Hugh was screaming because his sisters were screaming and he didn't want to feel left out.

"Let's turn round and go back home again," said Will.

"We can't. Isobel has to be baptised."

"Why?"

"Because she'll go to hell if she's not baptised."

"Francesca . . ."

"And my mother keeps tormenting me, wanting baptism photographs to show off to the Presbyterian Women's Association. Dorothy has promised to bring her camera . . ."

I opened the back door of the Range Rover for Ella to slide out.

"Do it in the dust."

Ella was screaming, "I need a potty. I need a potty!" when Dorothy's bakkie pulled up.

"God spoke to me this morning. He says He doesn't like

the look of that pimple on the side of your nose, Francesca."

"Why doesn't God talk directly to me and tell me?"

Isobel was wriggling and wriggling in my arms trying to latch on, Hugh had climbed like a spider onto my back and Ella was now lying in the dust in front of me in the throes of a full-blown tantrum, getting her pretty dress filthy, screeching at the top of her voice, "Potty! Potty!"

"God tries," Dorothy said kindly, "but I think there's so much background noise you can't hear Him."

She hauled Hugh from my neck, swung him up into the air and announced brightly and briskly, "Let's go into the church, Hugh, and see if we can find a potty for Ella. And if you're very good I might be able to find you both a couple of suckers in the bottom of my handbag."

"Suckers!!" Ella stopped mid-scream, leapt up off the ground and followed them into church.

Peace at last.

"Thanks, Dorothy."

At Isobel's baptism Pastor Bruce preached on the differences between men and women, the main point of which was that men were ready to have sex any time, any place, with anyone. Even minutes after a near-fatal car crash, while a woman was searching in her handbag for sticky plasters and smelling salts, it was not unlikely that a man might have sex on his mind.

"I don't think Estelle wrote that sermon for Pastor Bruce, do you?" said Dorothy.

"That man thinks with one organ and it's not his brain!" said Will.

Aunty Jean, one of the Mummy Gang, broke away from

the groupies pressing round Pastor Bruce to remind me to send an empty spaghetti box to school with Ella the following morning.

"If Ella doesn't have her spaghetti box she will not be able to do the 'craft'."

"Of course she'll have her spaghetti box. It's already inside the bakkie . . ."

On Sunday afternoon I met Margaret for the annual sale of Persian carpets in the Anglican church hall. There was an enormous selection of beautiful carpets, come by truck from Jo'burg, en route to desperate housewives in Zambia and Namibia. Margaret and I, with our years of international shopping experience, were able in less than five minutes to find the most perfect and unique carpet in the collection – a Mashoud (a heavy woven *kelim* from Iran).

"I think I'll buy it. It'll look good rolled up under the bed in the spare room with the Kashan I bought last year."

"Are you pregnant again by any chance?"

"Why do you ask?"

"You always buy expensive, useless objects when you're pregnant."

To compensate for the tedium of a sex-free pregnancy.

Monday was just another day in Africa. Will took Ella to nursery school while I breastfed Isobel on thermal leopard-print sheets, and Hugh lay snuggled into my back, drinking his milk bottle and hugging his Blankie. It was bitterly cold as we dressed close to the gas ring of the cooker in the kitchen and I was just remarking to Violet that I could see frost on the windscreen of the bakkie, when, with a sickening thud, the penny dropped and I suddenly remembered that Will had stuck his head round the bedroom door as he was leaving and told me he was taking the Range Rover because he thought it was leaking oil and he wanted the mechanic on site to look at it.

Ella's spaghetti box for her 'craft' was in the bakkie.

"Forgetting things again, madam?" Violet asked with a knowing smile.

Hugh and I gave chase with the spaghetti box. (If Ella didn't get her spaghetti box she might end up in analysis as a dysfunctional adult and it would be my fault for forgetting that my car was leaking oil.)

When I got to Aunty Jean's nursery school Ella promptly burst into tears and begged me to take her home.

"Please, Mummy!"

(This was the reason Will took her to school, not me. He was a great deal more brutal with the children's feelings. Sometimes he even said no when they demanded things but he always felt awful about it afterwards.)

Aunty Jean wrestled the screaming Ella away from me and briskly handed her over to Doris – a lovely big comforting nanny – who'd been employed exclusively to walk behind Ella and, every time she felt unhappy, to pick her and give her a hug.

Then I took Hugh to Kindermusick, which was run by another lady in the Mummy Gang, Elsa. Hugh was unsure if he liked Kindermusick, sometimes he participated in the music-centred activities, sometimes he preferred to have races up and down the hall on all fours, barking, with his best friend Peter de Villiers who'd been born on the same day as Ella and who was still being breastfed.

"What's that terrible thing on the side of your nose?" asked Elsa.

So I stopped at Village Spar on the way home to buy some toothpaste because Ex-Pat air stewardesses always used toothpaste to dry up their spots. (Toothpaste was also useful for brushing teeth, but since I'd forgotten to buy it we were brushing our teeth with salt.)

My little beggar friend came running over, with his hand out, asking for money.

I handed him some coins. "Now *impshee!*"

"You take the kid inside today? No baby-sitting money?" for sometimes I left Hugh in the car and paid the beggar boy to stand guard. A job he took very seriously and was very proud to be asked to do.

I shook my head. "No, thanks. Not today."

We bought toothpaste and I was strapping Hugh into his car seat and Hugh was kicking at me when suddenly, out of nowhere, a very tall, very thin man ran up, leant right into the bakkie, grabbed my bag and turned to run off.

Instinctively I grabbed him and held on, and he dragged me halfway across the car park until my knees were burning and bleeding and I had to let go. Once free of me he sprinted into the bush.

"He's got my bag!" I screeched at the top of my voice, and my beggar friend and a few of his associates gave chase but we never saw him again.

The Village Spar manager was very kind and gave Hugh a sucker and let me phone Will.

When Will arrived and saw the state of my bloody knees he was furious.

"You shouldn't have fought with him! He might have pulled a knife on you!"

"But my driving licence is in my bag, and it's against the law to drive without your licence! What am I going to do if the traffic police stop me?"

"Pull yourself together, Francesca."

The Village Spar manager said, "You must plead with the traffic police to be lenient."

Dorothy phoned while I was filling in an application form for a new driving licence, ticking a box to claim that I had no mental illness (!).

"I've made you an appointment for four o'clock."

"An appointment for what?"

"To get that thing taken off your nose."

"What thing?"

Next morning I was back in Village Spar buying Calpol.

Earlier, Will had taken Ella to nursery school, and I had been breastfeeding Isobel on the thermal leopard-print when I realised Hugh wasn't snuggled into my back drinking his milk bottle as usual.

"Where's Hugh, Violet?"

"Still sleeping, madam?"

We found him lying perfectly still on top of his bed, his eyes glazed, his temperature raging. He was too hot to move. I knew from experience that the shock would make him convulse. Hugh had raging temperatures on a regular basis, every three weeks to be exact.

"It's his ears again, isn't it? Make the room dark, Violet. Put some cloths into a bucket of cool water – not cold, not hot. Wring them out and put them gently on his body until I come back. I've got to go to Village Spar for Calpol. Ella drank a full bottle of it last week and I forgot to buy more."

I was racing through Village Spar when the manager took me to one side and whispered, "We found the bad man who took your bag, Mrs Dallas. He was in Morning Glory last night, boasting about where he got his beer money. We drank the beer he bought us and afterwards we followed him into the bush and beat him until he gave us back your bag. I am delighted to tell you that your driving licence is still at the bottom of it."

Just another day in Africa.

Chapter Eight

Ella was pulling at my arm screaming, "I've got to do a wee-wee, Mummy!" when Dorothy told me I had skin cancer.

Mummy has skin cancer. The three-year-old has to pee. In the great scheme of things what is more important? The toilet. Always the toilet.

"Tell me about the cancer in a minute," I said as Ella and I frantically retreated back out through the consulting-room door. "First we must go to the toilet."

"It's a basal cell carcinoma," I explained to Will, once the bath-time and bedtime manoeuvres were completed and Ella and Hugh were tucked up in bed. Isobel was tucked up on my breast. Will was dishing up our dinner. "That pimple Dorothy took off my nose last week, it's a type of skin cancer. I have to go back to the Mission Hospital to have a proper operation to get it all cut out or it'll spread. "

Silently Will handed me my dinner and a spoon. Lamb stew with butter beans. I'd taught Violet to cook when I was pregnant with Hugh. I'd taught her how to make six simple dishes and every week since Hugh's birth she had cooked them conscientiously and consecutively. Thursday was lamb stew with butter beans. Tomorrow would be cottage pie and broccoli. Will never complained about our monotonous nursery-food diet.

Perhaps he didn't notice it any more.

"Glass of water?"

If I were more insecure or immature I might have thought he didn't care. Tears might have blinded me as they did that balmy Omani afternoon he told me he was moving to Botswana. Three years in the African bush with three children under the age of three had dried up the easy tears. I simply raised my voice and repeated what I'd just said.

Finally Will said, "I thought it was probably a BCC. They're very common among white Africans, especially on the face where you're rubbing the dust away all the time. My mother had one taken off the side of her eye about thirty years ago."

"Did you give *her* any sympathy?"

Will shrugged. "My father was bitten by a puff adder and died instantly. My sister Kate died of cerebral malaria when she was twelve. I think, all things considered, my mother got off lightly with a little bit of skin cancer."

Before I could answer, a terrible howling started from Ella's room at the far end of the bungalow and my alpha-male husband leapt up like a sprinter under starter's orders.

"She needs the potty."

"Show off!" I shouted after his retreating back. "People die nasty deaths in Northern Ireland too!"

I'm not sure what possessed me to do a pregnancy test the morning I had to go into hospital to get the rest of the skin cancer cut out of my nose. Experience? Intuition? Dorothy insisted afterwards it was God speaking to me. (And me hearing Him.) Whatever the reason, I gave Isobel a quick nurse while the pregnancy test cooked. Will was right. Of course, this little princess should've been off the breast months ago. She had teeth now and was sitting unaided. Soon, Will teased, she would be able to crawl over to me and bite me if I didn't nurse her.

The test was positive. Of course. They always are with Will and me. Every time Will hangs his trousers over the bottom of the bed I get pregnant. Soon the Mummy Gang will be asking, "Why don't you take the Pill? Are you Catholic?"

"Will!" I called from the bathroom. "Surprise!"

Across the hall I could hear him remonstrating with Ella.

"No, Ella, you cannot wear your pyjamas to school. No, Ella, I'm sorry. It's simply not on." And then (assertively), "Ella, I'm not taking you into the nursery school again in those bloody 'Barbie' pyjamas," followed by Ella's high-pitched "Bloody, bloody, bloody!" as she escaped from him and ran down the hall to the safety of Violet who would let her wear anything or nothing, whatever made her happy .

I hid the pregnancy test in my wash-bag and shouted to my husband "May I suggest you use a different adjective with the 'Barbie' pyjamas in future? 'Inappropriate' or 'feminine'. Even 'pink and girly' will sound better when she's explaining to Aunty Jean why she's wearing Barbie pyjamas again . . ."

"Excuse me, Rra," I told the anaesthetist at the hospital, "I'm expecting a baby and I don't want a general anaesthetic. I want Doctor Dorothy to cut out the rest of the cancer under a local anaesthetic. With no drugs."

"Not even a Valium?"

"Not even a Valium."

It was nerve-wrecking but I'd been in nerve-wrecking situations before.

Like the first time I landed into the old airport in Hong Kong, bringing the 767 and two hundred passengers down over the top of Chinese washing lines with the blue sea winking at the end of the tiny runway. And Commander Andrew Cunningham, the ex-RAF boy racer who could do the landing in his sleep, or on his head, or with his eyes closed, or all three together at the same time, letting me get on with it all by myself while he studied his crossword.

Or giving birth to Isobel on the kitchen floor with no pain relief and an audience of Ella and Hugh, assisted only by Will who then tried to faint as the baby's head crowned. Violet wasn't in her room so we'd no-one to look after the children while Will got ready to take me to the Mission Hospital and by the time a bag was packed I was on my hands and knees, screaming, "It's too late. I can feel the baby coming!"

I tried not to panic under the glare of the theatre lights. It was very hot and very claustrophobic and the green theatre cloth which shrouded my body also covered my eyes but fortunately not my mouth.

"Nice lipstick!" said Dorothy cheerfully.

I'd been in nerve-wrecking situations before but none of them had involved the mutilation of my reasonably lovely face. Dorothy had been uncompromising during our pre-surgery consultation.

"Basal cell carcinoma is *only* caused by sun damage."

"But I *never* put my face in the sun. I'm much too afraid of wrinkles."

My palms were now perspiring. Pictures from my life began to drift soft and hazy beneath my sweating eyelids. I thought of strange, pointless, inconsequential things. Of a pink sundress I'd once worn on holiday. Of my resolve to remove Ella's and Hugh's milk bottles and make them drink out of a cup. Of strange old Aunt Grace who wore black to my wedding and who announced during the speeches, "Francesca's life is going to change utterly the Christmas she's forty. Mark my words, Francesca, the Christmas you're forty . . ." until Mummy, bleached white and looking very sad had grabbed her in a sort of half-nelson wrestling hold and frogmarched her out of the drawing room.

I'd just turned forty in March. At Christmas my life was going to change utterly.

Half a dozen injections only pinched as they went in; Dorothy cut me open with one smooth flick of her scalpel. There was a suction machine to get rid of the blood and her hands were clean when she'd finished.

"Finished," said Dorothy. "How do you feel, Francesca?"

"*Lekker.*"

If I'd remembered Aunt Grace's eccentric prediction at any other point of my life, even earlier that morning before being trolleyed into theatre shrouded in green, I might have spent an amusing half hour harmlessly fantasising about an utter change to more favourable circumstances. A lottery win or a spiritual epiphany. Made an easy leap from the sublime to the ridiculous and anticipated a jail sentence or the role of leading lady in a Hollywood block-buster movie.

So many possibilities. Yet in my petrified state, laid out on a theatre trolley shrouded in green, I could focus only on one. The fact that death changes everything utterly. I suddenly became convinced I was going to die. That Dorothy would miss a bit of the cancer and it would quickly and quietly spread into my brain and kill me. On my gravestone they would write: *She kept saying she had a headache and nobody listened.*

Or that I would die in childbirth, haemorrhaging uncontrollably under the Christmas lights, while Will ran in blind circles trying to pack our children into the Range Rover to take me to a hospital to get the bleeding stopped. Shouting, "You never bloody told me you were pregnant again!"

Malaria. Snake-bite. Cancer. There are so many things can kill you. Was one of them really going to get me at Christmas? And if I died, who would be kind to my children?

Will phoned as I was being wheeled out of theatre and back to my room.

"It's your husband," said the nurse. "He's phoned three times since you went to theatre."

My wonderful, patient, understanding, kind Will. So full of concern for his sick wife he'd taken the day off work to pace up and down our bungalow, hugging our children close, waiting for news of me. I could picture him chain-smoking and biting his nails. If I listened closely enough there was a Country and Western song playing somewhere in the background . . .

"Why are you not finished?" Will shouted at me. "What's keeping you?"

"What do you mean, what's keeping me? I'm only back from theatre. I can't just jump up and come home. My stitches might burst. My nose might fall off. "

"But you've been away since seven this morning! The water has stopped running, the dishes are piled up in the sink, the floors are filthy and there are ants marching in formation all over the house."

"Oh dear."

"And Aunty Jean says Ella peed herself in school, just stood in the middle of the classroom smiling while it ran down her leg. And when I put her down for a rest after lunch she coughed until she vomited up her milk bottle."

"Attention-seeking?"

"Then Hugh went into the fridge, took the butter and finger-painted it all over your new gold sofa in the living room. When I finally got it wrestled off him and put him down for a sleep he found a crayon and scribbled over his bedroom walls."

"So creative."

"Now they're refusing to eat their tea!"

There was a brief silence. Then a gasp.

Then in the voice a radio presenter would use to signal the end of the world he said, "Ella has just thrown her spaghetti bolognese over Hugh's head. It has stuck to his hair and we've no running water to wash him . . ."

He sounded close to tears. Even I realised that this was perhaps not the best moment to briskly remind him that he went out to work every morning and I stayed at home with the children. Instead I said, "Where's Violet?"

"Violet has been carrying Isobel around since you left. She hasn't even had time to cook dinner. That baby has got to come off the breast. Are you listening to me? She hasn't eaten a bite all day, nor taken a bottle. And the racket she's creating, screeching for you!"

"Yes, darling. Yes, I agree with you. Absolutely. She's coming off the breast today. It's at the top of my list."

"What list? I thought you'd just come out of theatre. When did you get time to make a list?"

"I made a list inside my head when Dorothy was slicing open my nose. Of things I must do when I come home. Getting Isobel onto a milk bottle is at the top of it."

Will dried his tears. "I hope getting Ella and Hugh off their milk bottles was next."

"Well, actually giving you a big kiss was next," I said, but he was too far beyond the point of rescue to want to kiss his wife. His sense of proportion had got switched off with the water.

"You'll be lucky. I'm ready to throw a naked Barbie." (An unkind reference to a particularly challenging evening a few days after Isobel was born. There'd been a thunderstorm with torrential rain which had knocked off the electricity and the running water, and the roof of the bungalow was leaking in a number of places and as night fell everyone became frightened and tearful – including myself – because outside there was a spooky, murky, yellow sky and inside the candles kept blowing out. And the phone lines were down, of course, so I hadn't heard from Will since morning.

When he'd finally got home from work, hours late, he found the three babies and myself huddled together in a dry corner of Ella's bedroom drinking long-life milk out of bottles and sharing the last of the Custard Creams. And instead of instinctively realising that we were all at the point of emotional collapse my husband importantly announced, "I'm lucky to be alive. The bridge has collapsed at Swiss Chalet. I had to drive miles to the ford on the other side of The Village to get across. Forked lightning hit the road just ahead of me. I could hear it cracking and fizzing. I could *smell* it. If it had hit me I'd have been electrocuted."

And I picked up the first thing to hand – a naked Barbie – and threw it at him.)

"Did you put *Rocky 2* on the video for them?"

Rocky 2 was their favourite movie. Hugh liked the scenes where Rocky is working out and Ella loved Rocky's baby.

"They've watched it twice. But even then Isobel was screeching in the background. And do you know what Ella said? She said: 'You're useless, Daddy. Your breasts have no milk for Isobel.' Let me tell you something, Francesca. No more children. I'm serious. Three is enough for anybody. In fact, three is three too many."

"You're absolutely right. Three is far too many, but there's not much we can do about that now. I'll check here at the hospital, I'll ask my friend Dorothy if you like, but I'm sure I've never heard of anybody sending one back."

"I'm serious, Francesca. I'm deadly serious this time. Don't think you can slip another one in without me noticing."

This really was not the moment to spring a fresh pregnancy on him.

"Which one did I slip in without you noticing?"

But he'd hung up.

Dorothy discovered me snivelling into the top sheet of my hospital bed and gently dried my tears with the cuff of her white coat.

"Are these the tears of Narcissus? That scar will heal in no time and you'll not even be able to see it."

"It's not my nose, Dorothy."

Dorothy sighed and sat lightly on the edge of my bed. "Then it must be trouble in paradise. Is Will not pleased about the new baby?"

"How do you know I'm pregnant? Have you been snooping in my wash-bag and found the pregnancy test?"

"What wash-bag? I don't need a pregnancy testing kit to know you're expecting. Apart from the fact that I've presided over your previous three pregnancies, God told me a couple of days ago."

"So you knew before I did."

Once I was dressed and ready to leave the hospital Dorothy arrived at my bedside with a wheelchair.

"Jump in. I'll wheel you down to my consulting rooms and book you into the Obs and Gynae folder."

"Thanks but I can walk, you know."

Dorothy pulled a face. "Don't be so independent and ungrateful. I nearly had to fight the porter to get this wheelchair for you."

I sat in the wheelchair and she pushed me to her consulting rooms.

"So this time you managed to get pregnant while breastfeeding. What are you going to try next?"

"I'm going to try to get pregnant without having sex."

"It's my understanding that has been done only once before."

We trotted briskly through the formalities. She took my blood pressure, took blood, palpated my abdomen.

"Unfortunately the scanning machine is at the Mission Clinic in Mahalapye. I can't really give you an accurate due date without it."

"Would it help if I told you the exact date conception occurred?"

"It certainly would."

"It was Will's birthday bonk. That was his birthday present. No condom."

Dorothy did the sums. "You've not told Will you're pregnant again, have you?"

I shook my head.

"Well, I wouldn't tell him just yet. From your dates, this baby isn't due until Christmas, and if your previous three pregnancies are anything to go by it'll be at least another couple of months before you show. Wean Isobel,

93

let your face heal, enjoy some recreational sex with your husband. Then act just as surprised as him when the bump appears."

"He'll be furious."

"Furious that you're pregnant or furious that you didn't tell him?"

"Both," I said but I could see her point. It's very tedious being married to a celibate husband and after three sex-free pregnancies in three years I'd reached the unhappy conclusion that there is no technique that can get a man into bed with you if he doesn't want to be there. It was fair to say that once Will discovered we were going to have another baby he would immediately begin to stay much later at work in the evenings, and would adopt the expression of a hunted animal when our paths did cross.

"A happy marriage is a fragile flower," said Dorothy and if it hadn't been sensible, pragmatic Dorothy speaking I'd have said she sounded distinctly wistful. "It needs good luck as well as good management to make it grow strong. Why don't you book a table for two at Swiss Chalet? I'll baby-sit if you like. I'm sure I can get Isobel to take a bottle from me if you keep her away from the breast all afternoon."

"That's very kind of you. Thank you."

"Will might be cross for a little while when he realises you've been holding out on the pregnancy news. But you've got the rest of your lives ahead of you for him to forgive you."

I came home from the hospital to chaos. The running water was still switched off, the dishes were still piled high in the sink and Hugh's hair was still caked with spaghetti bolognese.

Bending over made my nose bleed so I got down on my knees on the filthy tiles to kiss the children.

"Don't touch my face. Mummy has a sore nose. Kiss my hand instead."

Once my hand had been smothered in sticky kisses, Ella announced, "Daddy put Isobel to bed and he didn't change her nappy."

And Hugh who could hardly talk said clearly, "Stupid Daddy!"

"And he didn't give her a bobo, so I gave her my bobo and she drank it."

"With long-life milk in it, Ella?"

Ella nodded solemnly. "Yes, Mummy. She was crying and crying so I climbed into the cot and held it in her mouth and she drank it."

"What was Daddy doing when you were in the baby's cot?"

"Stupid Daddy was crying in the kitchen."

"Stupid Daddy!" Hugh chorused.

"Where is lovely, kind Daddy?" I carefully emphasised the adjectives 'lovely' and 'kind', and they pointed together to lovely, kind Daddy who was slumped, defeated, in front of *BBC World* with a beer in his hand. He couldn't even get off the sofa to greet me.

"I'm back from the hospital, Will."

In fact he could barely raise his head. But at least he didn't throw a naked Barbie.

Chapter Nine

The next morning Estelle drove up in a cloud of dust. Engine still running, she stuck her immaculately made-up face out of the open window of her battered bakkie and hollered, "Cooee, Francesca, *howzit?*"

It was seven o'clock. Will had just left to take Ella to nursery school – Ella had sat briefly on the potty before leaving but had preferred – inexplicably – to run into her bedroom and poo on the carpet. Hugh had run after her and stepped in it. Will, running after both of them, tried to sweep Hugh up to safety and the poo had fallen off Hugh's foot and smeared over Will's short shorts. Then Ella ran into the kitchen to Violet and said, "I've just done a poo in my bedroom and Mummy said 'Let's leave it for Violet to clean up'!"

Just another day in Africa.

I had not yet washed my face nor changed out of the

Mile High T-shirt I slept in. Hugh was still caked in last night's spaghetti bolognese. Isobel, who had been awake since five, was overtired and screeching with exhaustion from her cot.

I called to Estelle from the security door. "Park your bakkie under the jacaranda tree and come in for a cup of tea."

Violet, washing dishes in the kitchen, immediately stiffened and rolled her eyes.

"How many are there, madam?" she whispered, as Estelle, bearing a casserole dish and a homemade milk tart, tiptoed through the dirt yard towards me in her preposterous platform sandals. Behind her trotted a small boy with bare feet, a shaven head, and a stick of biltong clutched in his sturdy fist.

"Only Peter," I whispered back. "Everyone else is at school."

As Estelle and Peter approached the bungalow there was a heated clickety-clack of Afrikaans between them. Solemnly Peter handed me his part-chewed biltong, dropped his short trousers and, modestly turning away from us, peed into the jasmine bush which grows round our front door.

"Bravo!" cheered Estelle. "I told him that the rule is he gets a Smartie if he pees in the garden and a smack if he pees in the house." She shrugged her sequinned shoulders. "It has worked with the rest of the boys – it will work this time too."

She kissed me fleetingly on the side of my face with no bandages and pushed past me into the kitchen where

Violet was standing to attention waiting for her. Looking mutinous. For there was no love lost between my maid and Estelle.

Once, Estelle had brought all six of her sons to visit, and only three nannies to control them and it got ugly. The three nannies were so preoccupied with the three youngest boys – pushing them on the tyre swing, giving them drinks of water and carrying them backwards and forwards on broad African backs – and Estelle was so busy drinking bush tea and sharing church gossip ("Poor Bruce, he works so hard, we hardly ever see him any more") that the older boys ran wild, bouncing on the beds, swinging from the curtains and, as a grand finale, drenching Violet with the garden hose. Violet grabbed the boy with the hose and as they wrestled he bit her. Violet then put him over her knee and spanked him. He went crying to Estelle who insisted I have Violet flogged and sacked. Violet insisted Estelle leave or she would pack her bags and go back to Gweta, her village. I was rescued from the ghastly stand-off by one of the younger boys tripping on the hosepipe, falling and splitting open his head on the sharp edge of the tiled porch. The whole family has not been back since.

"Look, Violet," I said brightly, filling the kettle and putting it on to boil, "kind Estelle has brought us dinner. Is it beef stew, Estelle?"

Estelle nodded.

"Beef stew is your favourite, isn't it, Violet?"

"Yes, madam."

"And a milk tart for after. Milk tart is your favourite, isn't it, Violet?"

"Yes, madam."

"So no cooking today, Violet. No boring fish pie and carrots. Are you pleased?"

"Yes, madam."

Soon Estelle and I were seated on the porch with a pot of tea.

"Thank you for the stew. And for the milk tart. I know it's a tradition to bring food for the mother after she gives birth – I didn't realise it also happened after minor operations."

Estelle checked her big hair in the reflection of the French windows. "No operation on a woman's face is 'minor'. What can I do to help you? Will I host the playgroup at my house tomorrow afternoon?"

"Yes, please, Estelle," because the playgroup took a week to prepare for and a month to recover from.

Last time I'd made a lasagne, a quiche, smoked chicken and mayonnaise sandwiches, Fifteens, toffee shortbread, and a chocolate roulade (which didn't roll but tasted delicious).

"It's not enough," said Violet pessimistically.

I took her advice and baked a dozen potatoes.

"In Ireland we eat potatoes with lasagne . . ."

I'd also made five batches of play dough in five different colours for the children.

One child ate the play dough and vomited over his mummy. Ella brought her potty into the middle of the living room, and gave the poo performance of her life: "Come and hold my hand, Mummy. It's a really big poo!" Hugh, showing off, tried to climb a tree in the garden by climbing first onto his black motorbike, then on to Peter de Villiers' shoulders, then swinging like a monkey up onto the first branch, then falling like a stone onto concrete.

"Hugh's dead. Hugh's dead!" screamed Peter de Villiers.

I dashed to pick up my limp, lifeless son. As I ran past a fluffy blonde sucking her thumb she blew over onto the tiled floor. Peter immediately grabbed a plastic rolling pin from the play-dough table and battered her so violently round the head I had to produce a bag of frozen peas to numb the pain while Violet fed Hugh large spoonfuls of white sugar (for shock, she said).

"I never realised play dough could be so dangerous!" said Estelle brightly when the playgroup had gone home and she was helping me tidy up.

This morning Peter de Villiers was racing Hugh's black plastic motorbike round the pumpkin patch while Hugh stumbled behind him, sobbing, "Mine! Mine!"

I grabbed my son and hugged him.

"Hugh, listen to me. Peter is our guest. He's also your friend! You must share your motorbike with him. Go and ride Ella's motorbike. It's exactly the same as yours."

"Mine!" screeched Hugh, pointing at Peter. Snot and tears trickled down his face.

Estelle stood up. "Give me two minutes. Where's Ella's motorbike?"

She fetched Ella's bike and barked an order in Afrikaans at Peter. Peter dropped Hugh's bike, meekly took Ella's bike and rode away on it.

Estelle flicked some dust from her white jeans. "Kids!" Then she leant forward and whispered loudly, "Have you heard about Shirley?"

"Shirley Smith, the dentist?"

Estelle nodded. "Shirley with the big breasts. She has a lover. And he's married!"

Peter quickly tired of the black plastic motorbike as soon as Hugh got a bike to join in. Suddenly he appeared at his mother's side and announced, "Tit, tit, Mamma!"

Estelle lifted him onto her knee and plugged him on to her breast.

"Walls have ears," she mouthed quietly. "I will tell you when he finishes."

While Peter enjoyed his mid-morning tit-tit I rescued Isobel from the cot. She stroked my breast lovingly as she nursed. The bottle of long-life milk that Ella had so efficiently fed her the night before seemed to have done her no harm. Perhaps, under supervision, we could try to repeat the performance this evening? And heh, before we knew it Isobel would be effortlessly weaned.

After a couple more sucks Peter slipped down from his mother's knee and ran off towards the tyre swing, wiping his mouth with the back of his hand.

"Please tell me some more about Shirley Smith's lover."

"You know we're from the same town in Zim?"

I nodded. "Plumtree?"

"Shirley went home to Plumtree last weekend to put her mother in a retirement village and she told her mother who told my mother, who told me."

"She told her mother he was married?"

"That Shirley has no shame! She was always stealing boyfriends when we were growing up in Plumtree. Those big breasts – hard to miss, wouldn't you agree? She told her mother this one is married with children and he hates his family and cannot bear to live with them a minute longer and he's going to leave them and live with her."

"Shirley must have a very broadminded mother."

"That Shirley already has a reputation in Botswana as a marriage-wrecker," said Estelle in disgust. "You ask your friend Dorothy."

At this exciting moment Will's bakkie suddenly pulled up in our yard and Will jumped out, dragging Ella behind him. Ella's Barbie pyjamas were filthy, and she was screeching at the top of her voice.

"Will! What happened?"

"She peed all over herself again," said Will in a fury. "In my bakkie on the way to nursery school. And when I got her there and got her out she sat down in the dust and wouldn't move. When Aunty Jean tried to persuade her to get up and come into the classroom to get changed she spat at her!"

Estelle jumped up and said brightly, "Peter and I must go home and make Bruce some *koeksesters*. Poor Bruce, he works so hard, we hardly ever see him any more."

She gathered up Peter and bolted for her bakkie. Revving it up in her platform sandals she left the yard in a shower of red dust, Peter bouncing hugely in the front seat beside her.

"Please calm down, Will. Ella only peed on herself. She's only two and a half. It's not the end of the world."

I suppose he might have calmed down, and seen the funny side except Ella had by this time run over to me and buried her head in my T-shirt and started howling, "Bobo, I want bobo! Bobo is my best friend, Mummy!", Hugh had climbed up the back of the porch chair and started screeching "Stupid Daddy!" and I suppose with Isobel on my knee it looked for all the world as if we were ganging up against him.

Will pointed at Isobel, half hidden under the Mile High T-shirt. His face was a strange colour – bright red and deathly white at the same time.

"How many times have I asked you to stop breast-feeding her?"

"Will –"

He turned on his heel, climbed back into the bakkie and drove off in a shower of hot red dust.

Once he was out of sight Ella stopped howling and lifted her head out of my lap.

"I'm big trouble. Daddy says I'm big trouble."

"You and me both, darling."

Then Camilla phoned. "What are you doing tomorrow morning?"

"Much the same as today. Lurching from one crisis to another."

"Oh, what a bore for you! Listen, darling, I thought I might pop over and see you. I'm catching a flight out of London Heathrow tonight, and I'm booked on the Express up to Botswana tomorrow morning. Can you pick me up at the airport at eleven?"

When Will came home from work all the children had been

bathed and fed and were in bed sleeping. I had even bathed myself. Violet had lit a fire before she went home and our living room was cosy and tidy and child-free for a change.

The new Mashoud carpet was rolled out under a charming three-piece suite with elaborately carved legs and wicker on the back and arms, recently re-upholstered in soft gold chenille. I'd found the suite hiding at the back of the Rhodesian teak warehouse when I was pregnant with Isobel – it had been brought from Zimbabwe tied onto the back of a bakkie, left in for refurbishment and never collected.

"Colonial furniture! I have to have it!"

On the mantelpiece above the fire was a row of beaten scrap-metal photograph frames, some elaborately shaped like animals, some elegant, understated and unadorned. On the walls hung my collection of Botswana baskets.

The floor was swept, the toys were tidied away and the monster Rhodesian teak dining table, bought when I was pregnant with Ella, was set for two.

"We've even got real food this evening. Estelle brought a beef casserole. It's heating up in the oven."

"I'm in a hurry, Francesca. I have to pack. Let's eat dinner right away."

I watched him gobble his dinner in silence. Last night, after I'd come home from the hospital and put the children to bed, we'd sat down together on the gold sofa and first he'd poked at the wax in my ear, then he'd told me there was a bristle on my chin, then he'd run his hands repeatedly through my thin hair and asked me how much money I was spending . . .

I followed him to our bedroom and watched him stuff a sports bag with socks, soap and a toothbrush. Laid out neatly on the top of the bed was a folded pair of flannels, a shirt and a rugby-club tie.

"Where did you get those?"

"Don't you remember these long trousers? I used to wear them when I met you in your Crew Hotel in Oman. The first time I came to see you the doorman wouldn't let me in wearing shorts."

"Where are you going with them?"

He looked a bit shamefaced. I began to feel frightened.

"I have to go away tonight on business. I know it's a bad timing, but it's always bad timing with us, isn't it? There are some problems with the hospital contract. I have to go to Jo'burg to sort them out. I don't know how long I'll be away, maybe a week . . ."

I sat down on the edge of the bed.

"But Dorothy said she'd baby-sit. So we can go out for dinner together."

"Sorry," said Will. "I'm sorry, Francesca."

I was pregnant, I was breastfeeding, I was ministering daily to the demands of three very small children, my physical confidence level was at an all-time low . . .

He was leaving me.

"'*You've picked a fine time to leave me, Lucille*'," I said.

"I'm not leaving you. I'm going to Jo'burg on business. It's an emergency. I have a meeting first thing tomorrow morning. I'm flying down on the Express at ten o'clock tonight. I'll drive myself to the airport and leave the bakkie there until I come back."

He kissed me fleetingly on the side of my face with no bandages.

"Your stitches will be out by the time I get back," he said.

And he zipped up his bag and away he went.

Chapter Ten

I took all three children to the airport to meet Camilla's flight and just at that moment all three were playing nicely together. Each child had a naked Barbie. Isobel was sitting at my feet on the Arrivals floor chewing Barbie, Ella and Hugh were sitting beside her breastfeeding Barbie. People stopped to point and smile at the charming cluster of red heads, mine and the three children. Such a scene of domestic harmony was too unnatural to last. Hugh snatched Isobel's Barbie and Isobel began to screech, Ella started bashing Hugh and Hugh began to screech, I scolded Ella for unwarranted and unprovoked violence and she began to screech. In the space of thirty seconds the domestic harmony had subsided into screeching. I felt like screeching myself.

This was when Camilla burst through Customs.

"You look terrible," said Camilla. "Are you ill?"

I stared at my twin in astonishment. This was not the greeting I had expected.

"I've just had a basal cell carcinoma taken off my nose. It's been a stressful couple of days."

"It's not the nose. Well, not *just* the nose. You're so thin. I'm afraid to hug you, in case I break you."

"Hug me anyway. The kids are always climbing over me and bits haven't broken off yet. I don't think I've lost very much weight. My ghastly clothes still fit."

"They are ghastly. But you look so fragile. You need a *Handle With Care* sign on your back. And your lovely hair, it's quite faded and –"

I sighed. "You don't have to say it. You're right. Some if it has fallen out. Apparently that's quite common when you're breastfeeding."

"Please don't tell me Isobel is still on the breast!"

Ella and Hugh and Isobel stared in awe at Camilla – at her shiny, bouncy, strawberry-blonde hair, at the pale pink pashmina thrown casually round her aerobically toned body, at the rings on her French-manicured fingers and the bells on her pretty sandals. They'd never seen anything quite so eye-catching before. Not even Estelle de Villiers, with her big hair and sequins. They stopped screeching and began to crowd round.

Ella, who's very tactile, stroked the beautiful shawl with grubby fingers. "Soft, like my teddy bear."

Camilla smiled. "Your mummy brought me this back from New Delhi when she was a captain in command of an aircraft, a crew and two hundred passengers." She turned on me. "I suppose that seems like a lifetime ago."

Meanwhile Hugh was rubbing his face against the pashmina, leaving a snail trail of dust and snotters. "Soft, like Blankie."

"Blankie?"

"His blanket that he sleeps with."

Isobel had started to chew on Camilla's pretty matching leather luggage.

"Let's go," I said quickly before she noticed. I lifted Isobel into her back-carrier, secured her and hoisted her onto my back. I had tried to copy Violet at the start and tie the babies onto my back with a thin towel but it was never a success. As Violet had kindly remarked, my bum simply wasn't big enough to support the weight of a baby sitting on top of it. The white African compromise was a back-carrier – Game always had a supply of them for new mothers.

"Kids, put on your sunhats. Aunt Camilla will hold Ella's hand and Hugh's hand. Give Aunt Camilla your hand, Hugh. Hugh, put on your sunhat."

I led the way out of Arrivals into the blinding midday sun.

"Hat, Hugh!" I shouted. "I've got eyes in the back of my head, Hugh."

Camilla adjusted her expensive designer sunglasses and watched while I threw the children into their car seats in the back of the Range Rover. There was the usual battle with Hugh who likes to kick at me as he's being strapped in.

"Stop it, Hugh. Stop kicking. Hugh, I said 'stop kicking' or I'm going to have to tie your legs together."

Camilla watched in silence until I had the straps fastened. Then she climbed up into the passenger seat and said, "You do realise that you say everything to him at least twice? 'Put on your hat, Hugh. Put on your hat, Hugh. Hugh, I said put on your hat!'."

I poured milk out of a camping thermos into three bottles and screwed the teats back on.

"Pass these back for me. One each. And give Ella the pink teddy, Hugh the blue Blankie and Isobel that grubby T-shirt that says *Mile High Club* on it."

"She uses your T-shirt as a comforter?"

I started the engine. "I wore it in bed last night. She likes to smell breast-milk off it."

Within five minutes, as we drove along the straight road away from the airport all three children were asleep. Finally I had time to inspect my sister properly. She was beautiful, of course, and expensive and polished and perfectly groomed. The fairy godmother who attended our joint baptism and granted me the ability to breed like a rabbit had bestowed on Camilla every other gift she could think of including brains, sex appeal and plenty of money. And to Camilla's credit she'd used every one of the gifts to her best advantage. We were identical twins yet she looked ten years younger than me. She had a good job, a good husband and a good-sized bank balance. She could drop all and fly to the other side of the world to visit her sister when she felt like it. Lucky Camilla.

Yet there was an air of melancholy shrouding my sister. A strained listlessness. A lack of animation in her beautiful face. She'd worn the same look previously as her first two marriages began to fail. Could she be tired of James Snotter already?

"Phone James and tell him you've arrived safely," I

suggested when we were home again and her luggage was unloaded from the Range Rover. "Phone now before the kids wake up. They love to shout into the bedroom extension when I'm on the phone."

Camilla shrugged.

"James is at work," she said casually. "I'll leave it. Maybe later."

I know it was a really stupid thing to do, but once Camilla was in the shower I phoned Shirley Smith's dental surgery.

"I want to make an appointment with Dr Shirley Smith. Does she have any slots free?"

"I'm sorry, madam. Dr Smith has gone to Jo'burg for a dental conference. She won't be back until Monday. Is it an emergency? Would you like me to check Dr Mandela's appointment schedule?"

"No, thank you, I can wait until Monday. The pain isn't so bad."

Camilla's impromptu visit did not start well. First there was a problem with the milk.

"Don't you have fresh milk?" she asked when I made her a cup of tea.

"No fresh milk. And no bacon either. There's been Foot and Mouth Disease in the Transvaal for months. We have to drink long-life milk. You get used to it."

Camilla screwed up her nose. "Unlikely," she said after the first sip.

Then there was the problem with the stray dog across the street. She threw a stone at it.

"Why did you do that?" I said, for I fed the dog when Violet wasn't watching. "He wasn't hurting you."

"He was barking."

Then she shouted at the bright little beggar boy at Village Spar who asked me for money every time he saw me.

"But he's saving up to buy a kombi. He wants to have a taxi service when he grows up. I think it's good to encourage his ambition."

Then she had a tantrum in the post office when the lady behind the counter kept us and ten others ahead of us standing waiting while she drank her tea and chatted to her friend on her cellphone. "Aiee!" exclaimed the post lady at Camilla's foot-stamping and head-tossing and pointing and bad language. But it didn't make her serve us faster.

"Where do you get your patience from?" Camilla chided me when we finally got back out of the post office and into the Range Rover.

"Welcome to Africa."

But then she went too far. To my shame she shouted at Violet for boil-washing her pashmina and shrinking it to the size of a headscarf.

"You'll have to apologise for shouting at her. If you don't apologise, Violet will pack her bags and go back to Gweta, and you'll have to do all your own washing and ironing while you're here."

"I'm sure there's something the matter with her," I confided in Margaret when we went for a swim at the British Consul swimming-pool which was heated in winter. It's very grand at the British Consul.

"Why does there have to be anything wrong with her?

114

Because she stoned a stray dog? Because she scolded an irritating urchin? Because she threw a wobbly in the post office? I've done all those things myself on occasion. And I don't like the taste of long-life milk."

"She shouldn't have shouted at Violet."

"I think she showed remarkable restraint with Violet. I might have wrung Violet's neck if she'd boil-washed my pashmina."

"But it's only a shawl, and she has six more like it at home."

"Six? Really?" Margaret looked at Camilla, breaststroking in the swimming pool, with new respect. "All different colours? One for every outfit? Where did she get them?"

"I got them for her in New Delhi when I was flying."

"Lucky Camilla. I wish I had a sister like you."

"Violet says she saw her crying down behind the washing line this morning. Camilla never cries in private. Only crocodile tears in public to get attention. She must be really unhappy."

"Maybe she stood on a thorn," Margaret suggested briskly, "in those stupid flip-flop things she insists on wearing. She knew to bring boots, didn't she?"

"Of course, she knew. She's been here before. But she says she'll get a really silly-looking suntan if she wears boots. Her legs will be brown and her feet will still be white."

"She'll look even sillier if a snake bites her, or a scorpion stings her and they have to amputate her leg," said Margaret unsympathetically.

Margaret did not succeed in convincing me that my sister's uncharacteristic outbursts of bad temper were acceptable

115

in challenging circumstances. The baptism fairy who'd given her brains, sex appeal and plenty of money had also bestowed on Camilla beautiful manners and these had been evident all of her life.

"Yes, yes, of course I'll marry you, Adam. How sweet of you to ask," followed three years later by "I'm so sorry to be a bore, Adam. I feel terrible about this. Please give me a divorce and I'll never bully you again."

There had to be something seriously wrong if Camilla was cranky.

My children were the only people who did not receive the sharp end of Camilla's tongue.

Camilla was not known for her love of children but she spoiled and adored Ella and Hugh and Isobel even though they never stopped demanding things from her, especially Ella. "Come and wipe my bum, Aunty Cam," Ella serenaded her. "I've done a poo," and Aunty Cam rushed to administer assistance.

"Bobo, Aunty Cam," and it was filled up without a murmur of protest.

"Swing, Aunty Cam," and she pushed Hugh backwards and forwards in the tyre swing for so long he actually dozed off in it.

She was wonderful with them. Nothing was too much bother. The only thing she wouldn't do was rise with them at half past five in the morning when they woke up.

"Half past five is the middle of the night! You must be exhausted! No wonder you look so awful!"

"It's not that bad. You get used to it."

"You get used to it the way the soldiers got used to the trenches during the First World War!"

"I know they wake up early but they also go to bed early. It means Will and I have some time alone together when he comes home from work in the evening."

"Have you tried black-out curtains?"

"Of course. We hang big blankets in front of the bedroom windows, but it doesn't make a bit of difference. The tiniest chink of light wakes them. Or the faintest noise. The stray dog barking across the street, a rooster crowing, a car horn, Isobel whimpering to be fed."

"So you get up with them at half past five. Then what?"

"I bath them. I dress them. I fill their bottles with milk. I feed them toast and Weetabix. Then I make Will a cup of tea and he gets up at half past six and I get back into bed and breastfeed Isobel."

"Is there any reason why Will can't get up with them at half past five? And then make *you* a cup of tea? Or has he conveniently forgotten the magnificent speech he made the night before your wedding when he said he wouldn't marry you if you were going to end up pregnant, barefoot and chained to the kitchen sink?"

"I'm hardly that."

"Well, if I wake up even five minutes before eight o'clock," Camilla threatened, "I'm like a bear with a sore head all day afterwards."

So I got up with the children at half past five and kept them away from Aunty Cam's bedroom. We washed and dressed quietly in front of the gas ring in the kitchen. The children had breakfast, I loaded them into the Range Rover and we all took Ella to nursery school together. (And Ella did not pee on herself, she did not cry, she did not spit at Aunty Jean, and she most certainly did not wear her Barbie pyjamas.) On the way home we stopped at Village Spar for fresh bread, and Crotone butchers for fresh meat, and we were back in Tlokweng before Aunty Cam emerged, dazed and still half-asleep, from her bed at eight o'clock.

"I've always heard," I teased her, "that the more sleep you get, the more sleep you want."

Some people have a talent for asking intimate questions and finding confidential answers.

Mummy has a gift for it. As a child I watched her in admiration and amazement at church socials. She'd choose her victim and sit down beside him with a plate of Fifteens and toffee shortbread. There would be some banal conversation about the weather and the ploughing and then suddenly his life story would come cascading out and problems he may never have consciously realised he possessed would be aired and shared with my mother.

"Why do you always pick men, Mummy?"

"Two reasons. Many men live lives of quiet desperation – they think that nobody cares. Then the minister's wife sits down beside them and we start to chat and, frankly, they think God has sent me to help them."

"What's the other reason?"

"I'd never get chatted up otherwise . . ."

Mummy was such a success as unofficial philosopher and friend at church socials that once she had Camilla and me reared she went back to school and studied to become a professional counsellor. Now she has an office in one of the draughty manse bedrooms and her clients have to approach her and make appointments and pay. She emails Daddy when she wants a cup of tea.

'Meet u in the kitchen in 5. Put the kettle on' and he emails her back *'Do u think it'll suit me?'*

I do not have my mother's talent for benign inquisitiveness. All I could do was set the scene and hope my sister's problems would come flooding out.

"I've booked a table for us at Swiss Chalet. Dorothy says she'll baby-sit. Would you like to come out with me?"

"Only if you allow me to dress you."

"I don't look that bad, do I?"

"Yes, you do. Have you have any idea how *faded* you look, Francesca? "

What fun it was getting dressed up to go out with Camilla! For, naturally, the baptism fairy had also bestowed on her an impeccable taste in clothes.

"Gosh, you look fantastic!" I said. "And that outfit couldn't be simpler. It's only black trousers and a black polo neck."

"This outfit is deceptive in its simplicity – this polo neck cost a fortune."

"Will says I look like a spider when I wear black. Especially when I paint my eyes with black eyeliner and mascara."

"I notice you don't paint them any more."

"I had to stop when Ella was a small baby. My nipples hurt so much it brought tears to my eyes every time she latched on to nurse. The mascara and eyeliner usually ended up smeared in rivers down my face. I look like Ozzy Osbourne in all of Ella's baby photographs."

Camilla held up a delicious, green, bias-cut, devoré dress. "Try this."

I wriggled into the dress. "Don't wash this when you're here. It'll get ruined . . ."

The dress fitted like a glove but barely covered my knees.

"What a pity! It's too short on me."

Camilla was delighted. "You're such an old granny! You lived in the Middle East for far too long, covered head to toe in a shapeless kaftan. Everywhere else in the world the shoulder and the knee cap are *not* considered sinful parts of the body."

She offered me a pair of knee-high crushed velvet boots.

"I bought these to go with the dress. What do you think?"

I added a beautiful fine-spun, ruffled, woollen green cardigan from her luggage.

"African winter evenings are freezing. I'll get frostbite if our table isn't in front of the fire."

"Put on that double strand of pearls, and the pearl studs to match."

"Your good ones? That James Snotter bought you for your wedding present?"

Finally I was dressed.

"Excellent! I knew that outfit would suit you better than it suits me. There's an old-fashioned, timeless thing

120

about your face. It suits the simplicity of a strand of pearls. Pearls do nothing for me – I suit only the cold glitter of diamonds . . ." She picked up two thin limp locks of my hair. "I'm afraid there's not much we can do about your hair. You've obviously stopped using hair conditioner! The kindest thing would probably be to shave it all off and start again."

"That's rather drastic . . ."

"Let's use some mousse to thicken it up a bit and then pull it up into a chignon – I'll pull my hair back too . . ."

Finally we were ready. Camilla inspected me dispassionately. "That colour is great on you. It's a pity you don't have a full-length mirror to admire yourself. "

Ella was very impressed. She'd never seen her mother looking like a woman before. "Cinderella!"

Camilla agreed. "Your mummy is just like Cinderella. It's a pity Prince Charming isn't here to see you. Tonight you look almost like the girl he married."

"As good as that? Let's stop in Game, on the way to Swiss Chalet, so I can admire myself in a full-length mirror!"

"Let's stop in Game," said Camilla, "and *buy* a full-length mirror."

When Dorothy arrived and found my twin and me dolled up to the nines she said, "It's really quite amazing how identical you are now you're wearing the same quality of clothes, and your hair is pulled back. Amazing too that your figures are so similar when Francesca is three months pregnant. Are you pregnant too, Camilla?"

I looked at my twin in surprise. Could she be pregnant? It would certainly explain her curious mood swings . . .

Two tears sprang into Camilla's eyes. "Ten out of ten for observation, Dorothy."

Dorothy smiled. "Where's Will?"

"He's having a sleepover in Jo'burg," said Ella. "Without Mummy."

Chapter Eleven

When we got to Swiss Chalet I ordered a bottle of wine. A South African red called Kanonkopt.

Camilla's eyebrows shot up in surprise because all my life alcohol has made me vomit. Our pious parents kept no drink in the house when we were growing up so I never realised the full extent of the problem until I escaped away from them to university. Then my best efforts to fit in with everybody else had to be abandoned since a night out with my classmates always ended with my head down somebody's toilet, throwing up.

"Don't tell me you're cured of your allergy to alcohol?"

"I wish," I said ruefully. "But there's no point you visiting next door to one of the best wine-producing countries in the world if you can't get a drink of it." I pointed to the label. "According to my South African contact, Pastor Bruce, this is the best they've got."

She took a long, slow swallow. "He's the pastor? I think Adam Robinson and I might have lasted a bit longer if he'd not been so pious about drink. He said drinking alcohol would 'compromise his witness in the community'. And do you remember the scene he made about the Bible readings at our wedding? I wanted the one about Jesus turning the water into wine at a wedding reception, but Adam thought it would be 'inappropriate' so we had the one about love suffering long instead. How prophetic."

"Chronicle of a divorce foretold?"

"Never marry a man with high principles. They're fiendishly difficult to live with." She smiled at me and took another luxurious swallow. "I mean, *you* don't drink but you don't punish the rest of us, do you?"

"My abstinence is absolutely no fun at all. For the past twenty years I've always felt bored and left out at dinner parties after a certain time of the evening when everyone else is well oiled and laughing at their own unfunny jokes. However, the alternative is just as awful. Remember what happened when I had a glass of champagne on my wedding day?"

(The glass of champagne in the car that took us from the church to Lisglasson Lodge for our DIY wedding reception had seemed like such a romantic thing to do at the time. Less than ten minutes later, as the beautiful car swept through the gates and up to the house, I'd had to stick my head out of its window and vomit up the champagne in front of our guests.)

Finally Camilla was so far down the bottle she stopped complaining about the slowness of the service.

The steak arrived and I risked asking her, "Why did you come to Botswana, Camilla? Did you have a row with James?"

Camilla needed no encouragement at all to tell me – it all came flooding out . . .

"I can't talk to you when you're like this," said James Snotter in his pompous voice.

Camilla bit her lip. "Like what, James?"

James refused to look at his flushed, unhappy wife in her black bra, her stockings and suspenders and her black high heels. 'Dressing up' had been his idea. "My birthday present," he'd told her. It would make a change from a big feed in a suit and tie at The Rainbow's End. And some greasy fumbling and constipated heavy breathing under the covers with the lights out afterwards.

But he'd probably meant she should dress up in a nice frock for a pleasant meal together.

He'd come home from work to find Camilla in thin, sheer black chiffon. Silently smiling she'd led him into a living room filled with flickering candlelight, a roaring log fire, and music he didn't know the name of. Eyes bright with mischief she'd handed him a glass.

"Drink," she'd instructed and as he drank (he'd never drunk anything which tasted like that before) she began undressing him, gyrating slowly in time to the music.

"Have you been drinking?" he asked her and she'd silenced him with her hot, wet mouth.

Her strong, practised fingers had quickly unbuckled his belt and opened the flies of his flannels. When his trousers were puddled round his ankles and his Y fronts were bulging she'd slithered out of the sheer black chiffon, pushed him gently back on the sofa and climbed on top of him.

Well, he hadn't refused her, naturally he hadn't, he was a man after all and she was his wife, but he felt decidedly uncomfortable about the whole exciting episode. Yes, he accepted that Camilla had been married twice before, but once was to a minister and it was unlikely that she'd learnt those moves with Adam Robinson. It must have been with Sam Dawson. Husband Number Two. A gang member.

James was a member of a caring profession and he did not consciously hate anybody, but at that moment he hated Sam Dawson and the gang so much he could taste it.

"Dirty," he said when they were finally finished, "you're dirty."

Should I stay or should I go? Camilla thought.

And being Camilla she decided to go.

"Let me précis what you've just said. Your husband picked a fight with you because his birthday bonk was too good?"

"Yes."

"And he thinks exciting sex with his wife is dirty?"

"Yes."

"How long are you married?"

"Nearly four years."

"And this is the first time you've had exciting sex with him?"

Camilla started to look a bit shifty. "Where is this leading?"

"What have you both been doing in bed for the past four years?"

Camilla shrugged. "Nothing to boast about."

"That's not like you. Have you filed for another divorce yet? Citing unreasonable behaviour?"

Camilla shook her head. "Not yet. And I know that's not like me either. Ten years ago I'd have been out the door and down the road before you could say 'marriage guidance counselling'. Unfortunately I'm ten years older now. You know what happens to unmarried women of forty, don't you?"

I felt a chill and it had nothing to do with the bitter African evening.

"They either fall in love with God, like your friend Dorothy, or they fall in love with some other woman's husband. And I'm not temperamentally suited to either."

Her confession was cathartic. The calm after the storm. The relief after a painful extraction. Finally she became less self-obsessed and I was able to share my own sorry story with her.

"Do you remember what Aunt Grace predicted at my wedding?"

"About your life changing utterly the Christmas you're forty? I certainly do. It was almost as amusing as watching you vomit up the glass of Bollinger. I only wish we'd had a camcorder."

"Do you think she meant I was going to die?"

"Of course you're not going to die," Camilla told me with confidence. "If Aunt Grace was talking about anybody dying she was talking about herself. She was diagnosed about the time of your wedding. Sam Dawson got the unwelcome task of telling her. 'It's cervical cancer with secondaries in your liver and lungs. I'm afraid it's not looking good, Mrs Walsh.' She didn't bat an eyelid. 'Well, I have no intention of dying until I'm *organised*,' she told him and the stubborn old thing has outlived everyone's expectations."

"I should go home and see her," I said.

Camilla smiled sadly. "Better make it sooner than later. I don't know if she'll last until Christmas. She really is living on borrowed time. And it's not only the hip flask hidden under her pillow that's keeping her going now."

"What do you mean?"

Camilla mimed the rolling and smoking of a joint.

I had to laugh. "Aunt Grace is smoking dope? Where's she getting it? Please don't tell me she's growing it as well!"

Camilla shook her head. "I think Alex Flood is supplying it. He's always visiting her, doing her shopping, cooking for her. I know it's hard to believe when Alex Flood is almost as puritanical as yourself."

"I read," I said thoughtfully, "in the *Weekly Telegraph* recently that some doctors think Ecstasy tablets should be made available to the terminally ill. Whatever mind-altering properties Ecstasy has it can help people to talk about their fears of dying."

"Oh, do cheer up! When she dies you inherit everything. And Lisglasson Lodge is worth a fortune. Forty minutes to Belfast along the motorway and Sir Bobby Flood – Services to Rock Music – as a neighbour. I'm sure it's worth a million pounds."

"I'd rather have Aunt Grace than Lisglasson Lodge," I

128

said, for Aunt Grace had backed me up all my life, and taken my side in every argument, and praised every decision I'd ever made, even when I was wrong.

Hot tears welled up in my eyes and trickled, mascara-stained, down my cheeks. Camilla stopped eating and quietly rummaged in her pretty designer handbag until she found a hankie for me.

"I don't know why I'm crying. I've never been a cry-baby. It must be pregnancy hormones."

It wasn't like me to lose my nerve. I was the pregnant woman who'd breathed deeply and calmly through a hole in the side of my nose while Doctor Dorothy cut away the cancer spreading across my face.

"Your tears might be caused by pregnancy hormones," Camilla agreed, "but it's more likely the fact you're living in the African bush and there are no nice shops for miles. That's enough to make anybody cry . . . even me . . ."

"Tears of self-pity? You? I doubt it. You've always been far more resourceful than me, Camilla. You only cry until you've concocted a cunning plan."

I carefully wiped my nose, dried my tears and ate my steak.

Swiss Chalet twinkled in the firelight. It was a rustic, charming restaurant with a simple polished stone floor, wooden tables and chairs, and a thatched roof. The waiters wore gloves. One came over to fill up Camilla's glass. I waved across the busy room to the Mummy Gang who were making a lot of noise at one of the other tables. Estelle de Villiers was with them – she waved back.

"Is it a fancy dress party?" Camilla inspected the

Mummy Gang with distaste. I could tell from the way her nostrils were flaring that she wasn't impressed.

Once she'd finished eating, Estelle came over to say hello. She was looking particularly striking in a striped shiny shirt with diamante sparkles on the shoulders and a pair of skin-tight silver mock-crocodile jeans. Her eye shadow was all the colours of the rainbow, starting on the inside and working out in order – red, orange, yellow, green, blue, indigo, violet. On any other woman it would've looked as if she'd had a punch on the nose.

"We've been talking about you, Francesca! About how beautiful you look tonight! A creature from a fairytale. Your eyes are so pretty when you paint them with black eyeliner!"

"Thank you, Estelle." She was one of those rare women who are generous with compliments, and genuine.

"Did everything calm down with Will on Tuesday? His face was so funny when he arrived home with Ella and she was covered in pee-pee. I thought he was going to explode! Men get so upset about the silliest things! Bruce was very angry when he found Peter sitting on the toilet to pee.

'A man must stand to pee.'

'But Bruce, chicken,' I said, 'this small boy cannot reach the bowl.'

So Bruce fetches a Bible and a phonebook, and he builds them one on top of the other. Now we have a step in the bathroom and Peter must stand on top of it when he goes pee-pee!"

I could see Camilla eyeing her, thinking she'd been on the drink.

"I suppose Will is at home tonight," Estelle went on,

"hugging and kissing Ella's soft little red head and congratulating himself on having produced such a beautiful child?"

"Will's in Jo'burg," I said. "There's some sort of emergency with the hospital contract. He's having a meeting with the client."

Estelle's rainbow eyes immediately widened in alarm. "I thought the client always came to Botswana for meetings."

"Usually he does –"

"But *Shirley Smith* is in Jo'burg! Bruce met her at the airport – she told him she was going to a dental conference in *Jo'burg!*"

"Estelle, two and two make four, not six!"

Estelle frowned, confused. "English isn't my first language."

When she'd returned to the fancy-dress table Camilla said, "Who is Shirley Smith?"

I hesitated. Fatally. My twin leapt for the kill.

"Have you spoken to Will since he went to Jo'burg?"

I shook my head.

"You live in the African bush. You have three small children. You're pregnant. You've just had cancer surgery. And your husband hasn't phoned you in three *days*?"

Camilla took my phone from my bag and handed it to me. "Phone him."

"I can't," I said feebly. "I'm spineless. I'm sorry."

Camilla began scrolling down through the names. "You're not spineless. You love your husband. That's all that's wrong with you."

She reached Will's name and number. "Shall I call him?"

I nodded. I couldn't speak. I was so nervous I thought I was going to be sick.

Will's phone was switched off. What a relief!

Next morning I heard Camilla coaxing Ella and Hugh into her bed with promises of sweeties and storybooks. I lay on in my own bed, quietly nursing Isobel, listening to my sister reading Ella's favourite fairy tale, *Cinderella*, over and over and over again.

Ella came scampering into my bedroom. "I *love* Aunty Cam. Let's keep Aunty Cam and send Daddy back to the cold country."

Camilla followed Ella into my bedroom.

"Have you spoken to Will yet?"

"It's a bit early."

"*You're* up."

This time Will answered. "Why are you calling me, Francesca?"

"Why have you *not* called me?"

"I've been busy."

"Too busy to call your wife?"

"It's a long story," said Will. Now he sounded cautious. Edgy.

Ella started to tap me on the arm. "Excuse me, Mummy. Excuse me, Mummy," which is her little way of saying 'Hurry up and get off the phone and pay me some attention'. Up the hall, somewhere out of sight so I couldn't see if he was being eaten by a lion or just having a laugh, Hugh started screeching which is his little way of saying 'Hurry up and get off the phone and pay me some attention'.

Background noise. But I still heard it clearly. A woman's voice saying, "Come back to bed, Will, and let me get you a drink."

Before I could say another thing Will hung up on me.

"What am I going to do?"

"Phone him again. Tell him you heard the woman's voice. Ask him who it was. Maybe there's an innocent explanation. Maybe he's visiting his mother"

"His mother lives in Zimbabwe."

"His sister?"

"Dead."

"His ex-wife?"

"He doesn't have an ex-wife. Not that I know of anyway."

"Phone him again."

So I called the number again. And again. And again. A dozen times. But the phone stayed switched off.

"What am I going to do now? What would you do?"

"You could wait for him to come back and explain himself. Or you could you give him a dose of his own medicine. If he was my husband I'd pack my bags and go on a little holiday. I'd not tell him where I am, or who I'm with. Or whether I'm coming back."

"Pack my bags and fly away? Isn't that a bit drastic? What about the children? Should I take them too?"

"I'll mind the children for you," said Camilla gaily. "We'll kill two birds with one stone. I'll stay here and you go back to Ireland with my ticket and passport. You can visit Aunt Grace; you'll catch the end of the summer sales. You could get your hair fixed."

I opened my mouth to say I couldn't possibly leave my children to go back to Ireland to do some shopping and get my hair done. Then I shut it again and said nothing.

Chapter Twelve

Shirley Smith was not one of my professional forty-something friends. I knew her only on a professional basis. We'd first met when Ella was a baby. I was out with the Book Club, my first night out since I became a mother, chewing rare steak in Swiss Chalet. Barbara, whose literary tastes usually favoured practical instruction manuals and veterinary handbooks, had finally found a novel worth reading.

"I can't believe it's a novel; it's so real to my mother's life. She was brought up in the Congo just after the Second World War like the sisters in the book. Her father was a Southern Baptist missionary, just like the father in the book. But she *ate the monkeys*!"

Gosh, how exciting, I thought, I'll just finish chewing this bit of steak, then I'll ask her what book she's talking about.

It was at this point, while Margaret was exclaiming, "She did not eat monkeys, Barbara!" and Dorothy was asking, "Did she eat snake as well? I've heard snake tastes like chicken," that my tooth cracked and broke off. Not a back tooth, of course, that would never be seen, but an eye-tooth at the edge of my smile. I could feel it hanging, jagged. I licked it. It wobbled.

"Are your family still in the Congo?" I asked Barbara and the broken bit rolled out of my mouth and onto the table.

Barbara's answer was lost in the general laughter.

Margaret said, "I see that old wives' tale about a woman losing a tooth every time she has a baby isn't actually an old wives' tale after all," and Barbara, who'd once been a dentist in Zimbabwe before she woke up one morning and realised that she never wanted to look in another human mouth again said, "There's a very good dentist with a surgery at No Matata shopping centre, above Payless Supermarket. I use her. Her name is Shirley Smith."

I don't like dentists. Even before I met Shirley Smith. It's not exactly that I'm afraid of them. A dentist who barks, "Open your eyes when I'm drilling!" to a terrified eight-year-old would probably be struck off as a child abuser nowadays.

I don't like dentists but after five minutes of having a broken tooth my hitherto modest amounts of personal vanity began to exert greater influence than my natural aversion to dentists. If I didn't get it fixed, and fixed quickly, nervous members of the public would faint when I smiled at them. And naughty children would call me names, like 'Jaws', behind my back, perhaps even to my face. And my husband, when he saw it, would refuse point-blank to kiss me in case I left bite marks on his tongue.

So I made an appointment with Shirley Smith and she patched it up and informed me that I needed something major done, root-canal treatment or something, and I made an excuse and wriggled out of the commitment.

"It'll break again," she warned, "if you don't get it fixed properly."

She was right. The eye-tooth continued to break and break and break again every six months, and every six months I went back to Shirley Smith and she patched it up and said, "It'll break again, Mrs Dallas, if you don't get it fixed properly."

"What does she look like?" Camilla asked.

I thought for a moment. "She's hard to describe, because frankly she doesn't look like much. Older than me. Big breasts, short legs, average hair, average make-up . . ." I bit my lip. I was suddenly hopeful. "Maybe I'm wrong. Maybe she's not having an affair with Will. Will has never been attracted to large breasts. And to be brutal, unless you're a breast man, Shirley Smith is rather plain. If my husband wanted to have an affair would he not choose someone younger than his wife and better-looking than his wife to have an affair with?"

"Oh, innocent one!" Camilla said laughing. "You don't really believe that Will did the choosing? He probably never knew what hit him. No man can resist a woman who throws herself at him. Trust Aunty Cam. I was that slapper."

"Camilla!"

"Calm down, Francesca, the Puritan. I've never thrown

myself at a married man. Yet! I just happen to know that there's always an ugly, dumpy little dentist watching from the wings of every marriage. Waiting her chance. And in a quiet little backwater like this, with not much to choose from, I bet any man is better than no man and Will is not the only man she's thrown herself at."

On Monday morning I walked into Shirley Smith's surgery with my head held high. And my knees knocking but that had nothing to do with Shirley Smith or Will.

Shirley looked up from her notes and smiled kindly. "I heard about your nose."

Immediately suspicious, I said, "From whom?"

"You're the talk of Botswana. Doctor Dorothy's surgery is full of white Africans wanting lumps and bumps cut off. You've frightened us all. I had my own skin thoroughly checked when I was in Jo'burg last week."

"You went to Jo'burg to get your skin checked?"

"I go every six months, to the skin cancer clinic at the National Hospital. It's the best in Africa, maybe the best in the world . . ."

And on she chatted while she examined my troublesome eye-tooth. About her father and mother who'd emigrated to Southern Rhodesia from Scotland in the late fifties. Newly married they'd come together on a ship to Capetown, then overland by train to Plumtree.

"Plumtree is only a tiny little place. Everyone knows everyone else. My mother taught in the Boys' School. I went to the Boys' School too. Your husband Will was in my mathematics class. What a wild guy!"

I made a non-threatening, non-committal gurgling sound in the back of my throat, though frankly, I felt like biting her.

"Dad had a cattle farm and the bits and pieces of his fair, freckled Celtic skin that stuck out of the end of his long-sleeved shirts and short shorts and long socks got sunburnt every day in the African sun. By the time he was fifty all those bits and pieces were riddled with skin cancer and the tips of his ears and the end of his nose had been cut off."

Now I made a horrified, guttural sound in the back of my throat.

"It's a gene, you see," Shirley explained. "Skin cancer is caused by a hereditary gene. I've had to become intimate with my moles and they're checked regularly by a specialist dermatologist. I've already had a couple of things burnt off before they got a chance to spread. I've never sunbathed, of course, but there was no Factor 50 in Plumtree when I was growing up." She sighed. There were tears winking in her eyes. "Poor Dad. I'm sure skin cancer was the last thing he thought would kill him when he left Ayrshire for Africa in 1958."

Finally the dental work was finished and I was rinsing my mouth and waiting for her usual line, "It'll break again, Mrs Dallas, if you don't get it fixed properly."

But this time Shirley, with her face buried in her notes, said, "I suppose it was a bit of a shock about Will."

"Will?" I said stupidly. "You mean my husband Will?"

Shirley smiled out of her freckled face. Her eyes were pale blue and the lashes were almost white. She was wearing cheap earrings and there was at least a quarter of an inch of regrowth on the highlights on the top of her head. *Miaow!*

"Yes, Will. Will Dallas. Oh. He hasn't told you yet, has he?"

"Told me what?"

Did she not notice that I was behaving oddly? Or was I always a bit weak at the knees when I went to the dentist?

Shirley said, "Poor Will. It's so difficult for him. We talked about it yesterday. I guess he'll tell you face to face when he gets home. It's not really the sort of thing you can discuss over the telephone, is it?"

I should have bitten her when I got the chance.

What a lot of things had to be organised before I left Botswana. First I had to be sure my sister knew exactly what she was letting herself in for.

"Come, Camilla, I have to show you something."

I led her to the front door and pointed to the button above it.

"This is the panic button."

"What do I need a panic button for?"

"I'm not saying that it's ever going to happen, but if you just happen to open the front door some evening and discover an armed gang standing there and they point a gun at you and shout, 'Hands up!', put your hands up and hit the panic button. It lets off a hell of a racket. It might frighten them away. If not, the yellow security van should be with you in four minutes."

"You're not serious."

"There have been a series of armed robberies recently. The same gang. The same *modus operandi*. Like a Sherlock Holmes mystery – *The Mysterious Case of the Teatime Robberies*. They burst in. They frighten you. You give them whatever they ask for, they lock you in a bedroom, they escape. And it always happens about six o'clock."

"Why?"

"I don't know, and I'd advise you not to waste time asking if they do arrive. The popular theory is that if they do the robbery at teatime they've time to sell on the stolen goods before they catch the night bus back to Zim. And the police have no time to trace them."

"The robbers are Zimbabwean?"

"They're starving, Camilla. They're desperate. Don't fight with them."

Then I gave her my bum bag. "Forget your fancy handbag. This bum bag has enough room in it for a purse, keys and your cellphone. I know you'll look really unsophisticated but bag-snatching is an opportunistic crime and you're the perfect victim if you're preoccupied with children."

"Please don't tell me any more scare stories. You're making me nervous."

"Then don't put yourself in a vulnerable position. Use the bum bag while you're here, lock up everything and don't wear jewellery when you're out."

I was surprised and rather curious to see her so shaken. Camilla was a world traveller; her suitcases were covered in stickers. The burglar bars on my kitchen window were crammed with her postcards.

Camilla seemed to read my mind. "My jet-setting is a

fashion statement, not a lifestyle choice. And I always stay in Five Star Hotels."

Once the security arrangements were sorted out it was time to concentrate on the children.

"I don't know," I faltered weakly. "They're so small. I'm going to miss them so much."

"You're going to miss them the way you miss toothache." Camilla was brutal. "Make a list of the most important things I have to know. Violet can fill me in on the rest. And if it's a real emergency, I'll phone you."

"Don't do that," I said anxiously, for I have absolutely no sense of humour when it comes to my offspring.

"I'm joking. I'll phone Dorothy or Estelle or I'll ask Will. He's bound to come slippy-titty back again. Even if it's only to pack a bag."

I started the list.

1) Pour the milk down the side of Ella's Weetabix – don't splash it over the top or she won't eat it.

It was Tuesday lunchtime and I was giving Isobel one last nurse before I left.

Tears, salty and unasked for, slipped quietly off the end of my nose and splashed on the plump little hand stroking my breast with innocent ecstasy.

When she finished, Camilla took her from me and dried my damp tears with the Mile High T-shirt.

"You'd have had to stop anyway. You could never have continued to breastfeed her and carry another healthy baby."

142

"Of course, I could."

Camilla shook her head. "Your spirit is willing, but the flesh is weak. Have you had your blood analysed since you conceived?"

"Dorothy took blood last week, after I had the cancer operation on my nose. The results aren't back yet. But what's the blood analysis going to tell us that we don't already know?"

"You might be anaemic. After three pregnancies in three years your iron level is bound to be low."

"I'm sure it's fine. It always is."

"Do you feel pregnant?"

"What an unusual question! I don't know, Camilla. What does pregnant feel like?"

Camilla refused to be teased. "Tired. Perhaps a metallic taste in your mouth. Tender breasts. Nausea."

I shrugged. "I've had a bit of spotting, but I think that's normal enough during a pregnancy, isn't it? I had a bit of spotting with Hugh."

"You should rest more," said Camilla, "rest and eat. When you get to Ireland will you go into the surgery and see James for a check-up?"

"What an awful fusspot you are!"

My sister's flashy luggage, packed with her eye-catching, expensive outfits, was waiting for us at the hall door.

"Wear my clothes while you're here," I said. "I know you think they're ghastly but they were quite nice, quite Karen Blixen, when I bought them. Violet blames the water, and Will says it's the washing powder, I think it's the strength of the sun that has bleached them threadbare. I'm

143

sure you don't want your own lovely things ruined the same way after a couple of washes."

"And *of course* you must wear *my* clothes when you're in Ireland. I insist. It makes me feel quite ill to imagine that some ignoramus on the street might see you in your African rags and think it was me, glamorous Dr Simms, gone bush crazy. And you'd better stick some cabbage leaves in your bra – it'll help the breast milk to dry up."

Hugh, giggling madly, arrived in my bedroom with pale pink shampoo – the full bottle because I'd only just bought it – all over him. Ella was following in hot pursuit, also giggling madly, but with a certain sheepishness that two and a half has over one and a half, because Ella knew it was naughty as well as amusing.

"You won't be cross with them all the time, will you?" I was suddenly anxious. "I know they're naughty sometimes but –"

"I won't be cross at all," Camilla assured me. "You must stop worrying. It's not healthy."

"But there are so many things to worry about. I didn't sleep a wink last night thinking about them."

"Like what?"

"Like drowning. You won't leave them unattended, even for a second, in the bath, will you? Hugh's latest game is trying to breathe under water."

Camilla grabbed the book lying on top of my flight bag and shook it at me. "It was an accident. In the book. The little girl drowning in the duck pond was an accident. And the other baby died of meningitis. And the other baby was stillborn. These things *happen*, whether you're a careful mother or a careless mother."

I chose to ignore this advice.

"Violet is only allowed to do the ironing when you're in the house and it's your sole responsibility to keep the children away from the iron when she's ironing. And don't ever expect Violet to mind children and do housework at the same time. If she has to do both she might leave gas rings burning or the fire unguarded, or sharp knives lying around, or plastic bags littering the floor . . ."

I was still thinking up last-minute, anxiety-attack instructions as we loaded my bags into the Range Rover and strapped the children in.

"Always check that the seatbelts holding the car seats are actually clicked in. Ella opened them once and, when I braked, all the car seats, with all three children strapped inside, tumbled forward into the foot-well of the car. It's a miracle nobody was killed."

"I have to do a wee-wee!" Ella screamed as Camilla started the Range Rover, and drove gingerly out of the yard.

"Stop the car! If she has to do a wee-wee, always stop the car and let her out. From the scream that she has to pee till she actually does pee is about three seconds. Or you can bring a potty with you . . ."

By the time we reached the airport, and I'd checked in – with Dr Simms' passport and ticket, I was back full circle to my fear of the children drowning again.

"A baby could drown in a mop bucket. Don't let Violet leave the mop bucket unattended. And never let her have bleach in the house. Even if the toilet stinks of pee. I bought her bleach when she started working for me, before the babies were born, and she washed the dishes in it . . ."

Camilla was carrying Isobel in the back-carrier. She kissed me, then turned sideways so I could kiss Isobel.

"Bye bye, Dr Simms," she said firmly. "And listen. Buy yourself something frivolous to read in Exclusive Books in Jo'burg airport. That one about a beach perhaps. I read it when I was flying to Phuket a couple of years ago. Or the one about the clique of university friends who kill one of the guys in their gang and get away with it – I enjoyed reading that one just after Sam Dawson divorced me . . ."

I got down on the busy airport floor and hugged Ella and Hugh.

"I'm going shopping. I won't be long."

Ella stroked the scar on the side of my face. Camilla had taken the stitches out.

"Dorothy has done a lovely job. It could have been a real mess if she hadn't been able to cut along the natural line of your face. But this is excellent. Really tidy. Even you'll not be able to see it in a couple of months."

Ella said, "Mummy is flying away. Fly away, Peter! Fly away, Paul!" but she didn't seem unduly worried. It suddenly occurred to me that she was two and a half and I'd never spent a night away from her in her entire life. Even when I went into the hospital to have Hugh, I went in at six in the morning, Hugh was born at seven and I was home to bath her and put her to bed that evening. And, of course, I never got to the hospital with Isobel who was delivered on the kitchen floor.

Still I hesitated.

"Go," Camilla said, "before you upset them."

I took off Camilla's fancy designer sunglasses and turned at

146

the gate for one last look. From a distance my sister was striking in my *Out of Africa* clothes – today she was wearing a long loose sleeveless dress with a thin cotton T-shirt under it and a thin cotton shirt on top, and my wide-brimmed hat on her head and my Hi-Tec boots on her feet. Clustered round her were my three delicious babies: Ella in a faded pink sundress was still waving, Hugh had already pulled off his sunhat and Isobel had fallen asleep, slumped forward in the back-carrier. I watched while Camilla put Hugh's hat firmly and kindly back on his head and taking him and Ella by the hand led them away. From a distance you could never have guessed she wasn't their mother.

I bought the holiday reading Camilla had recommended. But I never got the chance to read it. I was asleep before the aircraft took off, sitting upright in an eye-mask, my feet resting on my flight bag – this had been my life for twelve years and old habits are hard to break. I slept, dreamless, until we landed.

By the time I'd disembarked in Belfast I'd stopped looking over my shoulder and trying to count red infant heads.

Chapter Thirteen

Most of my first hour in Ireland was spent signing forms and describing Camilla's expensive luggage which had got lost in transit.

"Don't look so glum," said the kind lady at the lost luggage desk. "It'll probably come in on the next flight. We'll send it home to you in a taxi when it arrives."

"If it arrives."

The next hour was spent crunching through the gears of Camilla's flashy two-seater sports car, and marvelling at how many clean new cars there were on the Ulster roads.

"Why would anyone buy a second-hand car?" Camilla had explained. "With a new car you can get free tax and free insurance and you can pay it off every month, direct debit from your bank account."

"Does Aunt Grace still have my old BMW?"

"I suppose so. But please don't let her out in it if you can stop her at all."

"Has she crashed?"

"Not yet."

"Where does Kathryn sit in the two-seater if I have to take her somewhere? Will I put her in the front seat?"

"Kathryn doesn't travel in my car. James has a people carrier to ferry Kathryn about."

Mummy was in the manse kitchen washing dishes, wearing a summer dress without a cardigan or a thermal vest because finally the manse had been given double-glazed PVC windows. She gasped when she saw me.

"Camilla darling, what has happened to your face? Were you attacked? Are you hurt? Oh, why does Francesca have to live in that dangerous place?"

"Mummy, it's me, Francesca."

Mummy dried her hands on a tea towel and narrowed her eyes. Suddenly suspicious.

"I don't believe you. I think you're Camilla and, as well as being attacked and knifed in the face, your hair has been pulled out in handfuls."

So I stripped off and showed her that there was no tattoo. Finally she believed me. Then she stopped bickering and went berserk.

"You can't just take a holiday away from your life!"

"Why not? Camilla is always taking holidays."

"This time she's taking a holiday in your shoes! How could you leave Will alone with her? She's stolen every boyfriend you've ever had!"

I didn't want to pick a fight with my mother the very first second I saw her so I said, "I've come home to see Aunt Grace before she dies."

Mummy's eyes filled with tears.

"Poor Aunt Grace! She's on a double dose of morphine tablets and she's refusing point-blank to go into a hospice. Stubborn old thing. I wanted to move in with her a month ago and she wouldn't hear of it. 'I can't think of anything that would kill me faster,' she said. Perhaps she was right. She's at the hospital this afternoon – I have to collect her at tea time. We'll go over and see her after you've had a sleep – you'd better go to Camilla's house to do that – it would be more peaceful for you and you really need a good sleep. You look dreadful, darling . . ."

So I spent my first afternoon in Ireland absolutely alone in absolute double-glazed silence in No 1 Bluebell Orchard, Camilla's house which she bought with the proceeds of the Sam Dawson divorce. No 1 Bluebell Orchard was very new and very beautiful and it absolutely outclassed the other four large detached houses built in what once was a bluebell orchard. It had en-suite bathrooms, wooden floors, a double garage and an enormous conservatory. It had central heating at the flick of a switch and a tumble-drier and a dishwasher and a microwave and a television and a video machine and a DVD player. It had an electric power shower.

There were no bluebells in the garden but the front door was painted blue.

I wandered, self-conscious and uncomfortable, through the immaculate rooms – outclassed, underdressed and overheated in leather trousers and a plain T-shirt. I needed

151

a full face of make-up, expensively highlighted hair and Camilla's understated and elegant clothes to harmonize with No 1 Bluebell Orchard where there was no dust, no grubby fingerprints on glass, no scribbles on walls, and no toys to trip over. No used tea bags abandoned in the kitchen sink, no scummy ring around the bath, no reproachful mountain of ironing.

"Mrs O'Hara comes in for two hours every morning to tidy up the house."

"Only two hours?"

"Mrs O'Hara spends two hours in every house in Bluebell Orchard every day. That's why we're classed as an *exclusive development*, because we have our own housekeeper."

Camilla's luggage never arrived so I was reduced to rummaging behind the mirrored slide-robes of the master bedroom to find something suitable to change into. So suitable in fact that when James Snotter brought Kathryn home from her childminder, Mrs Young, Kathryn thought I was her mother.

"Did you bring Mrs Young a wooden giraffe? You *promised!*"

"Good trip?" asked James, pushing past me and making for the stairs.

"But I'm Francesca."

James Snotter did not seem in the least surprised that his wife had gone to Africa and stayed there and sent her sister home in her place.

"That's nice. I'll get a locum to replace her."

He continued on up the stairs. I watched his retreating

rear end in amazement. It must have been very exciting sex indeed if he was still sulking about it.

Kathryn said, "Are you my new mummy?"

Kathryn and I went out to sit in the garden.

"What's this flower called, Kathryn?"

"I don't know, Aunt Francesca."

"Daisy. What's this one called?

"I don't know, Aunt Francesca."

Upstairs, clearly, I could hear James Snotter peeing in his en-suite toilet.

"Dandelion. What do you do all day with Mrs Young, darling?"

"First we take off our coats. Then we sit down in a row on the sofa in the kitchen and Mrs Young gives us our breakfast. And yesterday she spilt some on my pretty dress because I didn't open my mouth fast enough when she said 'Kathryn, open,' and I said, 'Mrs Young, you've spilt some on my dress and it's Mini Boden,' and Mrs Young said, 'Mini Boden, my arse, Kathryn Snotter. Just you open your mouth when I say 'Open' and no more will get spilt.'"

"And then?"

"And then we go to the toilet. And then we wash our hands. And then we dry our hands. And then we sit back up on the sofa and watch *Dora the Explorer* and *Maggie and the Ferocious Beast* and *Angelina Ballerina* and *Max and Ruby* and –"

"Stop!"

"And sometimes naughty Thomas gets off the sofa and Mrs Young shouts 'Get back up on that sofa right now, Thomas Flemming! If you fall over and get a bruise your mother will sue me. Get back up, Thomas Flemming, and don't move!'"

"What's Mrs Young doing when you're watching television?"

"Mrs Young is doing pilates," said Kathryn solemnly, "to keep her young and beautiful. Look, Aunt Francesca, let me show you," and she lay down on her back on the grass and waved her legs in the air.

"James," I said when he came back downstairs, "does Kathryn go to Mrs Young's house every day?"

"Not every day. Only five days a week. It's important that a child feels secure in her environment. A routine creates a feeling of security."

"What about summer holidays?"

"Pre-school children don't have summer holidays. I pay Mrs Young to look after Kathryn fifty-two weeks of the year."

"Even if Kathryn's not there?"

"Kathryn is always there."

James and Kathryn and I were sharing a delicious frozen pizza and some boiled potatoes when Mummy's modest car pulled into the cobble-locked drive and Mummy, looking furtive, jumped out.

"Convenience foods are just super," she announced, popping her head round the door of the dining-room. "Francesca, can I have a word, please?"

Bemused, I followed her out into Camilla's hall with its drag-washed terracotta walls and expensively framed Egyptian papyrus hieroglyphics, turned left into the cream sitting-room with its plasma-screen television and Arabic-door coffee table, through pitch-pine double doors into the conservatory.

"That bamboo swivel-chair cost six hundred pounds," said Mummy proudly.

"It's very fantastic. Do you want some pizza? Or potatoes?"

Mummy shook her head. "No, thank you. Now, I've thought about it all afternoon and I believe I have a solution to our little problem."

"What problem?"

"Francesca, stop being difficult. Your father is a *minister*. You simply cannot live here, right under his nose, with a man who isn't your husband."

"I'm not living in sin with James." I shuddered involuntarily at the memory of the sound of him peeing in his en-suite toilet.

"Well, I know that," Mummy whispered furiously, "and I wouldn't sleep with him either. But you're simply *naïve* if you think that everybody else – Daddy could lose his job –"

"I thought Daddy was ready to retire?"

"He is, and he'd really like his last few Sundays to be scandal-free. You know how *challenging* Camilla's divorces were on all of us. Don't you remember the Chinese Whispers?"

"I think you can only hear Chinese Whispers if you're listening for them." Then because she looked so downcast I relented and said, "What's your solution?"

"Aunt Grace. I'm sure she'd love you to stay with her. You've always been her favourite."

I looked at my mother in amazement. "What an excellent idea!"

Mummy beamed. "Let's go to Lisglasson Lodge right away and see what she says."

"Mummy and I are going to visit Aunt Grace. Can Kathryn come too?"

"Please, Daddy?" Kathryn took the final bite of her pizza and a careful sip from her glass of milk and wriggled and wriggled with excitement.

James checked his watch.

"Will you have her home again before eight? Eight is her bedtime."

"Yes, of course."

Mummy turned off the country road into Lisglasson Lodge's leafy avenue, and gingerly negotiated the familiar potholes. She had suggested some years back that Aunt Grace tarmac the avenue. "It will keep your car and your feet so much cleaner in the rain," and Aunt Grace, who had privately declared to me, "They will tarmac over my dead body!", had staged a heart attack in protest. When Mummy suggested she have her enormous single-glazed windows replaced by cosy double-glazed PVC Aunt Grace had rustled up some chest pains and a 999 call and an ambulance. There had even been an inelegant faint when it was proposed that the old Aga be pulled out of her kitchen and replaced by a brand-new shiny electric cooker. Now she had terminal cancer and my thoroughly modern Mummy had had to reluctantly abandon her best endeavours to modernise Lisglasson Lodge.

"I hope she behaves herself," said Mummy anxiously as we pulled up into the yard. "The last time Kathryn was here she went home shouting 'silly bugger' and James was furious."

Aunt Grace was out of bed, dressed and in the kitchen, shouting into her telephone. "I'm going to the BBC, you buggers! I've been invited on that consumer rights programme, whatever it's called, and I'm going to expose you thieving buggers on the television. Are you listening to me?" She slammed down the phone. "That told them!" she announced with satisfaction. Then she saw me. "Francesca! What are you doing here? You're early. I'm not dead yet."

"I heard you were going on the television. I'm star-struck and I want your autograph."

Aunt Grace beamed. "Let me tell you all about it. But first, I'll make myself a little drinkie. Did I see your tiresome teetotaller mother slipping away upstairs to look for a gin bottle under my bed? Too late, I've brought it downstairs. I've hidden it and she'll not find it. Ha ha ha!"

Kathryn said, "Daddy doesn't drink in front of me because he says it will set a bad example."

"What about your mummy?"

"Aunt Francesca is my new mummy."

Aunt Grace said, "Take my advice, girls – never shop in any retail establishment which sells itself on price alone. I have not won on the Lottery. I remain the same tight-fisted Presbyterian I have always been. I am, however, a tight-fisted Presbyterian who has had her fist burnt once too often and has come to the unfortunate but timely conclusion that cheap is never cheerful, only nasty . . ."

"What is she on about?" Mummy had returned from her gin quest angst-ridden and empty-handed.

"I am dying," Aunt Grace announced magnificently. "I am dying and I have accepted that there's very little I can do about the date of my death if the date is already decided. It's now too late to philosophise on the advantages and disadvantages of knowing when the great and terrible event is going to occur. There is no time for introspection. I have so much to do. I have loose ends to tie up. Affairs to put in order. Petty things to apologise for. A funeral to arrange."

The funeral plans included being waked in her own bedroom in her own bed with the curtains pulled back and the windows open and the breeze coming in from the wild-flower meadow, and Bobby Flood's album *Hellraising Woman* playing in the background. Then her body was to be cremated and her ashes scattered across the wild-flower meadow.

Under no circumstances was she to be buried in Derryrose graveyard.

With astonishing insensitivity my mother had protested, "Isn't that a rather godless way to go, Grace? Wouldn't you prefer a nice coffin?"

Aunt Grace had spent thirty years fighting off the claustrophobic good intentions of my well-meaning mother and playing cat-and-mouse with Mummy's best efforts at bereavement-counselling. She was battle-hardened. And she was not going into a nice coffin and into a nice grave beside Naomi's body.

Attack is always the best form of defence. With caustic flippancy Aunt Grace turned on my mother.

158

"I'm afraid my face wouldn't fit in your graveyard, Madeline. I could never spend eternity under stone chippings and plastic flowers."

(There were two wheelie bins parked against the graveyard wall and it was Daddy's duty at burials to tactfully bring them to the attention of the recently bereaved – "Of course, you can put fresh flowers on the grave, but please remember that the artificial efforts don't need changing as often.")

Gently Daddy said, "It's only your body that will be in the ground, Grace, not your soul."

"Well, then, it won't matter where my body is."

And she wanted me to scatter her ashes.

"It'll be like old times," said Aunt Grace (She'd been with me, on the flight out of South India when the landing gear stuck and we thought we were going to crash and burn in Abu Dhabi.)

"And I'm almost organised, but for this damned irritating business with my bedroom carpet – but I've got them snookered now, those thieving charlatans at Big Carpet, with their faulty carpet, their independent inspectors and their ambiguous reports. I'm going on the television to expose them!"

Aunt Grace's eyes were blazing. Kathryn's mouth was a perfect O. I resisted the urge to applaud.

Mummy came in from the garden with her arms full of Aunt Grace's washing.

"I changed your bed when you were at the hospital. And I've laid out a clean pair of pyjamas for you. Will I fold these sheets and put them on top of the Aga to air, or will I put them straight into the hot press?"

Aunt Grace rolled her eyes. "You are killing me with kindness, Madeline."

"Will I boil you an egg, Grace? Will I run you a bath? Would you like a hot water bottle?"

Aunt Grace looked suddenly old and ill and close to tears. "I don't want anything."

Mummy finished folding. She washed the gin glass. She brushed the kitchen floor. "Very well then. But we're going to have to go now. We promised James Snotter we'd have Kathryn home for eight o'clock."

"Go," said Aunt Grace faintly, "and leave me all alone. An old woman, dying . . ."

"Can I come back later?" I said. "Can I come back for a sleepover? Mummy's afraid I might have an affair with James Snotter if I sleep in the same house as him."

Aunt Grace perked up and sniffed disparagingly in Mummy's general direction.

"I only know your current brother-in-law in a professional capacity and I must say he's a very nice doctor. He has assured me that I'll not have to go into a hospice at the end if I don't want to. But really, your mother has lived such a *sheltered* existence . . ."

"How did you know I was Francesca?" I asked her as we were leaving. "You couldn't have known I was coming home from Botswana. I'm wearing Camilla's clothes, I had Camilla's daughter with me. *Mummy* thought I was Camilla!"

Aunt Grace said, "I've never understood why no-one can tell you apart. Francesca, darling, you have a halo. You've always had it, since you were a little girl."

"A halo? Like an angel?"

Aunt Grace kissed me. "I'll see you later."

"Aunt Grace's house is clean rotten," announced solemn, spotless Kathryn when we got into the car to go home. "And it's got a very funny smell, hasn't it? What was that smell, Aunt Francesca?"

"Yes," said Mummy, "what was that smell? Do you think she's started to burn incense?"

I shook my head innocently. "I have absolutely no idea. I thought it was furniture polish."

Chapter Fourteen

Camilla phoned. "She's full of Ginger, isn't she?"

"Ginger the pony?"

"Who else?"

Ginger had belonged to our cousins Frank and Philip. When Camilla rode Ginger it was poetry in motion. He was forward-going and honest, he trotted in elegant figures of eight, he always cantered off the right leg, and he never pulled or tried to run away with her.

Then I would get up on Ginger. I looked the same as Camilla, I weighed the same, my voice sounded the same, and I'd had exactly the same number of riding lessons. But Ginger would not move for me. I kicked him, I whacked him and I roared at him, and it didn't make the slightest bit of difference. Sometimes, to add insult to injury he would actually turn his head round, roll up his top lip and sneer at me while I broke sweat trying to kick him on.

If Camilla or Aunt Grace were in the field they would helpfully run at him, shouting ferociously and waving their arms. Then Ginger would take the bit firmly between his teeth, stick his naughty nose in the air, give an almighty buck and bolt.

"He's testing you!" Camilla would shout as we disappeared into the horizon. "Playing you up! You've got to show him who's boss!"

Ginger was always the boss. Once I'd finally got the pony under control I'd ride him back to Camilla and, reduced to frustrated tears, slip from the saddle and furiously hand the reins back to her. She'd leap easily into the driving seat and having barely touched him with her heel off they'd go, poetry in motion across the field again.

"Is Ella playing you up? What's she doing?" I tried to sound sympathetic, but I was secretly amused.

"Would you like me to start from the second you disappeared at the departure gate and she peed on herself in the airport or would you like me to fast-forward to the latest emergency when we couldn't find Hugh's Blankie before bed?"

"Tell me about Hugh's Blankie."

"First tell me how you can allow your son a comfort blanket without the safety net of a spare one? Hugh was on the verge of a panic attack, screaming, 'Blankie! Blankie!' and I said, 'Ella, where does Mummy keep the spare?' and Ella said, 'What spare, Aunty Cam? There's no spare.' And I said 'Do you know where Hugh's blankie is, Ella?' and Ella said 'Yes, Aunty Cam, I've hidden it,' and I said 'Go and get it, please, Ella – Hugh is crying,' and Ella said, 'No,

Aunty Cam. Blankie is playing hide-and-seek and you've got to find him,' and I said, 'Blankie is Hugh's best friend, Ella, and if he's lost Hugh can't get to sleep,' and Ella said *gleefully*, 'Aunty Cam, Blankie is hiding!'."

I started to laugh. "I should have warned you. Hiding Hugh's blankie is Ella's party piece. She tries it on with everybody."

Tested under the same circumstances Violet had put Ella over her knee and spanked her, and Dorothy had got down on her knees and prayed for divine intervention. Camilla it seems had tried a bribe.

"I said, 'I'll give you sweetie if you get me Blankie.'"

"Let me guess. Ella said, 'You'll have to show me the sweeties first, Auntie Cam!'."

"Yes, she did," said Camilla, in amazement. "I've never heard the like of it from a girl of two and a half! 'You'll have to show me the sweeties first.'"

"And did you show her the sweeties first?"

"I really had no choice in the matter, did I? Not when I'd already offered them. Fortunately I was able to find a couple of furry polo mints in the corner of your bum bag or I'd have been done for. I tell you, that is the first and last time I ever try to bribe a child."

"Have you never bribed Kathryn?"

"Kathryn is never naughty," Camilla boasted. "Kathryn was a contented little baby, then she was tamed as a toddler, now she's a well-adjusted, confident, gregarious little girl. At the risk of sounding pompous I think the Jesuits were on to something when they said 'Give me the boy till he's five and I'll show you the man!'."

I was not convinced. "Best of luck! Shall I post you out

your instruction books to assist with the reprogramming of the Dallas children?"

"No need to post them. I phoned Exclusive books in Jo'burg this afternoon and ordered them. They're being flown up in the Express tomorrow morning."

Aunt Grace said, "I've put you in your old room. Can you make the bed yourself? You can use the sheets on top of the Aga. My arms aren't really up to it."

"Shall I strip the sheets and sweep the mattress first?"

Will had stayed with Aunt Grace before we got married, and the morning of the wedding had stripped the bed to find the sheets full of mouse droppings.

"Which was considerably better than spending the night in the bed with a dead mouse at his feet and thinking it was a stray bed sock," I said.

"Or waking up on honeymoon to find a mouse drinking the milk out of the Teasmaid you've just been given as a wedding present," said Aunt Grace. "It was such a long time ago," she said, sudden tears welling in her eyes and her voice shaky. "I can't remember anything about Denis any more. I hope he's not waiting for me on the other side when I die. I'm really afraid I might not recognise him."

Uncle Denis and Naomi were killed by a bomb in the Wild West days of the early seventies in Northern Ireland. Two innocents in the wrong place at the wrong time. It was July, they were just back from Spain, and Camilla and I had been invited over to Lisglasson Lodge to admire Naomi's suntan.

"Look how brown I am!" Naomi pulled down her shorts

166

and pants so we could admire her white bottom. "I'm so brown I look like a Spanish senorita. And I can speak Spanish like a Spanish senorita. Listen. I want ice cream, *por favor.* Daddy, I want ice cream, *por favor.*"

Camilla and I were furiously envious, because the farthest we ever got on holiday was a cottage on the North Antrim coast, every year, and our daddy ran a beach mission in the sandhills when we were there, so it was just like Sunday School every day and this particular year it had rained a lot so we had no suntan, we didn't even have freckles.

"Ice cream!" said Uncle Denis. "What an excellent idea, Naomi. Let's drive into the village and get some ice cream for everyone. Do you want to come with us, Francesca?"

"No thanks," I said for a cloud had just crossed the sun and I was suddenly cold and needed my cardigan. I watched them jump into Uncle Denis' sports car, he beeped the horn a couple of times and they raced off down the avenue towards Derryrose.

Afterwards, Mummy said she'd been in the manse garden dead-heading roses when they raced past and she'd thought how irresponsible it was of Uncle Denis to allow Naomi to sit in the front seat without a seat belt.

There hadn't even been a warning as there usually was.

Derryrose village was festooned with red, white and blue bunting, a Union Jack fluttered from every lamppost, kerbs were painted red, white and blue. The Twelfth of July had been celebrated, the holidays were over, orange sashes and bowler hats were packed away for another year.

Uncle Denis parked. He and Naomi jumped out and walked along the street towards the Savoy. As they passed

Grubbs pub the bomb exploded. Uncle Denis was blown to pieces. Naomi had run on ahead towards the Savoy – she was killed by a piece of flying shrapnel. Camilla and I saw her in her coffin. She was still suntanned even though she was dead.

"What upsets me most," said Aunt Grace, "is that she never got her ice cream, *por favor.*"

"Of course, you'll recognise Uncle Denis," I told my aunt robustly. "Daddy told us the angels stuck him back together again in heaven. He'll be perfect; there won't even be join marks. And *I* remember him, so you're bound to remember him. He was tall, dark and handsome. He had a black leather jacket. I'd be more concerned that he doesn't recognise you, Aunt Grace. No offence, but your face was a great deal younger thirty years ago."

Aunt Grace cheered up. "You're absolutely right. He's never going to recognise me. Do you think I should try a face pack?"

"I bought a carpet in Big Carpet for my bedroom." Aunt Grace watched, amused, while I whipped and whipped at an egg white with a fork. "It was very pretty with little pink flowers on it. Five pound a square yard. I thought, well, I'm going to be dead soon and I want to be waked in my own bedroom and the old rug on the floorboards is threadbare and when I'm dead I don't want half the parish tramping in to see me and *criticising*. So I bought the new carpet in Big Carpet and they came and fitted it and I'm not exaggerating, it had started to unravel by the next morning. I phoned Big

Carpet and told them the carpet was faulty. 'That's not my fault,' says the manager. 'My dear,' I told her, 'I am a volunteer at the Citizens' Advice Bureau and I know my rights. The Sale of Goods Act 1994 states that I'm entitled to a full refund if the product I have purchased is not up to scratch. And frankly, how can I possibly have my wake in a bedroom with an unravelling carpet?'"

"How indeed?" I agreed. I was getting absolutely nowhere with the egg.

"I think you should start again with another egg," Aunt Grace advised. "I don't think you broke it cleanly into the bowl. I think there's yolk in it."

"Are you telling me you could do it better yourself?"

"Pass it over."

Deftly the dying old woman broke the egg, separated it and began whisking. Within a minute, as she talked, the egg was foaming.

"So the horrid young manager woman starts to huff and puff. She says she'll have to send an independent inspector to inspect the carpet and write a report and once she has read the report she can assess and evaluate and make an informed decision. And I said, 'Why don't you get into your company car and drive for fifteen minutes down the road until you reach my house and come and look at the carpet yourself? I'm sure you'll get expenses paid for your journey.' And she said no, she couldn't do that. It was against company policy. Her assessment would not be independent because she represented Big Carpet. So I waited four weeks for the independent inspector and finally, after I'd made many complaining phone calls, an independent inspector pulls up in his big car, takes the briefest of glances at the carpet, says, 'It's unravelling,' and leaves.

Three weeks later I'd still heard nothing from Big Carpet so I phoned them again and the rude young manager woman says she hasn't yet received the report from the independent inspector and I say that isn't really good enough because I'm dying and if she doesn't get a move on and get this faulty carpet replaced I'm going to be dead."

Finally the egg white was whipped.

"It's all in the wrist action," Aunt Grace told me slyly. "You've got to show it who's boss."

I smoothed back my aunt's hair and gently spread the egg white across her face.

Aunt Grace beamed. "This is such excellent timing. I'm going to look so well on television."

"Have you actually contacted the consumer rights programme? You're not just bluffing?"

"Of course I'm not bluffing. I'm Presbyterian. I don't bluff about money . . . I've spoken on the telephone to the most charming young man and he's coming to see me tomorrow with his own camera and we're going to do a piece together in the bedroom."

She winked. "It's years since I had a man doing things to me in my bedroom."

Before the egg white hardened she said, "We must remember to tell Madeline to add to my list of my final requests that I want my television performance videotaped and I want it played over and over on Camilla's plasma-screen television downstairs in the drawing-room at my wake."

After Uncle Denis and Naomi died, Frank and Philip were sent to the Masonic Boys' Boarding School in Dublin and Aunt Grace – suddenly alone after fourteen years of marriage and three children – rather adopted Camilla and myself. She cleaned out poor dead Naomi's room with frenzied zeal, burning anything that would burn in a large bonfire in the wild-flower meadow, and scrubbing and painting over everything else. Naomi's little white-painted wrought-iron bed and child furniture were replaced with the mouse-attracting double bed and an unfashionable enormous Edwardian wardrobe. When Camilla and I were children we climbed into the wardrobe and pretended the back had a door which opened into Narnia. Now I stored clothes in it – there were winter coats from twenty years ago, unsophisticated evening dresses from university and a handful of cotton sundresses, hardly worn and almost forgotten about.

"I'd almost forgotten about these. Do you remember them? I bought them for my honeymoon which never happened."

"Best honeymoon you ever missed, my darling," said Aunt Grace. "Where was it again? Mauritius? Mozambique? I'm sure it was somewhere beginning with 'M'."

"Maldives. An island called Paradise. Six wooden bungalows standing on stilts over the turquoise lagoon. White sand. Blue sky. A mischievous breeze. And nothing to do all day, and all day to do it . . ."

"What a wonderful memory you have! Remembering a honeymoon that never happened!"

"I'll never forget it."

"I'm sure these dresses would still fit you. If anything, you're thinner now than you were at twenty-four. Listen, darling, it's way past my bedtime and I'm dying on my feet. No pun intended! I'll go and get ready for bed and you try on the pink one – it's the prettiest – and come in and give me a twirl."

Aunt Grace was smoking in bed when I went to show off the pink dress.

"Do you want some?" A beatific smile had relaxed her face. Her fear of dying was back under control.

I sat down on the bed beside her. "Where are you getting it?"

"I have a friend who says I shouldn't have to suffer. Dying is a very lonely business."

I kissed the top of her head. "I'll stay with you. You won't be lonely any more."

Aunt Grace took another drag.

"I often wonder what Naomi would be like now. What she'd have grown up into. She was such a bold bad girl. Do you remember Marie Murphy washing out her mouth with soap when she started swearing? 'What can you expect, Marie?' I said. 'Doesn't Denis have a filthy mouth?'

'This child will be the death of me,' she used to say . . .

The years have just flown past since she died. Thirty years in a flash! I think about her every day. And tonight I feel really close to her, as if she was here in the room with me . . ."

I kissed my aunt again and went to my own bedroom. There's a time and a place for everything, and tonight was not the night to talk about myself. I'd ask her about the mad prediction she made at my wedding in the morning.

"Francesca!" she called me from her bedroom.

"Yes, Aunt Grace?"

"Did you ever tell your mother about the crash-landing in Abu Dhabi?"

"No, Aunt Grace."

"You should tell her, darling."

Next morning, very early, before Aunt Grace got up, I put on the pink dress and a pair of pink Marigolds. The television man was due before lunch. If he drove up to the front door he'd have to walk through the hall and up the stairs to get to Aunt Grace's bedroom. If he came to the back door he'd walk through the kitchen to get to the hall to get to the stairs. If he'd driven from Belfast he'd want to pee. Naturally I'd keep all the other doors in the house firmly closed but it still meant I had the hall, the kitchen, the bathroom, the landing and Aunt Grace's bedroom to clean and ventilate and saturate with domestic smells before he arrived. Strong coffee and baking bread and maybe I could mop the kitchen floor with Flash. A big bunch of lilies in the hall. Lemon-scented Cif in the bathroom. Potpourri. Scented candles. Air freshener. Anything which might blot out the stinking fog of marijuana that was hanging all over the house.

I was just back from the market, with a grotesque bunch of lilies and a plastic bag full of scented cleaning products.

Already Aunt Grace's kitchen smelt like I was hiding something.

"Hello, Francesca."

My back was turned to the voice but I knew it instantly. The hairs rose on the back of my neck, my stomach lurched and my legs went weak. Like a teenager.

Panicking I said, "I'm not Francesca; I'm Camilla."

The voice belonged to Alex Flood, the boy who'd almost been my boyfriend when I was seventeen. The boy Camilla had tried so unsuccessfully to seduce to find out if he was frigid or gay or if he just didn't fancy me. I hadn't spoken to him for years, but I could never forget his voice. I turned to find him carrying a grotesque bunch of lilies, a monstrous fillet of cod and a brown-paper bag with a bottle of gin in it. I knew that if I strip searched him I'd find a little tin full of hand-rolled cigarettes. Strip search? What on earth was I thinking of?

"Great minds think alike. Grace told me the television man was due at lunch-time."

"I never thought of fish. Well done. Fish stinks."

Our eyes met over the bunches of lilies.

"You've got green eyes," I said faintly. It was a stupid thing to say, but it just slipped out.

"So have you. The girl with green eyes. I *know* you're Francesca. You wore that dress in the Maldives. I remember."

Chapter Fifteen

The bomb in Derryrose shocked everyone. Of course, we knew that Northern Ireland was on fire. It was the early seventies and every day the news was full of it. Someone was shot; somewhere was bombed; the Army were on the streets; the politicians were talking; the politicians weren't talking. Bang-bang you're dead. But it hadn't affected us in Derryrose. Until now.

Now the news stories were about dashing Uncle Denis and there was a photograph of him, looking very young, with long sideburns, laughing on his wedding day. And about Naomi, looking very innocent, a lamb to the slaughter, in her school photograph.

After the Derryrose bomb Lord Laurence Glass abandoned his big estate, Lisglasson, and moved permanently to England. Lisglasson had been in his family since

Cromwell, but it takes only one hothead with a gun to kill you.

Lisglasson lay empty. The farmland was sold, the livestock were sold, the hounds were drafted and the sale of the estate became the stuff of legend. First there was an oil sheik who arrived by helicopter, then a country-house hotelier, then a representative from the National Trust who wanted the private chapel down by the lough but nothing else, then the Department of Agriculture with talk of an experimental farm.

Nobody committed. A thick, impenetrable hedge grew round the enormous house with its paddocks and kennels and stables and it might have slept for a hundred years. Until Sir Bobby Flood (Services to Rock Music) arrived for a viewing in a large limousine with tinted windows.

We were very, very excited by the rumour that Bobby Flood was in South Derry. He was the charismatic lead singer of Achilles Heel, a Belfast band who sounded a bit like Thin Lizzy. Aunt Grace played their best album, *Hellraising Woman*, so often I knew all the words by heart.

It was summer, I was seventeen, I was painting Aunt Grace's gate. A limousine slipped to a standstill beside me and the great Sir Bobby jumped out to introduce himself. He was at least forty-five, older than Daddy, but he was gorgeous – he had thick black hair, his jeans were very tight and his T-shirt clutched his biceps in all the right places. His eyes were green. I wasn't a fan of Achilles Heel – they were before my time – but everyone fancied Bobby Flood. He was the first rock star we'd ever had in Northern Ireland and everyone knew his romantic Cinderella story, his tough inner-city upbringing, how he wrote songs inside his head when he was working at the shipyard during the day and sang them in pubs and working men's clubs at night. How he loved the ladies and the ladies loved him. The drink. The drugs. The drying out. The knighthood.

"I'm your new neighbour," said Sir Bobby. "I'm Bobby Flood. Can I borrow a cup of sugar?"

Aunt Grace came running out of the house. Five minutes earlier Aunt Grace had been cutting grass in an old pair of jeans and an Achilles Heel T-shirt – now she was wearing a skimpy vest top, and her lovely red hair was shaken loose and she was wearing lipstick. For the first time in ten years, since Uncle Denis and Naomi died, her eyes were sparkling.

I met Alex a few days later. Such an inauspicious introduction to the first great love of my life. I was on Ginger, pink with futile kicking, when he rode up to me, dismounted and said, "Will we swap?"

He looked like his father; there was the same whiff of glamour and whiff of scandal.

"Oh, I couldn't possibly ride your horse. I'm hopeless. I can't make this bugger move at all."

Alex ignored my feeble protests. "Get off and let me give you a leg up."

The minute Alex put his strong hands round my calf to give me a leg up I knew something unforgettable was about to happen. It was like an electric shock – it fizzed up my leg and made my stomach lurch and my heart beat wildly.

"OK? Not frightened?"

Our eyes met.

"You've got green eyes," I said faintly.

"So do you," and he leapt easily onto Ginger and with one smart kick in her roly-poly stomach we were off across the field.

"Can you jump?" he shouted.

"No, of course not."

"Hold her mane and she'll jump it for you," and he popped over Camilla's fancy horse-friendly exit that she used to get onto Lisglasson parkland for her daily trespassing gallop.

I shut my eyes and managed not to faint as his mare leapt. Then I followed Alex. There was something magnetic dragging me along, which I didn't understand and didn't want to understand and didn't have to understand. I was swept away by it.

Cynical old boilers who have forgotten first love like to sneer at sublimated passion. It's so unfashionable nowadays to suffer desire and to do absolutely nothing about it. First love is expected to be a series of sexual complications and condoms.

"What do you mean?" said Mummy in horror. "You've been riding with Alex Flood? The rock star's son? What about your reputation, Francesca?"

"What reputation?"

When I was seventeen I never took my eyes off Alex Flood. When he was home from boarding school, we were inseparable. He even found me a quiet horse and taught me to ride. Suddenly I could be Plucky Prudence riding through the black bog on a wild horse to warn Major

Anthony Countless that the covert he was about to draw was poisoned. I was the ravishing Miss Sally galloping hard on the heels of Flurry Knox.

"Are you sure he's not got the wrong twin?" Mummy never understood. "Camilla's the horsy one. Would he not rather have Camilla?"

What nobody ever understood about Alex Flood was that he had one great passion in his life. Unlike his flirtatious sexy father, it wasn't fillies and fornication; it was fox-hunting. From the moment he arrived in South Derry with Sir Bobby and Lady Millicent, the only thing he cared for was to take on the country, and be the Master. There was a fanatical light in his eyes when he talked about it. A passion.

Camilla wasn't impressed. "I've seen that fanatical thing before. So have you! Does it not remind you of the travelling missionary who preaches in a tent?"

The travelling missionary came with his tent every summer. He stayed in Derryrose manse and Mummy always took us to his tent to make up the numbers. "It's only good manners, girls."

And Camilla was right. There was often a fanatical light in the travelling missionary's eyes when he preached on the evils of drink, or fornication, or working mothers . . .

"Beware of Alex Flood," Camilla advised. "The fellow's possessed . . ."

"She's just jealous," scoffed Aunt Grace.

Alex's idea of a big day out was to visit the long-established fox-hunting packs down the country and stand half an afternoon with the huntsman discussing his impossible dream of drafting a pack back to South Derry. Meanwhile I was regularly scolded for saying 'dog' instead of 'hound', 'tail' instead of 'stern' and 'barking' instead of 'speaking'.

I thought the whole thing was a bit of a joke. "What can you expect? I was never any good at languages."

Mummy, naturally, worried that the intimacy of the long drives together and the shared packets of crisps and Alex's habit of pulling over into a layby to listen to *The Archers* would result in an embarrassing and clumsy pregnancy.

"I hardly think that Alex is likely to become passionate while listening to *The Archers*!"

Camilla agreed. "Is *The Archers* not a very unusual thing for a young man to listen to? Especially a young man whose father is a rock star? Do you think he might be frigid? Or gay?"

Finally it became clear to everyone, including myself, that my reputation was not going to be given an opportunity to go off the rails. Apart from that first leg up Alex never touched me, we never flirted and he certainly never asked me to 'go' with him.

"Go where?" I teased Camilla. The lurching excitement I felt when I was with him got used to being kept tidily under control.

"Millicent says he's shy," said Mummy.

It was Camilla, always impatient, who grew tired of waiting for nothing to happen and decided to take my almost-romance into her own hands. But, when she pretended to be me and failed to seduce him and he bolted, I was forced to agree with her that perhaps there was something wrong with him.

"Maybe he is frigid, or gay. Maybe he just doesn't fancy me. It doesn't change the way I feel about him and the way he makes me feel."

"You need a real boyfriend," said Camilla bluntly. "Something steady and safe for your first outing."

"Someone I can show who's boss? Are we talking about horses or boyfriends, Camilla?"

After school I went to university and Alex went to England to work in the kennels of a very grand hunt and learn to be a huntsman. We kept in touch, occasionally, by letter and sometimes we saw each other, by chance, in the holidays.

"He rode past," said Aunt Grace, "about half an hour ago. He's gone to look for foxes in the little wood at the end of the avenue. Why don't you walk down and talk to him?"

"What would I say to him?"

I even found another boyfriend.

Sam Dawson, Mrs Doctor Dawson's son, who'd played hide-and-seek with us in Derryrose graveyard, was studying medicine at university, a year ahead of Camilla. Camilla was part of his medical gang and to my surprise, for he was very popular, and very good-looking, he couldn't keep his hands off me. I even went on a couple of holidays with him and his medical gang. One morning I woke up engaged to him.

"I believe you've got the hounds back at Lisglasson," I said to Alex in Aunt Grace's kitchen.

"I believe you've flown round the world twice," Alex said to me.

"I'm told you have four children."

"I'm told you have three."

"It's been a very long time."

"It's been sixteen years."

The last time I saw Alex I was leaving for the Middle East to join Ex-Pat Air. A new Delsey suitcase was in the boot of my BMW, Camilla had bagged the passenger seat, Mummy was in the back and we were waiting for Aunt Grace who had insisted that she come to the airport to wave me off but had forgotten to set her alarm-clock and was running late. It was early morning and Alex rode out of the mist. The magnetic attraction I always suffered with him bit hard and it took every ounce of my puritanical reserve to sit tight in the driver's seat until he'd gone away. I'm not going to pretend that it was coincidence that Aunt Grace overslept and kept us waiting until Alex just happened to ride by. Aunt Grace was the most subtle and kindest of match makers.

Alex said "Is Grace out of bed? The curtains are pulled back and the windows are open in her bedroom."

"Oh gosh," I said brightly, "I don't know. I do hope so. I'll just run up and check. I'm sure the bedroom carpet will need to be swept before the television man arrives."

And I scuttled out of the kitchen, blushing madly and feeling very hot in the most inappropriate places. What on earth was wrong with me?

When I found Aunt Grace peacefully dead in her bed my first selfish thought was for myself.

"Bugger!" I said because now I would never be able to ask her what she meant at my wedding, about my life changing utterly the Christmas I was forty. Now I would have to wait and find out for myself.

Then something painful and passionate bubbled up inside me and I wanted to beat my chest and howl and tear at my hair.

My darling Aunt Grace was gone away and I was never going to see her again.

"Alex, Alex!" Was that hysterical voice mine? I'd never lost my nerve in front of Alex Flood before. But then, no-one I loved had ever died before.

He ran straight up the stairs to me, two at a time and when he saw she was dead he put his arms round me, and held me close. I pressed my face into his shirt and felt, in the silence, his heart beating. I didn't speak and he didn't speak and gradually the painful, passionate grief subsided.

The etiquette of how to behave with an old lover is something I don't know much about. Camilla was always much better at casual relationships than me.

"Oh, we're just friends now," she always said.

"But how can you reverse? Once you let the intimacy out of the box, it doesn't go back in. It's out and it stays out."

Camilla shrugged. "Maybe there are different levels of intimacy."

"Is that a photograph of you?"

Alex pointed to a small photograph of a little girl in a silver frame on the bedside table.

I shook my head. "No. It's Naomi, and that's Naomi's teddy bear in the bed beside her. I always thought she'd burned everything. I remember the bonfire. She threw far too much paraffin on it. She was mad with grief. She screamed and screamed and screamed when they tried to close the coffin. And she's never set foot in Derryrose graveyard since. She didn't go to Camilla's first wedding."

"Naomi looks like you. You could have been sisters."

"I know. Poor Aunt Grace! I don't know if that was a good thing or a bad thing."

The television van pulled up to the front door. It was a great deal grander than I was expecting. I could read *News At Ten* on the side of it.

"I suppose we'll have to tell him she's dead," Alex said reluctantly.

"I suppose we will, but it's very sad to send him away empty-handed when it was one of her last wishes that she expose the thieving charlatans of Big Carpet on television."

We looked at each other. The television man was out of his van.

I said, "When a passenger dies on board an aircraft during a flight the drill is that you leave them in their seat until landing. Cover them with a blanket. Don't make a fuss. You never make an unscheduled landing and stop a flight just because there's a death on board."

The television man knocked on the front door.

"It's your shout," said Alex. "You're the boss. I'm going to answer the front door."

I tucked Naomi's old teddy in beside her and pulled the pink satin eiderdown up over my aunt. Darling Aunt

Grace and her ghastly taste in bedding. The pink eiderdown matched pink curtains and pink wallpaper. She'd had the room thoroughly revamped when Uncle Denis died – 'feminised' she called it. Pink was Naomi's favourite colour.

Then I went back downstairs. Alex and the television man were drinking strong cafetière coffee in the kitchen. A fish curry was cooking pungently on the Aga. Somewhere, really far back in the corner of my brain, I thought: 'I must shake his wife's hand when I meet her. What a good job she's made of him. When I knew him he couldn't boil water.'

I beamed at the television man, thrust my hand forward and said, "Good morning, how lovely of you to come. I'm Grace Walsh."

Both the television man and Alex half rose out of their seats.

"Hello, Mrs Walsh. I'm Jimmy."

Alex pulled a chair out for me and said, "Sit here, darling."

Shock and sorrow had made me a bag of nerves. My hands were shaking until Alex's fingers brushed against them when he handed me coffee, my legs were trembling until his foot rested lightly on top of my foot under the table.

Jimmy said, "We're in a very special position today, Mrs Walsh, and this is a very special broadcast. The managing director of Big Carpet has just been sacked. The official story is that he's been headhunted by a Japanese electronics firm but the word on the street is that Big Carpet has been inundated with complaints from the public about faulty carpets for the past couple of years since he rose to the top job. It's a huge human-interest story: *Fat Cat Brought Down By People-Power. News At Ten* are running it tonight. You're going to be on the national news with your carpet story, Mrs Walsh."

"Please call me Grace," I said faintly.

The news recording passed in a surreal blur. I sat on the edge of Aunt Grace's bed, shielding her while Alex helped Jimmy set up the shot.

"You've a lovely place here," said Jimmy as he fussed with the lighting. "It's not often you find an old house with all its period features still intact. The toilet in the bathroom is a genuine Thomas Crapper, did you know that?"

"I suppose it is," I said, laughing.

"And I notice the service bells are still hanging in the back hall. Do they work?"

I pushed a button in the wall near the bed.

"You'll probably have to go out onto the landing. If the door into the back hall is lying open you'll hear it."

"And that old Aga in the kitchen, Alex, did you get that converted to oil or was it already converted when you bought the place?"

"This isn't my house," said Alex smiling. "This house belongs to Grace. Doesn't it, darling?"

"Yes, it belongs to me. I inherited it from my aunt. She had the old Aga converted about twenty years ago."

Jimmy went over to the window to check the light again. "What a fabulous view across the meadow to the big estate! Does some lord live there?"

I shook my head. "Rock royalty. Bobby Flood. Lead singer with Achilles Heel. You're probably too young to remember them. Before my time too. They were huge in the seventies. Bobby Flood was the pin-up. Skin-tight jeans, black hair, green eyes. Girls used to have hysterics and faint with excitement at the sight of him. Didn't they, Alex?"

"I wouldn't know," said Alex smoothly. "I was at boarding school."

Jimmy was star-struck. Impressed. "My mother is a big fan of Achilles Heel. She has all their albums. In fact I bought her *Hellraising Woman* on CD for Christmas."

Finally we were ready to record.

"Just the facts please, Grace," said Jimmy and I looked into the camera and told it the facts about the faulty carpet, the independent inspector, the ambiguous report and the current stalemate with Big Carpet.

"Gosh, I'm impressed," said Jimmy. "One take. You're a natural."

"What a convincing liar you are," said Alex once Jimmy had finished and packed up and gone. "I believed every word you said."

"I didn't lie. I never tell lies." Then, because I didn't like his tone of voice I said, "Do you call your wife 'darling'?"

"I call my wife 'Emma'."

187

Chapter Sixteen

Aunt Grace's death was the talk of the country. By teatime her house was full of PWA ladies making tea and tiptoeing across the faulty bedroom carpet to pay their last respects to my aunt who lay serene and untouchable in her big bed with a posy of wild flowers twisted into her dead fingers.

"Poor old thing." They were kind and indulgent of the Hellraising Woman. "She's never been the same since the last time."

Mummy was over-excited and up to her neck in fastidious formations of ham sandwiches, weak tea in china cups, tray bakes and the bossing about of her friends, Lady Millicent and Mrs Doctor Dawson.

"Lady Millicent, please sweep the drawing-room floor before the rush, and put a row of dining-room chairs along the window. Mrs Doctor D, can you watch the sausage rolls don't burn in the Aga . . ." She took one look at me, bared her teeth and snarled, "What on earth are you wearing?"

"Aunt Grace thought it was pretty."

"Aunt Grace is dead. What are you thinking of? You can't serve tea at her wake in a pink dress. You're middle-aged, Francesca. You're a mother of three. I can hear the Chinese Whispers already – *mutton dressed like lamb*."

"Nobody is going to be looking at me."

"*Everyone* is going to be looking at you. If you've got nothing suitable to wear I suggest you quickly drive to the manse and pick something from my wardrobe."

Will's favourite bit of the *Weekly Telegraph* has always been the features about Western ex-pats who receive counselling from multinational companies when they move offices and move countries. Will loves to guess what the counselling involves – the differences in currency, the variations in weather patterns, perhaps the location of International schools for their children.

"Don't be so superior," I scolded him. "Just because your parents were pioneers!"

"Not just my parents. When you flew away to be a pilot with Ex-Pat Air – did you know anything about the Middle East?"

I thought hard. "Actually, no, I don't think so. I'd only ever been overseas once before. Two weeks in the Maldives. And that was a package holiday, so I suppose it doesn't count."

"And yet, at twenty-four, *without counselling*, you got on

an aircraft and flew seven hours across the world to take up a new job with a new company, in a new country."

"It was an adventure. If I'd had counselling I might not have gone."

Personally, my favourite *Weekly Telegraph* features have always been about ex-pats who need counselling before they return home, since it is generally the case that the world changes while your back is turned. Unless, of course, you are returning to South Derry. I had now been home for little more than twenty-four hours and, as far as I could see, absolutely nothing had changed in the sixteen years since I'd left. My mother was still wearing the grotesque pleated Black Watch tartan skirt and frilly blouse fancy dress that she always wears at wakes and Remembrance Sunday. Camilla calls them her 'dead clothes'. There are newspaper photographs of her wearing them at Uncle Denis' and Naomi's funerals thirty years ago.

When I got to the manse I phoned Camilla.

"Aunt Grace has died. Her wake is lurching between the sublime and the ridiculous. Upstairs we have *Hellraising Woman* and the smell of marijuana masked by the stink of lilies. Downstairs, there is a muddle of industrious effort and pious farce. I have been positioned at the front door in Mummy's best navy-blue Crimplene to meet and greet the mourners and have been issued with recent photographs of Frank and Philip so I recognise them."

After the Masonic Boys' Boarding School Frank went into the Royal Irish Rangers. I think I saw him once on television before the battle for Basra in Iraq but when I phoned Aunt Grace to tell her she said I'd probably mistaken Lt Colonel Tim Collins for him. Philip had joined the RAF as a photographer; he was now an officer.

"I hope Aunt Grace's soul is still hovering close enough to observe and chuckle fondly," I said.

"Lovely," said Camilla. "Listen, Francesca, I can't get the Range Rover to start. What do you think could be wrong with it?"

"You'll have to ask Will. Will keeps the Range Rover on the road. I suppose he hasn't come back yet, has he?"

Will grew up in the Wild West days of the seventies in Zimbabwe. Because of sanctions there were no new cars and no spare parts. Will liked to boast that he rebuilt his first Anglia with sticky-back plastic and toilet-roll holders and drove it up and down to South Africa to university with five friends, all of them contributing towards the petrol money.

I got an ache when I thought about Will. But I was going to have to get over it.

"Will's bakkie is at the airport. The spare keys are in a biscuit tin in the kitchen. Dorothy will drive you up to airport if you ask her nicely . . ."

The wake warmed up. Sir Bobby was reluctantly dragged away from a plate of toffee shortbread, and sent outside to direct the car parking.

A busload of mourners pulled up. "I'm starting to understand," said Mummy, "why Funeral Parlours have become so popular."

"Will Camilla and I send you to the Funeral Parlour?"

"Over my dead body."

She waited patiently until I'd greeted Paddy Murphy, a bachelor and professional wake-attender who would probably be back the following night for another free feed of sandwiches and buns.

"Go upstairs and sit with Aunt Grace. I'm going to have to send Daddy for more tea bags."

Everyone has their own way of grieving and not all them are pretty. Daddy was the youngest of six children and Aunt Grace was the oldest and as his mother had died shortly after he was born Aunt Grace reared my father. It was Aunt Grace who decreed he'd be a clergyman and Aunt Grace who encouraged him through Bible College and Aunt Grace who lobbied 1st Derryrose to take him on as their minister. Aunt Grace was the only mother Daddy had ever known.

"She's written out what she wants me to say at the funeral." He waved some crumpled pieces of stained writing paper peevishly in my direction and wiped a sneaky tear from the corner of his eye. "But her handwriting is dreadful and she seems to have spilt something on it and I can't make out the half of what it says. In this day and age you'd think she could have used a computer."

I was trying to read through Aunt Grace's funeral sermon when Lady Millicent introduced her daughter-in-law.

Emma Flood was small and dark. And of course she was very pretty. Alex and I didn't keep in touch after I went to Ex-Pat Air but thanks to the PWA and Lady Millicent who was always anxious to dispel the large question mark over her only son's sexuality – 'Back me up, Francesca. Alex isn't gay, he's shy,' – I knew the intimate details of Alex's first and only romance.

Emma and Alex met at a hunt in Tipperary. Alex was the whipper-in and Emma was having an eye-catchingly awful day. First she overrode the Master and the Master shouted at her. Then her horse kicked a hound and the huntsman shouted at her. Finally, at the covert side she shouted too soon and headed a fox and Alex shouted at her. Emma burst into tears.

"Finally," said Emma, "he looked at me."

They were married at the end of the season and he brought her home to Lisglasson. Emma built a cross-country course through the thousand acres of Lisglasson parkland; she bought two dozen flying armchairs and schooled them over the jumps. She taught Sir Bobby to ride and had him photographed – in his trademark tight jeans and dealer boots, and an Achilles Heel T-shirt – flamboyantly leaping a huge ditch full of water.

"She had me high on toffee shortbread," he told Aunt Grace afterwards.

The photograph appeared in every newspaper and magazine in Ireland under the caption '*The Flying Rocker*'.

Achilles Heel gave a sell-out tour soon after and Lisglasson Equestrian Centre became the in-place for the beautiful people to learn to ride. Most of them had never been to the scary North before, so Lady Millicent decorated a dozen bedrooms at the back of the house – (they looked fantastic in a twelve-page spread in *Hello* magazine) and the beautiful people paid for the privilege of sleeping there, and having Emma bellow, "You're on the wrong diagonal!".

Alex and Emma had four beautiful, adorable children and they all lived happily ever after.

"It's hard to believe we've never met before," said Emma Flood, "because I know all about you. Alex says you were a captain in command of an aircraft, a crew and two hundred passengers. And your mother never tires of boasting to the Girls' Brigade that you've flown round the world twice. Then you gave it all up and eloped to Botswana with a middle-aged Zimbabwean builder. And before anybody can say 'honeymoon baby' you've had three."

"Well yes," I agreed reluctantly, "but it sounds rather foolish when you say it like that. A textbook example of a desperate, ageing woman marrying in haste and repenting at leisure."

"On the contrary, it sounds rather romantic."

Mourners usually spend as little time as is decently possible in the self-conscious confines of the dead. Emma however made herself comfortable on the edge of Aunt Grace's bed and stroked my dead aunt's face with affection while she chatted.

"I used to sometimes meet your sister, the doctor, at the nursery school dropping Kathryn off. I have a Catherine too – they were both in Mrs Armstrong's class last year. What an old bat!"

"Who? Mrs Armstrong?"

Emma laughed suddenly. "Have I shocked you? I'm sorry. You see Camilla and I were always last and Mrs

Armstrong used to be very frosty when we breezed in ten minutes late. Again. 'Ladies,' she used to bark, 'your daughters are missing a vital part of their pre-school education!'."

"What did Camilla say to that?"

"I rather think it was water off a duck's back with Camilla. She just looked down her long arrogant nose at Mrs Armstrong and said, 'You're doing a marvellous job, Mrs Armstrong. Keep it up,' – so the old bat always had to vent her frustrations on me. And I'm always late for the most unfair reasons. The baby needs his nappy changed at the last minute. Or I can't find some vital piece of Catherine's pre-school equipment – like clean pants. One day we were halfway down the road and she pipes up from the back seat, 'Oh, look, Mummy, I've forgotten to put on my panties!' so of course we had to turn the car and go back and get them. Poor little Catherine had to stand up for me that morning 'Poor Mummy,' she announced kindly and firmly to Mrs Armstrong, 'she always tries her best.'" Emma hooted with laughter. "As a peace offering I brought some egg boxes and toilet-roll holders when I went back to collect her. 'From my recycling bin,' I explained, 'for arts and crafts. Arts and crafts are a vital part of pre-school education, don't you think, Mrs Armstrong?' and Mrs Armstrong said she was terribly sorry but they're not allowed to accept donations of egg boxes because of the risk of salmonella. And they're not allowed to accept donations of toilet-roll holders either –"

"Because of the risks of wee-wees?"

More hoots of laughter.

Mummy stuck her head around the bedroom door,

anxious disapproval written all over her funeral face. Especially at the sight of Emma, snuggled up beside Aunt Grace, giggling.

"Francesca, darling!"

So I lost my 'chief mourner' position in the bedroom and was unceremoniously demoted back to the front door. Emma gave Aunt Grace one last kiss and came with me.

"I've invited Kathryn Snotter countless times to play with my Catherine, but Camilla always turns me down. 'Oh, I couldn't possibly impose on you,' she always says. But she wouldn't be imposing. I even suggested that she come too if she doesn't like the idea of a little girl going off for a play date on her own."

"It's nothing to do with imposing. It's more to do with having to invite you and Catherine back to No 1 Bluebell Orchard and Catherine and Kathryn making the place untidy. When she's not at school, Kathryn Snotter spends most of her little life with Mrs Young, the childminder, in the village."

"I know you're identical," said Emma suddenly, "but Alex is right. You don't look alike."

"I have a scar on my face," I agreed, sighing, "and in Mummy's dress I look about a hundred years old."

"You have a halo," said Emma smiling, "even in that dress."

Back at the front door the flood of mourners had reduced to a trickle and Sir Bobby was reinstated beside the toffee shortbread. So he wasn't outside directing traffic when a flash Rover pulled up and Sam Dawson jumped out.

Sam Dawson, Mr Dawson, now consultant gynaecologist at the South Derry Hospital.

Sam Dawson, whose favourite joke when he got the job was, "It'll give me a chance to look up a few old friends."

I honestly didn't know what it was about Sam Dawson that made women flock to him.

There were better-looking men around. Taller men. Fitter men. Wealthier men. Nicer men. And Sam Dawson still won every time. Camilla and I always joked that if we could bottle his sex appeal we'd make a fortune.

"Do you know who that is?" I whispered to Emma.

"I most certainly do. That's *Ulster Tatler's* Most Eligible Bachelor. There used to be fights at the ante-natal clinic when I was pregnant because sometimes they'd try to fob me off with the registrar or the other consultant, or a midwife. 'I want Mr Dawson!' I used to screech. 'He's so charming, and he has such fantastic hands!' and they used to say 'Every pregnant woman in South Derry wants Mr Dawson – you have to learn to share.' In the end I had to go privately to get him."

"Is he still *Ulster Tatler's* Most Eligible Bachelor?"

"Oh yes. Voted on, I'm told, by romantic young women who dream of marrying a handsome doctor."

And nostalgic older women who'd been plucked by him in their youth.

"He asked me to marry him about twenty years ago," I boasted, "and I said yes."

"Alex said Camilla was married to Mr Dawson."

"She was. But first Sam was engaged to me, then he jilted me, then he was married to Camilla, then he jilted her . . ."

"Kinky," said Emma, checking her watch. "Listen, I'm going to switch on the television. Alex says the television guy promised you'd be on *News at Ten* tonight. Does Grace have a television? I've never seen her watching one."

"It's in the kitchen."

I had my back turned when Sam Dawson slithered up behind me, ran a confident and experienced hand over my buttocks and whispered, hot and wet into my ear "Love the dress, Camilla. Makes a change from the last time I had you. Was it really only a fortnight ago? It feels like forever. I can't stop thinking about the hard pink rosebuds of your nipples straining for me through sheer black chiffon . . ."

I bolted to the kitchen, blushing madly and feeling a bit sick. Was Sam really describing the same black chiffon Camilla told me she'd worn to seduce a thunderstruck and unappreciative James Snotter on his birthday?

I was away with Ex-Pat Air in the Middle East during most of Camilla's tempestuous marriage to Sam Dawson but I remember there was an evil-looking magpie perched on the limousine that took her to the church to marry him. If Mrs Murphy had been with us she'd have said, "One for sorrow, Camilla."

Camilla ignored the magpie. This was the happiest day of her life. She was going to be Mrs Doctor Sam Dawson. She didn't have to count magpies or pull the petals off flower heads – 'He loves me, he loves me not.' Not now she'd caught him.

It was only a little incident, too insignificant to foretell doom. I thought.

I caught the bridegroom red-handed and red in the face shagging a woman who was most certainly not his new wife over the bonnet of a car. In our matching cream suits Sam wasn't sure if his first act of marital infidelity was being witnessed by his new wife or her sister.

"Oh, bugger! It's only a bit of fun, darling."

Sam's 'bits of fun' became the most enduring feature of the marriage and it became clear that his wife was going to have to put up or shut up.

At first Camilla fought back. Hell hath no fury like a woman scorned. She meticulously shredded her husband's fancy suits and designer ties with a steak knife, she slashed the tyres of his BMW, she broke his bedroom window with a brick. Finally the police were called and there was an exclusion order passed against her and she was forbidden to come within a hundred feet of him.

Camilla cried her eyes out. She couldn't eat because her heart was permanently wedged in her throat; she couldn't sleep because she was hungry. At weekends, after work, she'd sellotape the bags under her eyes out of the way, get dolled up to the nines go to singles bars in Belfast and force herself on unmarried men. Glassy-eyed with drink and desperation she'd take one home, no names, no pack drill and call him 'Sam'.

And all the time she fantasised about reconciliation. How she would keep her husband at arm's length, tantalisingly close enough to smell her perfume, but not close enough to touch her.

"I should never have married him. Sam Dawson never loved me. He only married me because you wouldn't take him, Francesca."

"That's rubbish. We both know that Sam Dawson has never loved anybody, only himself."

"I can't forgive him for making a fool of me," she said but what she really meant was that she couldn't forgive herself.

At my own wedding Sam was in the crowd of well-wishers at the church throwing confetti, until Camilla picked up a stone and aimed it at his head.

And now Camilla was married to James Snotter. They had a daughter and she was expecting another baby.

Sam followed me into the kitchen. *News at Ten* was flickering from the corner, the PWA were washing up after a successful wake. Before anyone could speak, and with my back still turned to him so he couldn't see my face, I announced, "Have I mentioned that I'm expecting another baby?"

Then I spun round to face him. My face was partially in shadow but Sam could never tell who was Camilla and who was Francesca even when he was engaged to me or married to my sister.

"You stupid bitch!" said Sam softly and explosively, for only a consultant gynaecologist could be shocked when unprotected sex resulted in a conception. Then he shrugged, regained his composure and whispered, "It's never stopped us before, has it? Meet you Tuesday, same place, same time, same as usual . . ."

Then somebody, Emma I think, said, "Congratulations, Francesca!"

"You're Francesca!"

"Yes, Sam. Who else would I be?"

"Quiet, everybody!" said Emma. "It's coming on now. *Fat Cat Brought Down By People Power!* Oh look, Francesca, there you are . . ."

I'd never been on television before and I'd never been videoed with a camcorder, not even at my wedding, or at any of Camilla's, so it was a novel experience to see myself in three dimensions. Was I really so elegant? So attractive? So intelligent?

I really did look just like Camilla playing 'Confusion'.

No wonder Sam Dawson couldn't tell the difference between us.

Gosh.

"Pretty dress," said Emma. "Is it yours?"

"The pink dress? Yes, it's mine. From years ago. I found it in the big wardrobe in the spare room the night before Aunt Grace died. Aunt Grace said she liked it. I was going to wear it tonight at the wake, but Mummy thought it would be disrespectful to the dead."

"The dead can't hurt you," said Emma solemnly. "It's the living you should be more concerned about."

Chapter Seventeen

Aunt Grace was cremated on Saturday morning. I thought we should have brought Kathryn Snotter with us but James refused.

"No," he said.

"Not even to the service at Lisglasson Lodge before we go to the Crematorium?"

"Absolutely no way."

"But who's going to look after her? You can't expect Mrs Young to look after Kathryn at the weekend."

"I most certainly do. Childminding is not a nine-to-five job. A childminder has a moral duty towards the children in her care. Mrs Young knows I am a firm believer in the importance of stability and routine in a young child's life. She's Kathryn's primary care-giver and it's her duty to be available to Kathryn twenty-four hours a day, seven days a week."

"Well, I hope you've bought her a present. To say thank you. A bunch of flowers or something."

James shook his head firmly. "No presents. It's against my principles to bribe employees."

Mrs Young's grandchildren were cheerfully wrecking her house when I arrived with Kathryn and a large bunch of orange lilies on Saturday morning.

"I keep telling Valerie not to give them E numbers," said Mrs Young indulgently. "But I suppose I'm my own worst enemy. I've them totally spoiled. I can't help it. I only ever see them on a Saturday."

"Last Saturday Ross took off all his clothes and ran around naked," Kathryn told me solemnly and disapprovingly, "and Melanie doesn't flush the toilet when she does pee-pee. And she doesn't wash her hands after."

I said, "I'm really sorry about this, on a Saturday morning. Weekends are for families."

"Don't worry about that. This isn't the first Saturday Kathryn has spent here. She comes when Dr Snotter is golfing, and sometimes she even comes on Sunday if Dr Snotter is on call. Dr Snotter and I understand each other. I charge him double time at weekends."

Aunt Grace's funeral arrangements contrasted sharply with her flamboyant, sociable wake. Invitation was by ticket only, there was a fastidious seating arrangement, and many of the guests had been given speaking parts. Sir Bobby Flood was to sing "Always Look on the Bright Side of Life," James Snotter to read a poem and Aunt Grace would lie resplendent in the open coffin lined in pink satin, with her soul playing Peeping Tom through the drawing-room window.

"Intolerable detail," said Mummy irritably. "I think she did it to wind me up."

We were in the kitchen. I was polishing champagne glasses and Mummy was making buck's fizz.

"Pour the orange juice into the glass first. If you pour the champagne in first the whole thing will fizz up over you."

"How would you know?" she said rudely. "You don't drink."

"Well, forgive the observation," I snapped straight back, "but you don't drink either.

At least *I've* watched a thousand glasses of buck's fizz being made on the aircraft."

I watched, without surprise, as she ignored my advice and the buck's fizz reared up and attacked her.

"You could always tell an inexperienced air stewardess. She had orange stains, just like that, on her blouse."

Mummy slammed down the champagne glass. "Why don't you just say 'I told you so' and have done!" she said, and to my disgust she burst into noisy, hysterical tears.

I took a deep breath. This has always been the trouble between Mummy and me. Mummy hits the panic button at the slightest provocation and for forty years I've been breathing deeply and calmly and swallowing back the urge to bark, 'Pull yourself together!' at my own mother.

"Mummy, you need to go shopping. You need to buy yourself a new outfit. You've been wearing that pleated skirt and frilly blouse since Naomi and Uncle Denis were buried. It's time to take them off and wear something else."

Some day I'm going to have to thank Mummy for teaching me how to keep my head when all around are losing theirs and blaming it on me. Years of breathing exercises helped me stay calm under the knife when Dorothy was cutting cancer out of my face. They helped me stay calm the night Isobel was born on the kitchen floor. And they helped me stay calm during the four-and-a-half-hour flight back from South India when the landing gear was stuck on the 767 and my crew and I were preparing for a crash.

I'd just been made Captain and Aunt Grace was with me – she was my designated spouse. She could fly anywhere she wanted with me, in First Class, with a standby ticket.

We'd already been to Bombay – Aunt Grace had bought herself a pair of black leather trousers. We were flying south to Trivandrum, turning around and flying back to the Middle East, to Oman. As always, I'd phoned Will and told him what time to expect me.

The landing into Trivandrum was textbook. The passengers disembarked, the aircraft was cleaned; Marian the chief stewardess asked me if she had time to go into the terminal building to have a cigarette.

"Please go with her, Aunt Grace, and spend the rest of your rupees. It's against the law to carry rupees in and out of India, and I'd rather you weren't arrested."

"Where are your extra rupees?" she asked.

"If I had any, which I don't, I'd hide them in my bra."

On the take-off out of Trivandrum I realised immediately that there was something wrong with the landing gear. It hadn't retracted properly back up into the body of the aircraft. It was stuck. What would happen when we landed? Would it click into its proper position, or would it collapse under the weight of the aircraft? Would the aircraft slow down and stop normally or would we nosedive, belly-flop, skid and crash?

From the ground I was advised, "Fly back to the Middle East. Attempt your landing in Abu Dhabi. We'll have fire engines and ambulances waiting."

"Are we going to die?" Marian asked.

For four-and-a-half hours the crew and I rehearsed what we were going to do if the landing gear didn't click into place.

"Tell the passengers to stow absolutely everything in the overhead stowages. Handbags, books, bottles of water, everything. Tell them to take off their high-heeled shoes, take out their false teeth, put their spectacles away safely. Tell them it might be bumpy. Show them how to brace for an impact. Tell them to stay braced until the aircraft stops. When the aircraft finally stops, *and not before*, throw open the doors. The escape slides will inflate and we'll all slide to safety."

"Yes, Captain." Marian's lips were blue.

"How's Aunt Grace?"

"She's on her second gin and she's singing 'Fight the Good Fight'."

I tried to think of something profound as we circled the runway before landing. But I couldn't think of anything except the job I was doing. There wasn't any space in my head for a profound thought. I did my job. I landed the aircraft. The landing gear didn't collapse. We slowed down and stopped. It was one of my best-ever landings.

Afterwards Aunt Grace said, "I don't think we'll tell your mother about this, Francesca."

There was timid knock at the back door of Lisglasson Lodge. It was Mrs Murphy, Aunt Grace's old housekeeper, clutching her rosary beads.

"I've come to pay my last respects, if you don't mind."

"Of course, I don't mind," I said. "Aunt Grace is still in bed. I'll take you up to her."

Mrs Murphy's heart was broken when Naomi was killed in the bomb. She'd reared her from when she was a little girl: she'd baked her birthday cakes, bought her Christmas presents, scolded her, worried about her, loved her. When Aunt Grace and Uncle Denis were out partying and Naomi had bad dreams and woke crying, Mrs Murphy had lain beside her in her little wrought-iron bed until she'd gone back to sleep. The morning of the bomb Naomi had tripped and cut her knees and Mrs Murphy had cleaned out the cuts with salt water and put plasters on them

"*Gracias*," said Naomi who was just back from Spain.

Nobody knows for certain who planted the Derryrose bomb in front of Grubbs Pub. And it doesn't really matter anyway. The only important thing about the Derryrose bomb was that it killed an innocent man and little girl. The person who planted it has had to live with that on his conscience for the rest of his life.

Aunt Grace didn't need a housekeeper after the bomb. Mrs Murphy got a new job baking birthday cakes.

"What's she doing here?" asked James Snotter.

He was in the drawing room practising his poem for the service which would be held there later. Aunt Grace had wanted Alex to recite the poem but Alex had refused. So James Snotter had kindly stepped in though his voice was so boring I had little doubt we'd all be asleep by the end of it.

"She used to work here. She's gone to say a prayer."

"That's nice."

"Does James Snotter know what you did with your wedding dress after you married him?" I asked Camilla, for she'd given her pretty Regency-style dress with its extra big skirt to hide her extra big tummy to Mrs Murphy's pregnant granddaughter Niamh who'd had to get married in a hurry because Malachy, her fiancé, was going to jail.

"Of course, I never told him," said Camilla. "Niamh wanted to give it back to me afterwards, but I told her to keep it. I'm not planning to use it again."

The undertakers arrived and Aunt Grace was tucked into her coffin.

"Do you think we should put Naomi's teddy bear in with her?"

"No. Aunt Grace doesn't need it any more."

Aunt Grace always gave good parties and her funeral was

no exception. The drawing-room was filled with her favourite friends, there was a reassuring clink of crystal and the soft chatter of conversation. I waved across the room to Emma Flood but she was flirting with my cousins, Frank and Philip, and didn't see me.

"Before I say another word," said Sam Dawson with a wolfish grin, "are you Francesca or Camilla?"

"Does it matter?"

"It certainly does, darling," said Sam, running an experienced eye over me. "Listen, don't tell me. You know I love a challenge. I shall sit beside you at the back of the class and we'll play 'Guess the Girl' during the service." He raised his voice slightly as Alex walked past us, carrying a buck's fizz for Emma and a glass of tap water for himself. "And if I still can't tell, I shall have undress you, and examine you . . ."

I began to giggle.

"Flirting at a funeral," Alex reprimanded, "have you no shame?"

"I'm trying to guess," said Sam smoothly, "if this is Camilla or Francesca. I suppose you can tell, Alex?"

Alex smiled tightly. "I've no idea." And he walked on.

"I think he hates you," I said cheerfully.

"He's just jealous."

The service started and Daddy got up to speak first.

Sam whispered, "I'll know you're Camilla if you start to doze off. She always falls asleep when the Reverend starts to talk."

"We both do that. It's conditioning. Daddy used to

practise his sermons when he was trying to rock us to sleep in the big twin pram when we were babies."

Already I was beginning to feel the soporific effect of my father's voice. My eyes were closing and my head was nodding when the phone went in the hall. Sam followed me when I went to answer it.

It was Mrs Young. "I don't want to panic you, but Kathryn has fallen head first off the slide."

"I'm going to have to take Kathryn to Casualty," I said. "Mrs Young thinks she has a head injury. Will you tell James after the service?"

Sam kissed my hand. "Game over. Now I know you're Francesca. If you were Camilla you'd have expected James Snotter to take your daughter to the hospital . . ."

Kathryn was lying prostrate on the red-leather sofa in Mrs Young's kitchen. Her face was a horrible green and there were traces of vomit on her Mini Boden dress.

"I fell off the slide, Aunt Francesca."

I examined my niece's head carefully. There was no blood, no bruising, no bumps. "Do you think shock made her vomit?"

Mrs Young looked shaken. "Maybe it's shock. Maybe she's bleeding internally. Little children with head injuries just keep on running around and then 'Bang!' they're dead."

"You look quite shocked yourself."

Mrs Young started to cry. "I've been a childminder for seventeen years; there has never been a child hurt in my care before. Not even a bruise. I'm far more careful with other people's children than I ever was with my own. I never let them out of the playpen or off the sofa when they're here, I'm so afraid of them getting hurt and their parents suing me. But today, with Ross and Melanie running wild, I thought I'd relax the rules just this once . . ."

"So you let her off the sofa, and the minute your back was turned she ran straight to the slide and climbed up and fell off it from the top."

"My back wasn't turned. I was doing my Pilates on the kitchen floor and she wanted to slide and I said, 'Kathryn, don't climb the slide until I'm there to help you. I'll be with you in one minute when I've finished my Pilates. One minute, Kathryn Snotter.' But she didn't listen!" Mrs Young's voice rose. "If she'd been one of my own I'd have put her over my knee and smacked her with my Cement Hand and there'd not have been another squeak about climbing the slide without supervision. Even the threat of a smack would have been enough to stop her."

"Does James not allow you to smack?"

"It's not Dr Snotter who makes the law. Smacking is against the law."

"The law says we must spare the rod and spoil the child? That's new! I'm sure we didn't have that law when I was a child."

"No one likes to smack a little child," said Mrs Young. "But we used to say, when you were a child, that it only took one smack on a nappy at eighteen months to teach a child right from wrong."

I'd been to Casualty once in Botswana when Hugh fell into

the side of the stone fireplace in the living-room and split his head open. It was a few days before Isobel was due and I was supposed to be going out for dinner with the Book Group. One last adult conversation before the new baby was born and the mists of early motherhood descended.

My legs were swollen like bananas and Will had sent me to lie on the top of the bed. The Dallas family bathtime, the most fraught part of the Dallas day, was approaching and I needed all my reserves of energy to get through it without tears (the children) and the launching of naked Barbies (Will and me). So I was lying on the top of the bed, admiring my dusty feet and wondering if I would ever be able to touch my toes again, when Hugh and Ella and Will started screaming for me from the living-room.

By the time I'd dragged myself off the bed and up the hall, Hugh's forehead was protruding starkly white from the swollen sides of an enormous gash and Will looked like he was going to faint.

"You stupid man," I screamed at my husband. "I leave you alone with them for five minutes!"

If I'd had a naked Barbie, I might have stabbed him with it.

Meanwhile Ella who was two was using Hugh's Blankie to staunch the flow of blood and was shouting "999 Emergency!"

"Mummy, Mummy, Mummy!" screeched Hugh.

"Oh well. I didn't really want to go out this evening anyway."

We all went to the hospital together, which was just as well because, being pregnant, I couldn't go into the X-ray

Room and since Hugh wouldn't let the nurses anywhere near him Will had to hold him down on the X-ray table. Then Dorothy came from Swiss Chalet and stitched his head under general anaesthetic.

I took him back to the hospital a week later to get his stitches out, but he went berserk when the nurse approached him with a stitch-cutter, leaping out of my arms and running away from me down the hospital corridor, barefoot, with Blankie flapping behind him, screaming, "Help! Help! Help!"

"Come back tomorrow," said the smiling nurse, but I was too ashamed to go back and risk a repeat performance.

The night Isobel was born, half an hour before my waters broke, I sat on my son and Will cut them out with a penknife.

South Derry Casualty had one other child waiting on Saturday morning. A boy who was so constipated he'd started vomiting poo.

"Doctor Snotter says it's Ryan's diet," his distraught mother told me, "and he's been ever so helpful, making out diet sheets for him and giving us lists of food that he should eat. But Ryan doesn't like Weetabix and brown bread and fresh fruit and vegetables. And I must say I can't really blame him. I hate that healthy stuff and I won't eat it either. So then Dr Snotter prescribed Syrup of Figs, a teaspoonful every night before bed but it tastes disgusting and Ryan won't take it any more . . ."

The Casualty doctor was a charming Indian gentleman who said, "Hello again, Kathryn," when it was our turn.

"Again? Has Kathryn been here before?"

Dr Chada nodded. "Without even looking at her notes, I can tell you that she fell on a sparkler and burnt her face at Halloween. That she has stuffed beads up her nose, that she has swallowed a pound coin, and that she has a puncture wound in her armpit from bouncing off a bed and being impaled on a stiletto shoe. I cannot understand why this child is so naughty. She is looking for an accident every day."

"Today it's my head," said Kathryn importantly. "I fell from the top of the slide."

"Did you fall or did you jump, Kathryn?"

Kathryn smiled at the doctor. "I jumped. Head first."

I was horrified. "Is she saying she jumped head first on purpose? Kathryn, what on earth did you do that for? You could have been killed."

"She did it for attention," said Dr Chada.

"For attention? Do you think she needs psychiatric assessment, doctor? Counselling? Taking into care?"

"This child needs her mother," said Dr Chada.

Chapter Eighteen

On the way home from the hospital I said "What day is today, Kathryn?"

"It's Saturday, Auntie Francesca."

"On Saturday in my house in Botswana we eat Spanish omelette. Ella helps me to chop the potatoes into little boxes and we fry them with onions, and Hugh helps me to beat up the eggs and then we mix it all together and make an omelette. Do you like omelette?"

"I don't know. What's omelette?"

"Eggs, darling. Do you like eggs?"

"I don't know, Auntie Francesca."

I slowed the car and turned into the supermarket carpark. "Oh well, only one way to find out. Do you like shopping?"

"Shopping!" She was thrilled. "Can we take a trolley, Auntie Francesca? Can I sit in a trolley?"

When James got back from Aunt Grace's funeral the

Spanish omelette had been made and eaten and Kathryn –
enveloped in a new ankle-length Barbie apron – was washing
up.

"Look, Daddy, I'm helping!" She waved her hands in
new pink Marigolds.

"I'm sorry about the mess, but you can't make an
omelette without breaking some eggs!"

James felt his daughter's head professionally. "Did
Precash Chada X-ray at the hospital?"

I nodded. "It was clear. And he briefed me about head
injuries. I don't know, of course, I'm not a doctor, but she
hasn't vomited again and she hasn't been drowsy and she
says she doesn't have a headache. Do you think we
should phone Camilla and tell her, or will it worry her un-
necessarily?"

James was suddenly angry. "What's the point? Do you
think it would change anything? You don't know your sister
very well if you think it would change anything."

And to my embarrassment he burst into tears.

I took a deep breath. And swallowed back the urge to
bark, 'Pull yourself together!' at my current brother-in-law.
James had been a single parent for almost a fortnight and
the strain was starting to show.

"Kathryn, the onions have burnt Daddy's eyes. Will
you run upstairs to your bedroom and bring down your
medical kit so we can examine him and make him better?"

Fastidiously she removed the pink Marigolds and the
Barbie apron and bustled importantly out of the kitchen.
"Don't worry, Daddy. I can make you better."

When she'd gone upstairs James, almost hysterical,

shouted, "Kathryn's not my daughter! Don't pretend she is. Everybody knows she's not my daughter."

"I didn't know that."

He looked surprised. Then he repeated more quietly, "She can't be my daughter; the sums don't add up."

"What sums?"

James brushed away fresh tears. "When we got married Camilla told me the baby was due in December. But when she had the elective Caesarean section at Halloween – six weeks early – it was really obvious to me that Sam Dawson was delivering a full-term baby. Kathryn weighed over nine pounds."

"Perhaps Camilla got her dates wrong."

Kathryn returned with her medical kit. She was wearing a miniature white coat, and her mother's beautiful pointy-toed shoes that I had on at the funeral. There was a plastic stethoscope hanging from her neck.

"Sit down, Daddy, and don't be afraid. I'm here to help you. First I'm going to shine this pencil torch into your sore eye. Then we'll clean out your eye with some water. Then we'll put on a plaster. Then you'll wear a patch over your eye until it gets better."

"Kathryn!" I was impressed. "You sound like a real doctor."

Kathryn beamed. "I just remembered what Daddy told me when I squirted shampoo into my eyes in the bath!"

"Daddy says your birthday is at Halloween. That makes you special. I think you were found inside a pumpkin."

"Don't be silly, Auntie Francesca. Babies come out of the mummy's bum-bum."

Kathryn examined James' eye. "I think you need some eye shadow to make it better."

She sprinted out of the kitchen and back up the stairs.

"If Kathryn was conceived in January, I'm not her father," James told me slowly and painfully. "Camilla spent January in Barbados with the gang. She must have conceived Kathryn in Barbados. I'm not the father. I wasn't there."

A long silence stretched between us. James sat, defeated, with his head in his hands. Ugly, pompous James Snotter who'd diligently cared for Kathryn, to the best of his limited ability, every day of her life since she'd been born, yet was unable to enjoy the simple pleasures of parenting. He couldn't say the silly, proud things that Will and I were always saying like, "Ella looks just like you when I try to say no to her. The lip drops, her head droops, she has tears in her eyes, and I give in every time" or "Hugh's feet are exactly the same shape as your feet, Will." Because every time he looked at Kathryn he wondered who she was really like.

Finally I said, "From the moment she was born, you've been Kathryn's father. Does it really matter if it was your sperm that fertilised Camilla's egg?"

"It shouldn't," said James Snotter sadly, "but it does."

On Saturday night I had a hot date with my two best cousins, Major Frank and Flight Lieutenant Philip.

They'd turned up the morning of Aunt Grace's funeral – Frank from Iraq and Philip from the Falkland Islands – both looking exceptionally handsome in uniform.

"H?" Philip whispered.

"Hotel."

"F?"

"Foxtrot."

"Good girl!"

My cousins had smothered me in kisses, much to Mummy's pious consternation.

"I've seen nothing but sheep for months," explained the irrepressible Philip. "Come here and let me kiss you too, Aunt Madeline!"

"Boys!" exclaimed Mummy frantically. "Your mother has just died."

"Where's Will?"

The last time Frank and Philip had been home on leave together was for my wedding and since Will had done 'call up' during the bush war in Zimbabwe it's fair to say that my cousins had rather hero-worshipped him.

The night before our wedding, once Will had declined the services of Adam the pre-marriage expert, Frank and Philip took him out on the town. Thanks to my cousins, Will had one eyebrow shaved off and an unaccounted-for love bite on his neck the day he married me.

Now Frank and Philip had taken off their uniforms and were changing the oil in my old BMW.

"I service her every time I'm home," Frank boasted.

"And she's still taxed, insured and MOTed," said Philip. "Apart from empty crisp packets littering the inside she's spotless."

"Great, I'll drive her to church tomorrow."

"U?" said Philip

"Uniform."

"E?"

"Echo."

Frank said, "Did you ever apologise to Alex Flood for taking him to the Maldives, having your wicked way with him and then dumping him afterwards?"

"That's not what happened."

"That's *exactly* what happened. You broke the poor man's heart."

"Rubbish!" I was brisk. "And even if I did take advantage of him, I still respected him in the morning. He's happily married now with a super wife and four children."

"Then you won't mind him coming over for a drink later, will you?"

I made an unenthusiastic face. "Why don't you invite James instead of me? James Snotter, Camilla's current husband. He could do with a night out. I'll spend the night at No 1 Bluebell Orchard with Kathryn."

Now it was Frank's turn to make an unenthusiastic face. "I've heard he drinks Malibu and pineapple."

"I've heard he doesn't drink at all," said Philip.

"Alex Flood doesn't drink."

My cousins remained unenthusiastic. "But we like Alex. Alex hunts. You know what they say about hunting, don't you? Hunting is war without the gunfire."

"James Snotter is married to Camilla. I'd say that's the same as war without the gunfire."

Kathryn and I went to church together on Sunday morning.

I drove my old BMW and Kathryn wore her best dress with a feather boa, clip-clop shoes, and blue lipstick.

Before we'd even parked the car an enchanting child with dark shiny hair held back by a Barbie tiara came running over and announced, "My name is Catherine Flood and my telephone number is 79423456. Please will you phone my mummy and ask her can I come home to tea with Kathryn?"

And Catherine and Kathryn ran off to Children's Church holding hands and swinging jewelled plastic handbags.

I tried to speak to Emma after the service but she was rather red in the face and trying to round up her youngest son who was hiding from her under a chair in the Children's Church.

"Sebastian, darling, come out or the nice lady will have to lock you in," she pleaded while an audience of nice ladies unkindly smirked and nudge-nudge wink-wink whispered to each other, "That Emma Flood hasn't a clue. She can't control her children at all. I'm telling you if he was my boy he'd soon come out from under that table. Or else . . ." Etc, *ad nauseam*.

"How these people love to criticise me," Emma muttered desperately. "I do everything I can to give my children a happy home life. I read to them. I play with them. I provide a taxi service to drive them round the country to mini rugby and piano lessons and swimming lessons and ballet lessons and riding lessons and conversational French. Yet the minute I take them to church I am *judged* . . ."

Sebastian bolted from under the chair and began running, head down, arms pumping, for the door. There was only one thing for it.

I stuck out my foot and tripped him.

"Quick," I said as he fell, "give me your feather boa, Kathryn, and we'll tie him up and get him out to the car before he gets his breath back."

I picked up the little boy before he got a chance to run away again, threw him over my shoulder and we made a run for it. Kathryn, squealing with delight, and waving her feather boa in the air, ran after me. Now these people really would have something to talk about.

"Yes," said Emma Flood, "yes, of course, Catherine can come to tea tomorrow. What a wonderful idea. What time will I bring her over?"

"Perhaps you'd like to come too?"

"No need for that," said Emma brightly. "I have the hairdresser in the afternoon – why don't I leave her over then? It'll be nice for Catherine to have a friend to play with instead of television and crisps with boring granny . . ."

When Kathryn and I got home from church we found James Snotter passed out, snoring in a beer-soaked heap, on Camilla's cream sofa.

Kathryn screwed up her delicate nose. "Stinky Daddy."

We were dishing up lunch when James woke. His eyes were bloodshot, his hair was a mess, one of his eyebrows was shaved off and he had a love bite on his neck.

"How can I tell you've been out with those awful cousins of mine?" I said smiling. "They did the same thing to Will the night before his wedding. Got him drunk and took advantage of him."

James smiled ruefully. "I got off light. You should see what they've done to Alex Flood – they shaved his head!"

We sat down to dinner in Camilla's dining-room.

"I can't believe the price of beef," I said as I carved. "It's more than three times the price we pay in Botswana. But you've a fantastic selection of potatoes. Kathryn and I couldn't decide which to choose yesterday in the supermarket. In the end we picked the potatoes with the prettiest name, didn't we, Kathryn?"

"Kerr's Pink," said Kathryn, "but they're not pink. They're white."

"And we've got turnip because Kathryn says it's your favourite vegetable and we opened a tin of sweetcorn because Kathryn says Mrs Young lets her eat it with a spoon out of the tin."

James ate his dinner in silence. He chewed every mouthful carefully. Then he said, "You want something."

"What makes you say that?"

"Because your sister makes me Beef Wellington when she wants something."

"That's because Beef Wellington is the only thing Mummy ever taught us to cook! She told us that the way to a man's heart is through his stomach. I remember Camilla saying, 'And a cookery book can't make you pregnant'."

James refused to be charmed. "So you do want something?"

"It's only a little something. Kathryn and I have a friend coming for tea tomorrow. Please can we give Mrs Young the day off, so Kathryn can stay at home with me?"

James tried to protest. "I really must object. Mrs Young is Kathryn's primary care-giver."

"But I'm not used to being by myself all day." I was pathetic and pleading. "In Botswana I don't even get a chance to pee in private. I miss it. I'm lonely. I have a headache when the house is quiet."

Finally James said, "She can spend the day with you on one condition."

"Which is?"

"You have to spend the whole of the next day lying with your feet up. Reading a book. Watching a DVD. Resting and relaxing. I know you'll not thank me for saying it, but in my medical opinion as a doctor, you're never going to be able to carry another baby to term if you don't rest more. I'm going to phone Sam Dawson first thing tomorrow and arrange an antenatal appointment for you. I should think, at the very least, that you need iron injections. Have you had a scan yet?"

I shook my head. "What an old fusspot you are!"

James smiled ruefully and stroked Kathryn's cheek with his thumb. Kathryn kissed his hand. "I love you, Daddy."

"Kathryn, look what the onions have done to Daddy again," I said as James' eyes filled with tears. "Run and get him a hanky, darling."

When she was gone I said, "You could have a DNA test done."

James shook his head. "I did consider it at the time. But it wouldn't achieve anything. I know I'd forgive Camilla whatever the result. After all, what happened was before

226

we got married. And she's never ever given me cause to doubt her since. Until my birthday . . ."

He trailed off miserably. Then he said, "Why did you never waste your time with sordid, dirty little affairs before you married Will?"

"How do you know I didn't?"

Ever since Camilla offered to find out if Alex Flood was frigid or gay or if he just didn't fancy me, I'd made it a priority to do unto others as I would have them do unto me. I've made it a priority never to interfere in Camilla's marriages. I ask no questions. I volunteer no advice or opinions.

So what I said next to James Snotter surprised him even more than it surprised me.

"I think you should know, James, that Sam Dawson is sterile. Sam Dawson had a vasectomy when he was a young man. It's not common knowledge but I was his girlfriend at the time. That's how I know . . ."

Every fifteen minutes from the moment Kathryn woke up she asked, "When is Catherine coming, Auntie Francesca? Is it time yet?"

We made some chocolate Rice Krispie buns, and emptied half a dozen bags of crisps into a big plastic mixing bowl. Then Kathryn laid out all her dressing-up clothes – her Disney Princess frock, her bride frock and her Angelina Ballerina tutu on the top of her bed so Catherine could choose what she wanted to wear. And her tiaras and beads and bangles and rings and earrings. And her collection of clip-clop shoes and her make-up. "And my long gloves, Auntie Francesca, and my feather boa."

She neatly laid out her tea set and helped me make diluting orange to put in the teapot. Slowly the clock crept round to three o'clock.

"They're only a little bit late," I said at half past three. "Maybe they've been held up."

At four o'clock I said, "Maybe they've forgotten."

At half past four, with Kathryn in floods of tears, I phoned Lady Millicent.

"Catherine's here," said Lady Millicent. "Emma never said anything about an invitation to tea. Pity really. Catherine has been bored out of her brain all afternoon."

Camilla phoned.

"Is that my famous sister? Who is appearing every hour on the *BBC World News*? *Fat Cat Brought Down By People Power*."

"Was I really on *BBC World*? Gosh!"

"Yes, and I couldn't help noticing that you still haven't had your hair fixed."

I told her about Emma Flood standing me up. "Kathryn was really looking forward to it – she's cried all afternoon. I feel like crying myself. How could Emma Flood let us down?"

Camilla couldn't understand what the fuss was all about. "She probably forgot. The tablets make her forget things."

"What tablets?"

"Her tranquillisers. They're strong enough to sedate

one of those flying-armchair horses she has at the Equestrian Centre. Did James not warn you about Emma Flood? Or Mummy? She's Mummy's best customer. She has a fixed counselling appointment every afternoon at three at the manse. It's the highlight of Emma's day. One whole hour to talk about her favourite subject – herself."

"She told me she was going to the hairdresser at three. I was actually going to ask her who cut her hair!"

"James calls her 'Mrs Rochester'. He's convinced Alex has a padded room for her at Lisglasson. Before she started paying Mummy to listen to her, she'd get totally fixated on a subject and rant on and on about it every time you met her until you were ready to stuff a sock in her mouth and phone the men in white coats to come and take her away."

"What sort of subject?"

"Recently it has been the poor quality of the school dinners in the primary school. Before that it was super bugs in National Health Service hospitals. Before that Tony Blair and the war in Iraq. She was like a walking tabloid newspaper when the twins started primary school and she discovered that all the Protestant ministers in Derryrose go in on Tuesday morning to teach Religious Education to the children who belong to their church. Daddy does the Presbyterians, and there's a Free Presbyterian minister, a Baptist, a Brethren, a Church of Ireland and probably a couple of others. And the kids who don't belong to any church stay in the classroom and read library books. 'But there's only one God,' she kept saying. 'Doesn't it say in the Bible – *repeatedly?* that there is only one God? Why can't there be just one religious lesson? The twins don't want to be Church of Ireland any more. They're insisting that we all become Presbyterian because dear Reverend Simms brings the Presbyterian children sweeties . . ."

"But she seemed so nice and normal when I was talking to her!"

"You can never judge a book by its cover. You should know that! You've always got your nose stuck in a book!"

"One more question. Does your husband know you're pregnant again?"

"Sorry. Got to go," said Camilla.

And she put the phone down on me before I had time to ask her the same tired question I asked every time we spoke:

"Is Will back yet?"

Chapter Nineteen

I was dreaming. It was a bright winter morning in
Botswana. The air smelt of wood smoke. Inside our dusty,
untidy, noisy kitchen Violet was giving Isobel breakfast.
Isobel had started to talk. She was saying, "Mama, Mama!"
Ella and Hugh were outdoors. Ella was wearing her Barbie
pyjamas. Hugh had no sunhat. They were walking, hand in
hand, barefoot past chickens, goats, donkeys, dogs and
queues of spotless people waiting for the kombi to take
them to work. Finally they walked to Tlokweng Speedy
Motors, and Mr JLB. Matekoni, the owner, came out of the
garage to meet them.

"*Dumela, Rra,*" said Ella in her funny, clipped African
voice, "Good morning, sir. I want to speak to the No 1
Ladies Detective," and Mr JLB. Matekoni took them
round to the back of the garage to where his wife, Precious,
had her office.

"*Dumela, Mma,*" said Ella, "Good morning, madam. We have lost our mother. Can you find her?"

I woke feeling homesick. They say that once you've lived there you can never shake the red dust of Africa from your shoes.

This nightmare was James Snotter's fault. Good as his word he'd pulled strings and organised an emergency antenatal appointment for me and good as my word I was lying in bed relentlessly relaxing to please him. But already, and it was only half past six, it was clear that I'd got the heavy end of the stick. Bed is so boring when you're in it by yourself. I was used to having Isobel tucked up on my breast and Hugh snuggled into my back. I was used to being woken at least twice every night by a little voice calling, "Mama, mama!". I hadn't had more three hours, unbroken sleep in the past three years. Now I was getting a full night's sleep every night and I was exhausted.

Emma phoned. Stricken. "I'm so sorry, I meant to phone you last night but I was so engrossed in *I'm a Celebrity, Get me out of Here* that I completely forgot. We're hoping to get Sir Bobby into the jungle in the next series."

"Why were you going to phone me?"

"I was trying to think of a delicious excuse for not bringing Catherine over to play with Kathryn yesterday afternoon, but everything I thought of sounded *shifty*."

"You could have told the truth."

"Oh no," said Emma emphatically. "I couldn't possibly have told you the truth."

"Is the truth really so awful? Does Catherine have nits? Fleas? Worms? Is she not yet properly toilet-trained? Does she bite other children? Perhaps Kathryn Snotter bullies her? Perhaps she doesn't like Kathryn Snotter. Perhaps you don't like Kathryn Snotter –"

"Stop!" said Emma. "It's none of those things. It has nothing to do with Kathryn Snotter or my Catherine. It's you. I didn't want to see you."

My cousin Philip stuck his head round the bedroom door. His compassionate leave was over. He was back in uniform. Frank and he were taking the first shuttle back to London.

"T?" I heard.

"Tango."

He laughed. "What I actually meant this time was would you like a cup of tea?"

He brought it to me and sat down on the bed beside me while I drank it.

"I wish I hadn't promised James Snotter that I'd rest. I hate lying here. It's so boring. Pregnancy isn't an illness."

"Adrienne said exactly the same thing when she was pregnant with our third baby. 'Pregnancy isn't an illness. I haven't time to sit with my feet up' – she was actually making a list in the labour ward when she was having wee Naomi: *'Jane has ballet at three. Grace has ballet at four. Do Grace's homework with her in the car when you're waiting for Jane. Go over her reading at least ten times; she's hopeless at reading. There's Irish Stew in fridge for tea. Lift something out of the freezer for tomorrow.'*

And when the consultant came to break her waters she said, "Philip has to pick up the girls from school at 1 p.m. Is there any chance we can get the baby out before 1 p.m.? Can you stick your hand in, break the water bag with your nails and pull her out? Please?"

I laughed. "When I was having Isobel on the kitchen floor last November, and Ella and Hugh were standing watching Will says I was shouting at him. 'Wipe Hugh's nose. He's got a runny nose!"

"Adrienne has never been to Northern Ireland, has she? You never even brought her back here to meet Aunt Grace after you got married."

Philip shook his head. "There's nothing here for Frank and me. Mum should have sold up and moved away after the bomb. She could have come to Dublin with us. She could have married again. She could have made her life move on, but she never did. I'm glad she left the house to you, Francesca. You're welcome to it. Mum couldn't move forward and Frank and I can't move back."

He kissed me, then stood up and saluted.

"B?"

"Bravo."

And he was gone.

"I've been looking forward to this," said Sam Dawson when I was fast-tracked past his fan club and through to his consulting rooms in South Derry Gynae.

"I bet you say that to all the girls."

Sam smiled. "Certainly do, darling," but his eyes

lingered just a little too long on my face and I noticed the faintest flicker of what we used to have, years and years ago, so long ago I can only remember it with affection.

During the Troubles, Northern Ireland was an ugly place and it became fashionable for my generation to cross the water to mainland universities and to blend in with all the other small fish. Camilla and I did not follow the fish. We went to Queen's in Belfast where we were quickly absorbed into Sam Dawson's gang. We already knew Sam from Derryrose because his mother, Mrs Doctor Dawson, was friendly with our mother and we'd played with him when we were children. Privately we'd always called him Sam the Sissy because he'd played with our dolls and when we were dressing up he'd always picked the nurse's uniform – leaving me to be a fireman and Camilla to be a cowboy. (One of Mummy and Mrs Doctor Dawson's favourite child-rearing theories was about 'conditioning of the sexes'. In an effort to prevent 'conditioning of the sexes' Sam was made to wear pink and Camilla and I were given Meccano and Airfix as birthday presents.)

At Queen's we were dazzled to discover Sam the Sissy was known as 'Sam the Seducer,' and he was notorious for deflowering every virgin he could get his hands on. Camilla and I couldn't understand why, since our idea of sexy was Bobby Flood with his tight jeans with his drug problem. Even Aunt Grace fancied Bobby Flood – and she was brazen about it.

"Are you quite sure Millie Mouse has gone to visit your mother? Excellent! Girls, I'm just popping up to Lisglasson for a cup of sugar." (Bobby's wife had always been known as Millie Mouse before she became Lady Millicent.)

And Grace would jump into Uncle Denis' old sport car and roar off down the avenue to Lisglasson.

Sam Dawson managed to worm his way – insidiously – into our affections. He drove us up and down to Queen's at the weekends in his brown Mini Metro, he roughed up his very clean Barbour coat when we teased him about it – "*So* Presbyterian, Sam" and he threw away the pin in the collar that said 'Barbour' to humour us.

Belfast was a curious town when I was a student. It was too small and too violent for most tastes, so we had to do without big bands like U2, and famous faces like Sebastian Coe, and be grateful for Achilles Heel and Steve Ovett. Dorothy Perkins was our most chic clothes shop, and lasagne and potatoes at Romeo's was the height of gastronomic sophistication. The Medics Ball was the social highlight of the university year.

Camilla was already safely engaged to Adam Robinson and her big white wedding was less than eighteen months away. Regretfully she waved her modest diamond cluster in Sam's face.

"I can't go. I've been invited to a Sunday School party at Adam's church."

So Sam asked me to the Medics Ball.

It was my very first ball. Aunt Grace lent me an evening dress: it was from the sixties, it was psychedelic, the front plunged in a V to my waist.

"Won't my breasts fall out?"

"Only if you're dancing on tables!"

I know Sam the Seducer thought his patience was to be

rewarded that night when he saw me in Aunt Grace's dress. I know Sam the Seducer thought my name was going to join his long list of deflowered virgins.

He wined me and dined me.

I vomited all over him.

"I'm so sorry. I think I might be frigid."

Amazingly Sam Dawson and I became an item at Queen's. Girlfriend, boyfriend. I liked him. I really did. It wasn't Sam's fault that I've never been attracted to Viking blonds in Barbour coats. I've always preferred my men dark, with a bit of stubble, in tight jeans. And maybe sometimes, when we were kissing in the dark, I nearly called him 'Alex' by mistake. But only sometimes. And his brown Mini Metro was better than no car. And it was flattering to be the girlfriend of *Ulster Tatler's* Most Eligible Bachelor. All the girls in my class were pea-green with envy.

The humour was very black in Belfast when I was a student and we made our own fun. Camilla and I longed to get caught up in a bomb scare – and get on the television – so we loitered around the Europa Hotel, the most bombed hotel in Europe, waiting for something to happen. Sometimes we took tea in the foyer, full of nerves and excitement. The afternoon the Europa was bombed I was at a hairdresser a few streets away and we were evacuated before the stylist had finished and, thanks to the bombers I was left with a really silly-looking 'Flock of Seagulls' hairdo with one side considerably longer than the other side.

"Let's go away for a dirty weekend," said Sam.

"Can Camilla come?" I asked, for I knew that Mummy would never let me go unchaperoned.

"Why not? We'll ask all the usual suspects. Go in a gang."

That was how Sam's holiday gang started. Six of us in a caravan in Portrush on the North Antrim coast in March. Squashed round the Formica table, huddled inside cheap sleeping bags, playing snap with a pack of cards. Arguing about whose turn it was to venture outside into the gale-force downpour to fetch drinking water. Head-banging at Tracs Disco on the seafront beside the Amusements. Standing on a street corner eating chips from a van on the way home. And flipping a coin to see who would sleep in the double bed in the caravan and who would have to sleep on the bench seats.

That Portrush weekend was where all the trouble started with Camilla and Sam. It was less than a fortnight till she married Adam Robinson and she'd told her fiancé she was having a hen night. I know Adam fondly pictured her eating lasagne and potatoes with a couple of Scripture Union girls in Romeo's, before going on to watch *Karate Kid* in the New Vic. He could never in his wildest imaginings have supposed she'd spend her hen night in the clutches of Sam the Seducer. An experience I think she never fully recovered from.

Camilla was horrified with herself afterwards. "What do you mean you're not jealous? How can you not be furious with me? He's your boyfriend and I'm a slapper and I'm absolutely furious with myself."

"Well, *I* wasn't planning to lose *my* virginity in a caravan full of medical students so why would I be cross with you, Camilla? You know you're not the first hen Sam has plucked since he started going out with me. And you won't be the last. It is his hobby after all. I'm told he's really quite an expert. Practice makes perfect and all that."

"I'm going to take blood first," said Sam Dawson. "Roll up your sleeve, Francesca, or take off your shirt. Whatever you prefer."

I rolled up my sleeve.

"What is this obsession with blood tests? Camilla was nagging at me in Botswana that I needed blood tested, then I come to Ireland and James Snotter nags me that I need blood tested. Now you want to test blood."

Sam gently stroked the inside of my arm where he was to take the blood.

"You don't know Sinéad Murphy."

"Is she Mrs Murphy's daughter?"

"Mrs Murphy's granddaughter. She was James's patient. Expecting her first baby. Routine blood test. She was riddled with leukaemia. She was more surprised than anybody. There wasn't a symptom. She felt a bit tired, flu-like. She thought it was morning sickness."

"What happened?"

Sam sighed. "You can probably guess. She refused to abort the baby and have chemotherapy. She said she couldn't kill the baby to save her own life. And they both died."

Once Sam had taken my blood and my blood pressure, he said, "Now, Commander Simms, I'm going to scan your tummy. If you'd just like to take off all your clothes and lie down on the bed . . ."

I laughed. "You are incorrigible! No, thank you, doctor. I'll just keep my clothes on if it's all the same with you. It's twenty years since you last saw me naked. I don't want to spoil the memory."

"But I think you're still beautiful. Maybe even more beautiful now than twenty years ago."

There was an awkward pause.

I said lightly, "Love is blind, Sam."

Before I ever fell in love with anybody I used to marvel that my mother could bear to go to bed with my father who was almost bald and had a narcissistic tendency to sweep his last few thin strands of hair over the shiny and freckled dome of his head. He had not always been bald, of course. When Mummy and he married he was as redheaded and as tall and slender as Camilla and me. But he'd been cursed with a sweet tooth and a lack of self-discipline.

For forty years wee bun after wee bun disappeared down Daddy's throat at church socials and parish visits, and lodged accusingly round his midriff. The ladies of 1st Derryrose provided an inexhaustible supply of excuses for his big belly as they plied him with still more wee buns.

"You've a sluggish metabolism, Reverend Simms. And you've big bones. Have another wee bun . . ."

After forty years, and the only exercise he'd ever taken was to climb three steps up into his pulpit on Sunday morning, Daddy had turned into a fat, pink little pig.

What was most alarming about Daddy's physical decline was that Mummy never seemed to notice. Derryrose Manse was full of bedrooms yet every night Mummy slept in a double bed beside him. I also noticed that though there were a number of comfortable armchairs in the living-room they always cuddled up together on the sofa to watch the television.

"Doesn't it bother you that Daddy is fat and bald?"

"Is he, darling?"

"Look!" I showed her a photograph of my unfortunate father. "Fat and bald."

Mummy studied the photograph carefully. Finally she said, "That's not Roger. That's his father, your Grandpa Roland."

"What does Daddy look like?"

"Daddy is taller. And a great deal thinner. And he has a head of thick red hair, like yours. I was so pleased that you and Camilla inherited Daddy's hair. And his wonderful green eyes. Daddy doesn't have piggy little eyes like that ugly old man in the photograph."

I tried my best but I never could work up the enthusiasm to make a fool of myself with Sam Dawson. I never counted the hours till I saw him. I never stared at his hands and imagined them touching me. I never went weak at the knees when he looked at me. He never made me speechless with nerves and desire.

"You're just using him," said Camilla in admiration, but that wasn't right either.

Sam and I were very happy together and I accepted

without hesitation when he got down on one knee during my Finals and asked me to marry him.

We set a wedding date, my mother helped me choose a (suitable) wedding dress, we put a deposit on a house in Belfast and I got a job offer with a chartered engineering practice, and was employed as a graduate engineer on the latest rebuilding of the Europa Hotel. Mummy was thrilled; Daddy was thrilled; the Dawson parents were thrilled.

Aunt Grace was not thrilled.

"You're making a big mistake," said Aunt Grace.

"I'm not listening, Aunt Grace."

"Why do you have to get married? You haven't even finished university. Don't you want to see the world before you settle down?"

"I can't hear you, Aunt Grace."

The most exciting part of our wedding plans, for Sam and me, revolved around the honeymoon destination. With Sam's holiday gang I'd backpacked and inter-railed most of the way around continental Europe. I'd learnt to sleep standing up on trains, and brush my teeth out of a carriage window. I'd learnt that no one would bat an eyelid if I used the toilet on the train when it was standing in a station in southern Europe, but I could and would be arrested for doing the same thing in northern Europe. I knew the currency of every country, and its approximate exchange rate with pounds sterling. Now I was ready to try something different.

"Let's go on a package holiday honeymoon. With everything paid for and previously organised by somebody else. And let's fly. I've never been on an aeroplane."

"What a good idea," said Sam. "We'll fly away to a desert island in the sun. Alone together. With nothing to do all day, and all day to do it . . ."

"You'll get bored," said Aunt Grace ominously when I told her we were thinking of the Maldives. "He's so boring, Francesca. The only exciting thing that man does is flirt with other men's wives."

"I always feel nervous at this point," I said, when Sam slathered some jelly on my belly and slithered the ultrasound probe across it. "Just in case there isn't a baby."

"Or just in case it's twins?"

My antenatal appointment was finished. I walked slowly back to the BMW. The first photograph of my twins, from the ultrasound, was cradled gently in my hand. I had a foolish urge to rock them gently backwards and forwards. Babies are little miracles and today there were two of them, bouncing oblivious in a bubble inside me.

Medically frank to the point of rudeness Sam had said, "Have you considered family planning?"

"Don't you think it's perhaps a bit late for that?"

"Allow me to make a suggestion, Commander Simms. Elect to have a Caesarean section with the twins and I'll tie your tubes while I'm in there. As far as sex is concerned, you'll never be able to tell the difference. There will not, however, be any more babies."

"Thanks, Mr Dawson, I'll think about it."

Sam shrugged. "I've never liked condoms either."

When I got back from the hospital Emma Flood was waiting

for me. Standing on Aunt Grace's doorstep in floods of tears brandishing a photograph. I had an almost irresistible urge to turn the BMW and drive away. But I restrained it and got out of the car and walked towards her. Attack is the best form of defence.

"Emma, you'll never guess. I've just been to the hospital. I'm expecting twins!"

Emma's tears checked immediately. "Oh, how awful!" she said. "My head nearly went when Ralph and Oliver were babies. I begged Alex to go for the snip. Of course, he never listened to me and now we have four unmanageable children instead of two. What on earth is your husband going to say when you tell him you're pregnant with twins?"

"My husband? What's he got to do with it?"

Emma thrust the photograph at me. It was a singular photograph, carelessly taken at a curious angle, of a couple kissing. The man was definitely Alex Flood, the girl's face was lost in shadow. The only really clear thing about the girl in the photograph was the pink dress she was wearing.

"Alex carries that photograph in his wallet," said Emma, "and I never, never guessed who it was until I saw you in the same dress on the television. Why is my husband kissing you, Francesca?"

244

Chapter Twenty

There are no excuses for what I did to Sam Dawson. It was a dirty, low, despicable act and the fact he forgave me is only proof that love is eternally optimistic, as well as blind.

Camilla says I was getting my own back. Teaching him a lesson. The boot was on the other foot. Any old cliché. But then Camilla has always been obsessed with Sam's inability to forsake all others and stick with the one girl. Or maybe she has always been obsessed with Sam.

Sam and I decided to marry on Boxing Day because we'd noticed when you asked people how their Christmas went they invariably sighed and replied, "Very quiet". So we thought, with the arrogance of youth, that we'd get married at Christmas and give everyone something to talk about. We got our wish. There was no wedding but they're still talking about it.

Getting married was such fun. There were so many pleasant things to think about. The candlelit service. My white satin, fur-trimmed wedding dress. The wedding cake. Chauffeur-driven limousines. Church music. And, of course, the super honeymoon to finish us off.

And so many decisions. Should the Christmas tree in 1st Derryrose be tastefully decorated, or seasonally decorated? Should we sing Christmas carols, or regular wedding hymns? (I wanted 'Fight the Good Fight' but Mummy thought it wasn't suitable.) Should I carry a bouquet of flowers, or a muff?

"Will Sam Dawson wear a morning suit, or dress as Santa Claus?" asked Aunt Grace.

By September all the wedding plans were finalised. There was only our package holiday honeymoon left to book. I took the brochure to show Aunt Grace.

"Two weeks in the Maldives. In a wooden bungalow perched on stilts over a green lagoon on an island resort called Paradise."

"Very photogenic," sniffed Aunt Grace. "Have you shown it to Alex?"

"Alex?"

"He rode past about half an hour ago. He said he was going to look for foxes in the little wood at the end of the avenue."

In the beginning, after he dumped me, I ached for Alex so I went home to Derryrose every weekend in the hope of casually bumping into him. I saw him sometimes, riding past the bottom of Aunt Grace's avenue and once or twice he stopped and we struggled with polite and shallow chit-chat.

Gradually the ache subsided and soon I became so busy tripping through Europe with Sam's holiday gang that Alex Flood got tidied away in a memory-lined box with '*unconsummated teenage passion*' scribbled on the lid.

"I'm sure Alex isn't interested in my honeymoon plans."

But as usual, at the mention of his name the box started to rattle and suddenly I felt nervous.

"Oh, really, Francesca!" Aunt Grace was suddenly cross. "I've struggled long and hard to keep my mischievous nose out of your affairs. So let me spell it out to you this once and I'll never mention it again. Alex Flood has a thousand acres of parkland to ride at Lisglasson yet any time you visit me he is, without fail, loitering in the little wood at the end of my avenue."

I was getting into my swanky new BMW – a present from Sam – when I saw Alex ride past the end of the avenue. Just a flash of him on a grey horse, like a figment of the imagination.

Aunt Grace's parting words, 'There have never been foxes in the wood at the end of the avenue' were ringing in my ears.

Before I could take a deep breath and pull myself together the lid came off the box, Sam and the wedding flew straight out of my head and I hunted Alex Flood in my swanky new BMW, and ran him to ground.

He had dismounted and was standing quietly in the little wood. Watching me. I got out of the car. Summer was over and it was raining. I was foolishly dressed in a pink sundress and thin sandals bought cheap at the end of the sales. After today they would be neatly folded away for my honeymoon.

Our eyes met across the boggy copse. Alex began to walk towards me. His eyes were the same colour as his old coat. My mouth was dry, my stomach lurched, my heart beat wildly. To hell with nettle stings and briar scratches – I slipped unhesitating through the barbed-wire fence. The magnet which had pulled me after him over stone walls and through ditches when we went riding together was now dragging me through the sodden undergrowth towards him.

By the time we'd met halfway my silly, pretty sandals were ruined with muck and my summer dress was almost see-through in the rain.

"I believe congratulations are due," said Alex. "Grace tells me you're marrying Sam Dawson. That's the fellow you used to call Sam the Sissy. How nice for you! Will you also be known as Mrs Doctor Dawson, or will you be Mrs Doctor Dawson Junior or Mrs Junior Doctor Dawson?"

He was jealous. It was written all over his face. I could smell it from his skin. If I kissed him I would taste it. Today I knew he most certainly would not bolt and run if I touched him.

"The wedding is on Boxing Day," I said. Testing him. Teasing him.

"I'll be hunting on Boxing Day."

I was so nervous I couldn't even smile. My heart was thumping so loud I couldn't hear the wobble in my voice. Staring at my feet, shivering with rain and adrenaline, I said, "I'm not here to invite you to a wedding. Do you have a passport, Alex?"

Later that afternoon I booked a two-week package holiday in the Maldives. To a wooden bungalow perched on stilts over a green lagoon on an island resort called Paradise. The passengers travelling were Francesca Simms and Alex Flood and we were leaving the next day.

"You can't," said Camilla.

"Can't what?"

"Can't *possibly* take Alex Flood to the Maldives instead of Sam."

"Sam who?"

Emma set her teacup down with a bump. I'd brought her indoors and made her a cup of tea because I considered it more civilised that we were preoccupied with domesticity – filling the kettle, measuring tea leaves into the teapot, sniffing the milk. The alternative was to stand on the front doorstep and painstakingly describe my love affair with her husband. I suppose I could have told her to mind her own business – Alex Flood and I went to the Maldives together years before she ever met him – and I might have, but for the photograph now lying accusingly on the kitchen table between us.

"Camilla took that photograph. She drove us to the airport and took the photograph of us before we left. She must have given it to Alex."

Emma had listened quietly until now. Now she interrupted. "I can't believe you."

"You don't believe me that Camilla took the photograph?"

"I can't believe that you chose Alex when you could have had Dr Sam Dawson. I know who I'd have picked. And it's not my husband."

249

"I think Sam was quite surprised too. He said, 'Best of luck, Francesca. I always thought Alex Flood was gay.'"

"You know it was me, don't you?" Camilla said at the airport. "It was me who tried to seduce you when we were seventeen."

"Yes, I've always known that."

"And you know it was me spread the rumour you were gay?"

"Yes, I know."

"Don't you hate me?" She was curious.

"I don't care anything about you, Camilla, no matter what you say about me," said Alex which I think must be the nastiest and most hurtful thing anybody has ever said to Camilla.

"I've never been on an aeroplane before," I announced to change the subject.

"Aircraft," said Alex.

Camilla was suddenly spiteful. "You'll like flying. You'll recognise it. Take-off feels just the same as being run away with on a horse."

Camilla was right. I did like flying. With Sam's holiday gang we'd always taken trains and boats and buses. Only now did I fully realise what I'd been missing all my life. I was on my first aircraft for five minutes (the Airbus A320 shuttle to Heathrow) when I realised that I wanted to become a pilot.

"I'd love to be pilot," I whispered to Alex as we burst through the dank clouds over Aldergrove and flew into blinding sunlight.

Alex grunted, uninterested. Much of Alex's unconventional childhood, before he was packed off to the safe confines of boarding school, had been spent taking long holidays overseas with his mother (Millie Mouse, the Longsuffering Wife) while big bad bonking Bobby Flood went on tour with Achilles Heel.

"I should think it gets boring after a while. A pilot is little better than a glorified bus driver."

I was undeterred and abandoned him with his nose in a novel and took up residence in the flight deck and spent most of the long-haul non-stop direct flight from London to Colombo admiring the control panel of the Boeing 767 and asking the Captain and First Officer questions. By the time Alex and I were boarding our third aircraft – an ancient Tristar, absolutely jam-packed with European holidaymakers – to fly from Colombo to Male (the capital island of the Maldives archipelago) I was determined to send my CV to Ex-Pat Air.

"The Captain says they're the best airline in the world to work for. Best destinations. Best perks," I said as we threw our bits of hand luggage into the overhead stowage. "The head office is in London but they're based in the Middle East, so you get a tax-free salary, and they fly all over the world. This month alone that Captain has been to New York, Manila and Colombo. Manila is in the Philippines in case you didn't know. You need A Levels or a degree to be considered but no previous flying experience is necessary. And they're recruiting at the moment . . ."

I tailed off, suddenly embarrassed, as a large woman in a straw hat attempted to squeeze past us and I was crushed against Alex. I could smell the heat of his skin through the exquisite thin cotton of his shirt. Until today I'd only ever seen Alex dressed in riding clothes and his old coat and I suddenly realised that I liked him better in his wellies. When he was dressed like the rest of mankind going on holiday I wasn't quite sure what to do with him.

Even that stupid photograph Camilla took of us together, kissing at the airport, I'd ducked my head at the last minute and he was actually kissing my ear by accident, not design.

Alex threw his novel at me. "Read that before you decide to become a pilot. He crashed and burned."

I looked at the cover. "He deserved to. He was flying away with another man's wife."

"So am I," said Alex softly.

So we were both shy and we were both on our best behaviour and we kept apologising to each other. I was actually changing my clothes in the bathroom. And although there was only one bed in the wooden bungalow it was enormous and there was absolutely no chance of us accidentally rolling together in the middle of the night and touching. The tension was almost unbearable. On the inside I wanted to weep and gnash my teeth and pull my hair; on the outside I was saying, "Pass the bread rolls, please."

There's very little to do in the Maldives if you're not having sex. On the second day we took a bouncy boat to a diving platform on the outskirts of the atoll.

"Doesn't look too safe," said Alex pessimistically and

prophetically, but he was impressed with the coral. It was the best he'd ever seen and the platform was the deepest he'd ever snorkelled from. I'd never snorkelled before and I wasn't a marvellous swimmer and I'd have felt a lot safer at the start if Alex had held my hand . . . But quickly I became proficient at treading water in flippers and spitting salt water out of my breathing tube. We swam in circles pointing at things – a red starfish, an enormous yellow, black and white angel fish, psychedelic purple and green parrot fish. I was just deciding to buy a sarong from the resort shop with *'Fish of the Maldives'* printed on it when the sky suddenly darkened and huge cold raindrops began to splash onto the surface of the warm water.

"It's a tropical storm," said Alex. "It has blown up too quickly for them to send the boat out for us from the resort. Maybe it'll blow over . . ."

I followed him away from the mesmerising coral and, on his instruction, wrapped myself around the diving platform.

"I'm sure it's very sturdy," said Alex calmly, "but if anything happens you're to swim with the current. The storm will blow us to the island" which wasn't especially reassuring since the island was wiped out with grey lashing rain.

"Hold tight," said Alex and even then, even when the storm hit and I was being thrown about in the high waves, swallowing unromantic amounts of seawater, trying not to panic and becoming unpleasantly cold, he didn't touch me.

Suddenly the storm blew over and the bouncy boat reappeared from the resort. Drenched and bedraggled I limped past the dining-room where everyone else was cleaned up for lunch.

When we got back to the wooden bungalow perched on stilts over the green lagoon I said politely, "I'll wait outside if you want to get changed for lunch," and went out on to the terrace. My legs were shaking. I'd been so preoccupied keeping my head above the cold water as we clung to the diving platform during the storm that I hadn't realised until now how frightened I'd been.

I've heard since, from optimists, that drowning is a nice way to die. You get the chance to watch your life pass in front of you as your lungs fill with seawater.

Two huge tears welled up in my eyes and splashed quietly down my face.

Suddenly Alex was kneeling in front of me, wrapping a towel around me, pushing my wet hair off my face, holding my hands between his.

"I'm so sorry," I said. "I've brought you all this way and now I realise I can't do it. I thought I could but I can't."

"I can't do it either," he said and he started to kiss my hands. Not old-fashioned courteous, asexual lips-brushing-fingertips kisses but warm wet kisses on the palms and the shock of it ran through me as if I'd touched an electric fence.

"Oh," I said faintly. I couldn't have pulled my hands away if it had been to save my life.

"So then you realised he wasn't gay?" said Emma.

"I always knew he wasn't frigid or gay." I smiled at the memory of it. "And I always knew he fancied me . . ."

After all the years of longing, and all the romantic fantasies of how it would be with him, it was inevitable that the first time would be frantic and unsatisfying. A disappointment. We clashed teeth when we kissed, he poked me in the eye when he was pulling off my swimsuit, I couldn't stop shaking, and he kept his eyes tightly shut until it was over.

And yet, it was passionate, primitive and unrehearsed. It was beautiful. Afterwards we lay together on the hard floor of the wooden bungalow perched on stilts over the green lagoon with our fingertips touching and said absolutely nothing at all to each other.

I spotted Sam Dawson in the Arrivals Hall at Aldergrove before he saw me. He was wearing his old Barbour that we'd roughed up together. What was he doing at the airport? He spotted me and began to wave enthusiastically. "Francesca! I've come to take you home."

"How did you know when I was coming?"

"I asked Camilla. You don't mind, do you?"

I watched Alex walk away through the crowd in the airport. Only a minute earlier we'd been holding hands. Two minutes earlier at the baggage carousel we'd kissed. I could still feel the imprint of his lips, the roughness of his black stubble against my cheek. He walked away from me very tall and straight, with his head held high. His black hair gleamed in the fluorescent glare of the Arrivals Hall. I opened my mouth to shout, "Alex, come back and get a lift with Sam!" but the words got lost somewhere between my heart and my mouth.

I went home with Sam. Back to our house in Belfast. All my

things were still there and he'd made us dinner. His best lasagne with baked beans in the meat. And potatoes. I felt a degree of affection towards him, the plonker.

Most men would have been jealous and angry, even heartbroken. Most men would have made a point of finishing with me before I got a chance to do the dumping. But Sam wasn't most men. The beautiful thing about Sam, the thing I admired, was that Sam knew how to dish it out and he knew how to take it. He'd been deflowering virgins, 'plucking hens', since we started going out together. Why shouldn't his fiancée go on holiday with another man?

"You've taught me a lesson," said Sam. "Please come back and I'll never look at another woman. Come back now. Let's forget it. It never happened."

But I couldn't go back. We broke off the engagement, I gave him back his ruby. I moved out of the house in Belfast and he moved in a lodger – a really pretty blonde girl. We stayed friends.

Mummy tried to be brave about it.

"Of course, everybody's at it these days. A broken engagement is nothing these days. It's not as if she's actually taken her marriage vows. It's much better not to get married if you have doubts. And Mrs Doctor Dawson still wants to be my friend . . ."

But she wore such a face of personal suffering and pained disappointment that in the end I went to live with Aunt Grace.

Aunt Grace advised me to lie low until the Chinese Whispers died down.

"I don't understand what all the fuss is about. It's not as if you've killed anybody. You've probably done Sam Dawson a favour – he's just been voted *Ulster Tatler's* Most Eligible Bachelor. Again."

Camilla admired what I'd done. "If you don't love him, you can't marry him." It inspired her to walk out on Adam Robinson.

Mummy began to suffer from agoraphobia.

Alex never once tried to get in contact me. Even when Boxing Day came and went and I wasn't married to Sam. He just walked on, and out of my life. Lady Millicent told Aunt Grace that he'd gone to Tipperary to work as a huntsman. "It's a wonderful opportunity."

It's a long, long way to Tipperary.

I stayed locked away in Aunt Grace's house, nursing the shame of having thrown caution to the winds and having it thrown back in my face. I couldn't eat, I couldn't sleep, I couldn't even cry.

Aunt Grace said "Do you think it's better to have loved and lost than never to have loved at all?"

"Not yet."

Our two weeks spent together in the Maldives might never have happened.

I burned all the photographs and applied to Ex-Pat Air as a pilot.

When I went to Ex-Pat Air, Sam married Camilla.

Chapter Twenty-one

Daddy's forty-year ministry at 1st Derryrose was almost at an end. In less than a month he would be three-score years and ten, the official Presbyterian Church retiring age, and a younger minister would be called to replace him. It was generally believed that Reverend Adam Robinson, now happily remarried to the heavenly Rachel and with a family of little Robinsons, was listening intently and with great determination for the voice of God to direct him to 1st Derryrose, and not just because the local town had a very excellent grammar school.

When this happened my parents would be cast adrift to fend for themselves. The free house would go, the company car would go, for the first time in their innocent lives they would have no-one to account to, only each other. In the long years between his retirement and death the best Daddy could hope for was a voluntary job visiting hospitals, and the odd guest appearance back in Derryrose when the new minister took his holidays.

Daddy, by nature, is a stoic with the enviable talent of accepting things he cannot change – the changing seasons for example, the march of time, Mummy. No one thought to ask him if he minded leaving 1st Derryrose where he'd been an important and much-respected member of the community for forty years. If we had asked he'd not have known what to answer us. Mummy was a different matter entirely.

"I think it's simply outrageous that we are expected to move out of South Derry! Your father and I are far too old to uproot. All my friends are in South Derry, and my counselling practice."

"And your daughter Camilla and your granddaughter Kathryn?"

Mummy shrugged, uninterested. "Them too, I suppose."

"But being a counsellor," I teased, "you must appreciate the psychological implications of you and Daddy outstaying your usefulness in South Derry. It's only human nature that the congregation of 1st Derryrose would still come running to Daddy in a crisis. Instead of a new man."

"I can't say I'm going to miss that bit of manse life. I know I shouldn't say this, but it's such a bore being at the mercy of every Tom, Dick and Harry in the congregation. And I'm most certainly not going to miss having to keep the house spotless every second of every day in case one of them turns up on the doorstep wanting something."

We were sitting at the scrubbed pine kitchen table of my

parents' holiday cottage on the North Antrim coast. They'd bought it when Camilla and I were babies. Family legend has it that Daddy did the sums and told Mummy they could afford the cottage or another baby and Mummy, though not terribly keen on the picturesque but impractical cottage, but even less keen on another baby, chose the lesser of the two evils and agreed to the cottage.

We spent every summer holiday there, squashed in for a fortnight, miles from the shops but a short bicycle ride to the beach. Even as a fun-seeking teenager Camilla hadn't complained about such isolation because the beach attracted surfers, an exotic and quite rare species in the seventies in Northern Ireland.

Temporarily released from the respectability and responsibilities of his profession, Daddy indulged himself annually in a DIY orgy. On sunny days Mummy pitched her deckchair and watched with love and indulgence from behind her sunglasses while the overgrown garden was cut back to expose apple-trees and washing lines, a gloomy privet hedge was uprooted, and the house and outbuildings were whitewashed.

"What an improvement, Reverend," said the Flying Donkey from the farm next door. "That wee house was nearly derelict till you took it over."

Mummy agreed. "You've done a marvellous job, Roger. It's just a pity that the cottage sits right on the edge of the road and the Flying Donkey only has to relax her foot on the accelerator to get a clear view of whether our Sunday roast is burnt or not."

So Daddy applied to the DOE for permission to move

the road over a bit, just far enough to build a stone wall, or plant a hedge to stop the Flying Donkey shamelessly staring in through our windows when she was capping cattle. But the grey men from the DOE said there wasn't enough traffic on the little road to justify the moving of it and they refused his application.

Mummy has never learned to take no for an answer.

"And what would they know? A hundred years ago this road was only a grassy lane and one donkey cart went past a week. Now we have enormous contractor tractors racing past in the silage season with lights flashing and radios blaring. The whole house shakes . . ."

Today the boot was on the other foot and it seemed my parents were losing again. Today we were at the cottage to assess the very real possibility of Mummy and Daddy moving from South Derry to spend the rest of their lives in their holiday cottage which we have always joked is better than a caravan but not by much.

Daddy had planned to build a new kitchen at right angles to the existing cottage in the long years between his retirement and death. The kitchen windows would look over a field down to the sea instead of onto the road. There was a gate into this field at a lovely sweeping angle, with white-washed round stone pillars and wrought-iron ornamental gates shaded by a spreading chestnut tree. It was Daddy's intention to preserve these last remains of old decency and to use the gate as his new 'site access'. Or it was, until the grey men from the DOE saw the plans and refused to pass them until they'd come and seen for themselves.

Mummy was uncharacteristically nervous when the grey man got out of his car. "What will work better with that sort of man? Young and lovely? Old and flirtatious? Dog collar?"

"Why not all three? There's safety in numbers."

But the grey man was impervious to charm. He informed us that the stone pillars, the wrought-iron gates and the spreading chestnut tree would have to be bulldozed away to make a spanking new 'site access', lying at a precise right angle to the road with visibility of 60 metres up and down on either side of it.

Daddy said, "You can't be serious! That chestnut tree is a hundred years old. We can't uproot it!"

Mummy said, "I don't understand. I'd understand if we were on a main road, but you've been telling us for years that there isn't enough traffic on this road to take it seriously."

But the grey man from the DOE wasn't finished. "The tree will have to go as well as everything else that's more than 50 centimetres tall and closer than 2.5 metres from the side of the road."

(This included not only the whitewashed pillars but the porch of the cottage and the privet hedge around the old-fashioned orchard where we sunbathed naked as children.)

"I don't want to discourage you, but I think you should seriously consider bulldozing the stone cottage away and starting again. The government are giving out grants for replacement dwellings – you could build a lovely new bungalow on the cleared-away site with plastic windows and central heating and a fitted kitchen."

Mummy's eyes lit up. "What about a timber-framed bungalow, Roger? I've heard they're very warm –"

"No," said Daddy.

Mummy sighed despairingly. "That's the trouble with you, Roger. You're a *romantic.*"

The grey man from the DOE said, "You've a nice spot here. My wife says she'd love to live in the country with a big view across the fields to the sea."

Daddy was tart. "The things you plan to do to my hedges and trees, your wife will soon be able to see across the fields to Scotland."

But the grey man had already jumped into his grey car and driven off.

"What are we going to do now?"

"Phone your architect and see can he do anything."

"Or sell," said Daddy sadly, "and move to a flat in Portstewart. There's a new development on the cliff walk – it's being made into a retirement village for the clergy."

"So every Reverend Tom, Dick and Harry can knock on my window when they want something?"

I said, "It's a pity you have to move out of South Derry. You could've moved into Lisglasson Lodge and lived there."

"Aren't you going to sell? House prices have shot away up since the ceasefire. I'm sure Alex Flood would give you a million pounds for it. Even without central heating. He's been trying to buy Lisglasson Lodge from Aunt Grace for years. Everyone knows that Emma can't bear sharing a house with her mother-in-law. And without being too indiscreet, may I say Millicent isn't so fond of her either."

"Lisglasson is hardly a house. It's bigger than most airport terminals."

"Size is relative, darling."

Then Daddy said, "I really don't think you could expect Will to move from Southern Africa to South Derry when his hospital contract is finished."

"Why not? Will's mother is from South Derry after all."

We locked up the holiday cottage and drove silently back to South Derry. I could tell from my parents' rigid backs and sidelong glances that my disinclination to sell Lisglasson Lodge was the icing on the top of their awful day. It was not mentioned again but what was left unsaid hung heavily in the BMW between us.

Thirty years before, Aunt Grace had cleaned out Naomi's room with frenzied zeal. She'd burned everything that would burn, and she redecorated, but she never succeeded in cleaning away the sense of loss that engulfed Lisglasson Lodge. My orthodox parents didn't believe in fairies or banshees or the luck that comes with a four-leaved clover so on principle they refused to believe Camilla and me when we insisted we'd seen Naomi's ghost.

"You're at an impressionable age," Mummy told us firmly and dismissively. "Pubescent girls always have vivid imaginations. I was *convinced* I was adopted when I was a teenager . . ."

But I knew she was worried sick by Naomi's ghost because I overheard her muttering "God forgive me, Roger, I would not believe Camilla's oath, but if Francesca says she's seen a ghost . . ." and Daddy muttering back, "Then there must be a ghost . . ."

They even tried to persuade Aunt Grace to allow an exorcist to bless the house.

"A haunted house isn't good for Roger's reputation," Mummy explained to my grief-stricken aunt.

"I wish I could see her." Aunt Grace was suddenly vicious. "I sit here every night waiting to see her. And I see nothing. Not even a shiver on the stairs. It's much much worse to see nothing."

No one ever spoke about it again. Camilla and I continued to see Naomi. Sometimes she was bouncing on Aunt Grace's pink bed, sometimes she was running across the landing from Aunt Grace's room to her own bedroom, sometimes she was on the stairs.

Mummy started her counselling courses and talked loudly about developmental hormones and Freudian theories and the Peter Pan complex. She made a point of never sleeping over in Lisglasson Lodge.

I have never understood Mummy's anxiety. As Emma Flood said at Aunt Grace's wake, the dead can't hurt you – it's the living you should be more concerned about.

Next morning was breezy and I took Aunt Grace's ashes outside to the wild-flower meadow.

Mummy and Daddy had offered to help.

"No, thank you. It's not on the list of final requests. She didn't want an audience at her final scattering. Only me to do it. I don't think anybody should be there. Only me."

"I can't understand." Mummy was genuinely bewildered. "Why did she pick you, Francesca? Camilla and you, you're identical –"

"Love is blind."

This is the poem James Snotter read at Aunt Grace's funeral:

> *Do not stand at my grave and weep.*
> *I am not there, I do not sleep.*
> *I am a thousand winds that blow.*
> *I am the diamond glints on snow.*
> *I am the sunlight on ripened grain.*
> *I am the gentle autumn rain.*
> *When you awaken in the morning's hush*
> *I am the swift uplifting rush*
> *Of quiet birds in circled flight.*
> *I am the soft stars that shine at night.*
>
> *Do not stand at my grave and cry*
> *I am not there; I did not die.*

A man was watching me. He was tall and dark and he was wearing short shorts, long socks and boots. It wasn't the sort of outfit normally associated with South Derry men.

Boiler suits and black suits are more common in South Derry. There was only one man in my life who'd ever looked like that and I recognised him immediately. I walked back up the meadow to meet Will.

There's something about Will that makes me happy. I can't

explain it. It happened the very first time I met him in Mutrah Suq, when Aunt Grace fainted on top of him and his eyes met mine and something warm and comforting and familiar flooded into my nipples and groin and the pit of my stomach.

Will said, "This is no place for a lady," and I said, "I'm not a lady," even though he wasn't talking about me.

Until very recently I'd always thought my marriage to Will was the success story of my life.

It was happening again, the warm, familiar, comforting happiness as I walked up the wild-flower meadow towards him.

I should've felt angry. The last we'd spoken I'd heard a woman's voice inviting him back to bed.

And I could have been sick with fear. There was a very good chance he'd followed me halfway across the world to tell me he was leaving me for a large-breasted dentist.

Of course, he could have saved the price of the flight and phoned me to tell me that.

"Will! What a pleasant surprise! Were you just passing?" I said, which is what he'd always said to me when he met me at Seeb Airport, any time of the day or night when I was a captain in command of an aircraft, a crew and two hundred passengers and I flew in for a stopover, bug-eyed with exhaustion and eyeliner.

Will said, "On Monday afternoon I was sitting in the lobby of the Pleasure Palace hotel in Jo'burg, waiting to be summonsed into a conference room to explain again to the anxious client why the building of a 300-million-*pula* private hospital in Gaborone was running one hundred million *pula* over budget and eighteen months behind the agreed completion date of Phase One. Trying to explain that the operating theatres designed by the client's architect are not big enough to hold the operating equipment bought by the client's representative. Trying to explain that the vast majority of my workforce are African ladies who work with a baby strapped to their backs, when out of the corner of my eye on the muted television set, I spot my wife on the *BBC World News*, sitting on the edge of a pink nylon bed, talking into the camera . . ."

"How did you know it was me? If the volume was turned down. It could have been Camilla."

"You were wearing my wedding ring, Francesca."

Chapter Twenty-two

Some women use sex as a weapon. Camilla has a talent for it. She discovered this the week after she married Adam Robinson, having returned from her first honeymoon – Paris – in floods of tears.

"Premature ejaculation."

"I suppose he's excited. A romantic city. A new wife. His first week on the job . . ."

"But he's hopeless. He hasn't a clue."

"Why didn't you take a test drive before you bought the car?"

"Because Adam is a Presbyterian *minister*." She had the grace to look shamefaced. "And Sam Dawson was a very good teacher."

"Well, I feel sorry for Adam. A cuckold on his wedding night. I suppose your wretched husband was expecting you to be as inexperienced as him. Look on the bright side, Camilla. You can train him up the way you want him."

Camilla sighed. "I suppose I'll have to. There's no point leaving him – we haven't got all the wedding presents opened yet."

Adam Robinson, lucky chap, was suddenly liberated from a life of furtive masturbation and the occasional, unsatisfying rumble under the duvet with a reluctant wife who was wishing she was in bed with Sam Dawson. I refused point blank to listen to the details of what Camilla did to Adam Robinson, I only know that she supplemented her shameless imagination with ideas from women's magazines and diagrams in her anatomy textbook.

"Oh really, Francesca," she sneered when I stuck my fingers in my ears at the word 'vagina,' "it's not as if you don't have one."

"I would prefer not to advertise it."

There are various vulgar expressions for the hold my sister had over Adam Robinson. Suffice it to say he utterly adored Camilla, gave her absolutely everything she demanded and allowed her to bully him mercilessly. He was devastated when she left him, and I think he went rather off the rails with his pre-marriage classes and his eccentric insistence that the husband of a modern marriage be the head of the household. And his advice to young husbands that no wife be allowed to read women's magazines. It was years before he pulled himself together. I've noticed, however, that his new wife, Rachel, always wears an enigmatic and fulfilled smile on her sweet obedient little face. I think she has Camilla to thank for that.

Will and I were in bed. Two faces on the same pillow with noses touching. Even today, with so many unasked and unanswered questions hanging between us, I could think of nothing nicer than making love to my husband before blast-off.

"I'm very upset with you. That's why I packed my bags and came back to Ireland."

"It must be bad if you came home to your mother."

"You went to Jo'burg and didn't call me."

"Why did you want me to call you? Was there something wrong?"

"No . . . but then when I called you, I heard a woman's voice saying 'Come back to bed, Will, and I'll get you a drink.'"

Will stopped kissing the back of my neck and sat up in bed.

"Don't stop!"

"You think I was in bed with some other woman when you called me?"

"Were you?"

And that was the end of our lovemaking.

Will and I sat in Aunt Grace's kitchen waiting for the kettle to boil on the Aga.

It's at pivotal points like this in my life that I wish I could take a stiff drink. Tea takes so much longer to prepare.

"I was in hospital."

He ran his big rough hand through his hair. Will had thick black hair when I met him, so thick and black my mother once suggested he dyed it. It's a great deal thinner and greyer now since he married me and the children were born, and he wears it cut up very short, almost shaven.

"I had a malignant melanoma. Remember that horrible thing on the top of my head that looked like an open sore and wouldn't heal? Dorothy couldn't cut it out of my skull; it was too deep. She sent me to have radiotherapy at the National Hospital in Jo'burg."

A malignant melanoma. The most aggressive form of skin cancer. It spreads into the lymph and then you're dead.

He bowed his head to show me a perfect naked square on the crown of his head where I'd indulgently assumed he was growing a bald patch. My hair was falling out. Why wouldn't his hair fall out?

"Will, I wish you'd told me. Why didn't you tell me?"

"I tried to tell you the night after you got the BCC taken off your face. Then I thought I'd save you a lot of worry by *not* telling you. You phoned when I was in hospital. It was a nurse talking to me. She made me turn off my cellphone, and she confiscated it in case it interfered with hospital equipment."

"But Camilla said –"

"What is Camilla doing in Botswana?"

"She arrived the morning after you left. She came on a flying visit, she'd had a row with James and she came to cool down . . ."

"What did Camilla say?"

I frowned, trying hard to remember. "I can't remember what she said. She said something that made me doubt you. I've never doubted you before."

"You never doubted me until your clever sister sowed the seeds of doubt."

The tea was postponed. Will and I were back in bed again. Two faces on the same pillow with our noses touching. He wouldn't tell me another thing about his melanoma, not even if it had spread, or if he needed more treatment. Just that it was a real stroke of luck to get the meetings with the client in Jo'burg scheduled for the same weeks as his cancer treatment.

This is the reason my mother, married to her safe husband, didn't want me to marry Will.

Mummy doesn't approve of men who stare unflinchingly into the face of death. Men who free fall and bungee-jump and hunt leopard and swim with sharks. Who smoke and drink and refuse to wear a seat belt. Mummy thinks Reverend Adam Robinson has a duty to warn women about alpha-male husbands at his pre-marriage classes and advise that they come with a health warning and a guarantee of early widowhood.

"He'll make you miserable every day of your life," she predicted pessimistically at our wedding. "He's not a team player."

Aunt Grace, as always, took my side. "He'll make you miserable but if you don't marry him every other man you meet afterwards will be a disappointment."

Aunt Grace had tried other men after Uncle Denis. An architect, a history teacher, a bank manager.

"Pointless," she complained. "They are tonic water without the gin. Pointless."

We were progressing nicely through the repetitive rigmarole of our lovemaking. Will had run his fingers along the accordion pleats of my rib cage, he'd rubbed himself along my stomach, and he'd kissed my lips until they were bruised. Now he was running his tongue along the inside of my thigh.

"Please kiss my breasts . . . Isobel's milk has dried up . . ."

"Rise and shine, Francesca!"

Mummy was at the bottom of the stairs.

"Sleepyhead! It's almost lunch-time. I've made a delicious macaroni cheese with ham and peas. Can I pop it into your Aga to warm it up? Bottom right-hand oven, is that the warming-up oven? I was expecting James and Kathryn for lunch but they've gone to the holiday cottage for a couple of days and there's far too much for Daddy and me. Do come downstairs and join us!"

Will stopped kissing me, jumped out of bed and furiously began pulling on his clothes.

"Slow down! We're allowed to be in bed together. We've got a licence."

But that was the end of our lovemaking. Again.

When Mummy saw Will, the friendly smile died on her face.

"Roger and I were wondering when you would turn up."

At lunch Mummy said, "I phoned the architect. I told him about our interview with the DOE, and how they've insisted we bulldoze away the stone pillars at the holiday cottage, and the spreading chestnut tree, and the porch and the privet hedge. 'There's not a thing I can do to help you, Madeline,' he said. 'The Civil Service is on strike today.'"

"I'm not doing it," said Daddy stubbornly, "I'm not bulldozing away that beautiful tree. And I'm not bulldozing away the privet hedge. It attracts butterflies and honeybees. Bulldozing them away would be a desecration. I'd rather sit out my last few years in a religious retirement village."

"Why do you have to retire?" asked Will

"Because that's the rule. Presbyterian ministers retire at seventy."

I said, "But you're not ready to retire! Seventy is the new forty. I read it in one of Aunt Grace's women's magazines. Everyone is getting younger. You're not old now until you're ninety."

Mummy grimaced. "So that's why she used to go clubbing with a bottle of gin in her handbag . . ."

Will suddenly announced, "I know of a church with a vacancy, and I've come to Ireland on a mission from God to invite you to fill the post, Reverend Robinson."

My poisonous mother said, "Have you finally found God? Oh, Will, 'there is more joy in heaven when one sinner repents . . .'"

"I'm sorry to disappoint you, Mrs Reverend Simms –

I'm only here to deliver a message. God spoke to Francesca's friend Dorothy. He wants you to spend your retirement years preaching blood, fire and fury to the church in Botswana. Dorothy says God isn't a bit fussy about your age."

Nobody spoke. Mummy and Daddy and I stared at my husband in amazement. We all knew that Will was many things, none of them good, but he wasn't a liar.

"But Bruce de Villiers is the pastor at the church in Botswana."

Will smiled at me. "Oh, ye of little faith, Francesca! Big bad bonking Bruce has chucked his lovely wife Estelle and their six sons and run off with Shirley Smith, the large-breasted dentist. I saw them with my own eyes, in the Pleasure Palace Hotel, when I was having meetings with the client in Jo'burg. Shirley Smith and Pastor Bruce all over each other like a rash. Shirley and I shared a taxi when she was going to the skin clinic to get her moles checked."

"So Shirley knows about your –"

"Meetings with the client," said my husband firmly because, spoilsport that he is, Will would never give Mummy the opportunity to cry crocodile tears into a lace handkerchief and say, "Cancer. I told you so. All that smoking and drinking and refusing to wear your seat belt. What can you expect, William?"

Mummy was thoughtful. "Me. Madeline Simms. A missionary. In darkest Africa. By special invitation. Gosh, how exciting! Do they speak English in the outlying villages in Botswana or will I have to learn a new language? I've always been very good at languages. I have an 'O' Level in French."

"French is only spoken in countries previously colonised by the French or the Belgians. Like Congo. Or Morocco. Botswana was a British Protectorate in colonial times. Everyone speaks English in Botswana."

Mummy was crestfallen.

"It would be polite to know some of the local language," I told her kindly. "Think how popular you'll be in Ulster Presbyterian pulpits when you come home on furlough and you can speak an African language! Violet will teach you. Or Ella. Ella knows more Setswana than me."

"What do you think, Roger?" Then, before Daddy had a chance to speak she announced: "We'll do it!"

After lunch she left us to do the washing-up while she raced to telephone Lady Millicent and Mrs Doctor Dawson and tell them that God had called her personally to be a missionary in Africa.

I was amazed by her enthusiasm. Especially since she'd been so bored the one time she'd come to visit us when Ella was born.

Only my father didn't seem at all surprised.

"Aren't you amazed that Mummy wants to go to Africa to be a missionary?"

Daddy shook his head. "God works in mysterious ways."

Will and I were back in bed. Two faces on the same pillow with our noses touching.

Picking up where we'd left off.

"So you didn't come to Ireland to see me! You came because Dorothy told you to come."

"Well, both. But, you know, I didn't even realise you were in Ireland until I saw you on *BBC World News*. I thought you were in Tlokweng, sulking about something."

"Sulking? Me?"

"I phoned you when I got out of the hospital. I spoke to Camilla. She said you were at the dentist. I phoned the next day and Violet said you were at the airport – I assumed you were seeing Camilla off. And any time I phoned after that I always got the answering machine. Then I saw you on *BBC World News* and I *still* couldn't get through on the phone – finally I phoned Dorothy and that's when she told me that you were in Ireland. She said you'd gone to get your hair done. Then she told me that God wanted the Reverend and Mrs Reverend to become missionaries."

He wasn't leaving me. He had no intention of leaving me. I took my husband's nipple in my mouth and bit it.

"Ouch!"

"Will," I said in desperation, "please stop making small talk and get on with the job, or I'm going to climb on top of you and do it myself."

But instead of resuming the delicious, repetitive rigmarole of our love-making, Will sat up in the bed, folded his arms across his chest and looked stern. The way he looked when he was trying to get Ella to do what he asked.

"You're not going to tell me, are you?"

"Tell you what?" but I knew from his tone of voice that I was caught.

"That you're pregnant. Didn't you think I'd notice?"

I could feel my face falling into the stubborn shape Ella's took when she wasn't getting her own way. My lip dropped, my eyes filled with tears. Attack is always the best form of defence so I said, "Are you not going to tell me?"

"Tell you what?"

I touched the tiny, tender fresh scars hiding in the thicket of my husband's pubic hair.

The scars were tiny but I knew my husband's body intimately and they had not been there the last time we made love. And I didn't have to be a doctor to know that tiny scars in that place could only have been made during a vasectomy operation.

"Didn't you think I'd notice?"

Chapter Twenty-three

When we were children Camilla and I weren't allowed to read our horoscope. Horoscopes, my father explained, were one of the many honey-traps set by Satan and his devils to seduce the innocent. Horoscopes were cleverly dressed up as a bit of fun, but before we knew it we would be sucked into the occult and sent hurtling down the broad road that leads to Hell.

I had no reason to doubt my parents who were good-living and well-meaning so I never confronted them about the horoscope thing or argued with them when they wouldn't allow us to dress up as witches at Halloween or send our friends Christmas cards with Santa Claus pictures on them. If Mummy and Daddy preferred me to wear a golden angel false face at Halloween and send Christmas cards of the Three Wise Men that was fine with me.

Camilla, as usual, honoured her parents with a pinch of

salt. She did not dress up as a witch, but wore a (witch's) cat false face, and she did not send Christmas cards of Santa Claus, but of snowmen wearing Santa hats. And she did not buy horoscope books, she read them in the shop instead.

"I'm an Aries. What can you expect?" she explained after she'd tried, unsuccessfully, to seduce Alex Flood.

And when I flew away from South Derry at twenty-four, halfway across the world to start a new career in a new country, she blamed that on being an Aries as well.

"Aries are adventurous, pioneering and courageous. That's your bit of Aries."

"Is there anything bad about us that I ought to know?"

"Selfish, impatient and quick-tempered. That's my bit of Aries."

So thanks to my sister I know I'm an Aries, a passionate woman who quickly grows sullen and sour when my husband won't sleep with me. And thanks to my sister I know that my husband is also an Aries, a selfish man who will not sleep with his wife when she's pregnant.

It's the fault of Aries that early-morning sex arguments are commonplace within my marriage.

"What sort of a husband won't sleep with his wife because she's pregnant?"

"What sort of a wife doesn't tell her husband she's pregnant?"

"What sort of a husband sneaks off and has a secret vasectomy?"

The phone rang. Will sighed.

"I suppose that's your mother again, to give us some more riveting information about the fabulous game lodges in northern Botswana, which one has a viewing deck and which one has air-conditioning in the bedrooms. Does she really think she's going to be able to afford to go on luxury safaris when she's a missionary?"

"It was your idea she read a holiday brochure."

But it wasn't Mummy. It was Emma Flood inviting us to the Opera House in Belfast to watch *Private Lives*.

"I've booked a table for four in the Europa. They have a pre-theatre special offer, two courses from their à la carte menu and a free champagne cocktail for £20. I've booked it for six o'clock. It'll give us oodles of time before the theatre starts."

It was only a foursome to the theatre. Nothing to get excited about, but perhaps I would sit beside him. In the cramped theatre seating our bodies were bound to touch. Accidentally.

All my life, Alex Flood had been disappearing around a corner ahead of me: he'd been at the end of a dead telephone line; he'd written to me one of the 14 million letters the Royal Mail loses every year. When I wake up fitful and restless in the middle of the night I know I've been dreaming about him.

Even when I was a captain in command of an aircraft, a crew and two hundred passengers, even when I was in Botswana with the Dallas family circus, Alex appeared unbidden, and unasked-for in my thoughts, an itch that had never been satisfactorily scratched.

Will watched my face with amusement.

"Why are you smiling like that?"

"Oodles of time to do what? Play footsie with Alex Flood under the table?"

I gave him the bad finger. "Oodles of time to ask Emma if Alex sleeps with her when she's pregnant . . ."

For some reason Will thinks the story of Alex Flood and me is an enormous joke.

"You had to take him to the Maldives to have sex with him?"

"I'm not proud of what I did."

"Oh, my poor darling! *You* didn't do anything wrong. I've never met the bloke but I'm going to have to take Camilla's side on this one. He might not be frigid or gay. But he's certainly mad."

"Why do you say that?"

"Because no man in his right mind would let you slip away."

"Will! For a man who won't sleep with his pregnant wife, you sound almost romantic."

Will laughed. "I love women. Fat, thin, tall, short . . . Name that woman, I've slept with her. And forgotten her. Hundreds of them."

"There's no need to boast."

"Then I met you."

Will and I drove to Belfast in my old BMW.

"I suppose the Europa is one of those pretentious places where you have to wear a tie and the waiters are pompous and it takes two hours to get fed," said Will.

"I know for a fact they'll check if you're wearing underpants before they let you in."

"We'll have to buy some then."

It was sixteen years since I'd been to Belfast and it was difficult to remember that it was no longer a war zone. So I still anxiously scanned the West Link for petrol bombers, my heart raced when an ambulance screamed past, and I broke sweat when a rude man in an anorak stood on his horn and waved his fist at me because I slowed down at an orange light.

"You're jumpy," Will observed from the passenger seat.

Thanks to the ceasefire, crazy bombed-out Belfast had real shops, even shopping centres and I didn't have to open my bag for the security guards before they let me in to them.

We bought Will his underpants and I tried to buy a pot of eye gel.

"This stuff is a miracle in a pot." I showed my husband the page torn from Aunt Grace's women's magazine. "It has only just been released. I don't even know if it has come to Belfast yet."

There was only one assistant behind the miracle counter, a woman talking on a telephone. We waited politely and fruitlessly for her to finish her telephone call and acknowledge us. She'd probably been quite pretty once but I noticed she was now a victim of too much sun-bed, too many blonde highlights and definitely too much make-up, most of which was caked in the crow's feet round her eyes.

"If *she* has it she's not using it," muttered Will.

"Do you have this?" I showed her the photograph.

"I'm on the telephone," she snapped at me.

I noticed lipstick on her teeth before she turned her back on us to continue her conversation.

"Ignorance training," Will whispered.

"You're right. And to be honest, close up she's not much of an advertisement for the miracle in a pot."

We were turning to leave when the woman finally finished her conversation.

"That was a client! I've got to go and make up an order for a client," and she was gone, striding across the department-store floor without giving us a second glance.

"Now do you understand why I'm jumpy? There might be a ceasefire in Northern Ireland but you don't have to scratch too far beneath the surface to find someone who will shoot to kill."

Alex and Emma were almost an hour late to the Europa. Will had drunk all four free champagne cocktails and we'd ordered and eaten our starters and I was beginning to despair that he wasn't coming. And Emma, of course.

"Chin up, Francesca," said Will kindly as the restaurant rapidly filled with beautiful people, and not one of them was wearing a tie. And not one of them was Alex Flood.

Finally I heard them arriving.

"I'm sorry we're late," I heard Alex say to the maître d'. "My wife couldn't decide what to wear."

Then I heard Emma, nervous and strained, laughing like an overwrought hyena.

"I tried on absolutely everything in my wardrobe. Even my wedding dress. But everything is covered in baby sick or Weetabix or felt-tip pen. And the twins have cut up all my knickers with their craft scissors. I had to ask Lady Millicent for a frock . . ."

Emma said, "The last time Alex and I went out together was last Christmas. We went to the Tyrone Crystal showroom in Dungannon to look for a crystal bunny rabbit to give to Lady Millicent for Christmas. She collects them. She must have a hundred."

"She has ten," said Alex, "all bought by you. One for every Christmas since I married you."

"Ten. One hundred. It's all the same," said Emma gaily. "Anyway we got away without the children because three of them were at school or pre-school and Granny said she'd baby-sit the baby, which is absolutely unheard of, but that particular morning her watercolour class had been cancelled because Deborah Slim, the tutor, had 'flu. I don't know if she was suffering from *real* 'flu, probably not. People say they have 'flu and quite often they only have a runny nose –"

"So you were in the Tyrone Crystal factory," I prompted, "and . . ."

"Well, we went to the factory, and they have a really beautiful coffee shop and café. I suppose you could call it a delicatessen, couldn't you, Alex? Upstairs, with a view of the factory floor, and all the crystal twinkling in the spotlights."

"For God's sake, Emma," said her husband, "hurry up, and get to the point."

"Alex and I decided to have some lunch. To celebrate

the fact that they had a crystal bunny rabbit for half price in the discounted seconds because it had the tiniest hairline fracture along one of its ears. Lady Millicent will never notice, and if she does we'll say the children dropped the box."

"So you had a romantic lunch together."

"I wanted lasagne," said Emma, "but unfortunately they were sold out of lasagne by the time we got to the front of the queue. We had to have the soup of the day. It was leek and potato soup which I have to say has always been one of my favourites. And our children love it too. We grow our own potatoes at Lisglasson, you know, in a plot behind the green-houses. We also grow leeks in the vegetable gardens but I've never had much success with leeks. They always succumb to rust in the autumn –"

"Emma," interrupted Alex, in a dreadful voice, "please finish your story before your soup goes cold . . ."

"Ha ha ha!" laughed Emma. "I'm not having soup tonight, Alex. The leek and potato soup at the crystal factory was served in plain white bowls. With sterling-silver soup-spoons. I suppose Tyrone Crystal don't make crockery. Or cutlery. I've never heard of crystal bowls, have you?"

"Only in fairytales."

"And the soup was really hot."

We waited for the rest of the story.

Then we realised that was the story.

"Gosh," I said.

Alex's green eyes met mine across the starched tablecloth. "I must apologise for my wife – she's such a terrific bore. I can't remember the last time she said something interesting."

"That's because I don't have a life. I spend all day every day mucking out horses, and grooming horses and exercising horses and talking to horses at the Equestrian Centre. I think I'm turning into a horse sometimes. Ha ha ha! I have no identity any more and no money of my own. I have to ask Alex for money when I want to buy tampons."

"It's the tablets," I told Will when we were walking across the street to the Opera House and Alex and Emma were still in the restaurant gobbling up their main course. "Her tranquillisers. I think they make her a bit stupid. Camilla says it was either tranquillisers or her head stuck permanently in a brown-paper bag. She collapsed into the surgery one morning after the school run – she was convinced she was having a heart attack. Chest pain, a tingling round her lips, numb fingers. Breathing so fast she was nearly blacking out. She hadn't been able to find the car keys to take the children to school, and the twins were going to be late again for Ms Gordon's class, and Catherine was going to be late again to Mrs Armstrong and, well, let's face it, anybody would start hyperventilating at the thought of Sarah Gordon and Mrs Armstrong waiting for them. And while Emma was pulling the house to pieces trying to find the car keys the children ran outside into the rain without coats and got soaked, and she had to find them dry clothes before they left and that made her even later. And the reason she couldn't find the car keys – Alex had taken her car and not told her . . ."

"It's her husband," said Will. "I'd be on drugs if I was married to him."

Will sat thoughtful and quiet through *Private Lives*. At first I thought it was because Emma had dozed off on his shoulder and was fast asleep, dribbling, and he was afraid to disturb her. But when we got into the car to go home he said, "Would you have married him if he'd asked you?"

"Alex? I don't know. Maybe when I was twenty-four. I don't know now. He's rather nasty to her, isn't he? You're never nasty to me. Even when I deserve it."

"Have you ever had sex in a car, Francesca?"

"You know I haven't."

"Will we stop on the way home?"

My BMW purred quietly and patiently behind a tractor and silage trailer down the winding country road that takes you from the motorway to Lisglasson Lodge. It was almost eleven o'clock but still light.

"How amazing! If I was flying above the clouds there would be streaks of red and silver in the sky . . ."

"If you were flying above the clouds you wouldn't be stuck behind this tractor. Can't the driver see there's a hard shoulder on this part of the road? There'd be plenty of room for us to get past him if he pulled over onto the hard shoulder. Why doesn't he pull over and let us pass?"

"Because it's an Ulsterman driving. Only tourists give way in Northern Ireland."

Finally the tractor peeled off up a long concrete lane and we were left alone together in the gathering dusk. Will slowed down as we drove past Lisglasson's magnificent electric gates because there was just enough daylight to see right to the end of the straight mile to the enormous house which was floodlit like an airport. Then we continued along the fortified walls and over a modest cattle grid and past the little wood at the end of Aunt Grace's avenue.

Will stopped the car and switched off the lights.

"What do we do?" I asked, suddenly nervous. "Front seat, back seat?"

"Depends."

"Depends on what?"

"The size of the car and the size of the woman."

He leant towards me in the dark, and slipped one hand up under my dress. I felt the roughness of his hand on my inner thigh, then suddenly my car seat was tipped back, my pants were torn off me, my thighs were parted and my husband was on top of me and inside me.

"Will . . ."

It was all over in seconds.

"Sorry about that," said Will, rolling back onto the driver's seat and smoothing my dress back down over my thighs. "I know it was probably the worst sex you've ever had in your life, but I'm so afraid of hurting you in your condition . . ."

"You didn't have time to hurt me." I stifled an urge to laugh. "And I can tell this is not *your* first time in a car. Is that why you never wear underpants, Will? In case they get in the way of an opportunity?"

Will shrugged. "Sneer if you like, I don't feel sexy when I'm buttoned up. I nipped into the Men's Toilets and took my new ones off before we left the Opera House. You probably didn't notice – you were too busy sharing a glass of tonic water with Alex Flood."

"Tonic water without the gin. While Emma knocked back the gin."

Will shook his head, suddenly sad. "I hope she still thinks the big house and her father-in-law's millions are worth it. It's quite obvious Alex doesn't love her. I don't think he even likes her. He couldn't take his eyes off you all evening. And he almost elbowed her out of the way to get sitting beside you in the theatre."

"I think she walked into that marriage with her eyes wide open."

After I told Emma the whole story about Alex and me in the Maldives she said, "He's never looked at anyone else, you know. Never. Never before you and never after you. He never looked at me either. He's only ever had eyes for you."

"It's a pity," said Will as we drove up the lane to the Lodge. "Some other lucky man could have made her very happy."

I was brisk. "If you're going to be unhappily married you might as well be unhappily married to the only son of a rock-star millionaire. Sir Bobby has a villa in the Caribbean, a chalet in Switzerland, a castle in Tuscany and a penthouse in New York."

Chapter Twenty-four

Next morning Will and I bought our tickets back to Botswana, departing Sunday afternoon after Daddy's farewell service at 1st Derryrose, with probably just enough time to show our faces at the tea and buns in the church hall after the service, if Daddy's closing sermon didn't take longer than fifteen minutes.

"But you've only just arrived, Will!" Mummy protested. "Why do you have leave again so soon? You came on a flying visit the last time too. You just jetted in, married Francesca and swept her away to Botswana. When are you going to give South Derry a chance?"

I tried not to stare at my mother but there was definitely something different about her, and her sudden civility to Will was only the tip of the transformation. We were at the manse helping her clear out, and it seemed with every bin-liner bag of dead clothes that she labelled *'charity'* and every box-load of theological textbooks she labelled *'Church House'*, the strained piety and anxious religiosity in her face were smoothed away and she was beginning, for the first time in her married life, to look happy. Mummy had lived in a manse goldfish bowl for forty years, trying to set a moral example and trying to please all of the people all of the time. Now, finally, she'd stopped listening for Chinese Whispers.

"Now, Will," said Mummy lightly, "Roger and I are going shopping to the Sales this afternoon and we need some advice. Do African men wear short shorts, long socks and boots even in winter?"

"What are you going to do about Lisglasson Lodge?" Daddy asked. "Are you going to sell to Alex Flood?"

"Alex has never once said to me that he wants to buy Lisglasson Lodge."

"But that was the reason he took you out to dinner and the theatre, to talk to you about it."

"It was never mentioned. He must have changed his mind."

"Well, that will be a first, because if there ever was a man who made up his mind about something and stuck to it – *intransigently* – it's Alex Flood."

I looked at my father in surprise. For forty years I'd always innocently assumed that Daddy, by virtue of his profession and his modest nature, was utterly out of touch with reality. When I was growing up he was either locked away in his study working on a sermon, or gone away to minister to the needs of his parishioners and Mummy, though she had no stomach for it, had reared Camilla and me and taken on the full burden of parental responsibility – including the boyfriend thing – while Daddy was affectionately dismissed as a vague man who enjoyed stuffing his face with wee buns. Even now he was fondly indulged in his awful habit of calling every one of Camilla's husbands by the same name – Adam. (When Camilla was standing at the front of the church taking James Snotter to be her third lawful wedded husband, and Daddy asked her if she would take "Adam Robinson," Camilla had vehemently answered, "Never again!")

Will said, "I saw Alex Flood riding past the front of Lisglasson Lodge this morning. He went into the little wood at the end of the avenue."

"Never chase a man or a bus," I said sharply, as a goose tripped over my grave. "There's always another one coming. Eventually."

"You'll wait a long time to sell Lisglasson Lodge to anyone else for a million pounds," said Daddy pessimistically. "A million pounds is a lot of money."

"Yes, Daddy."

"Perhaps you could swallow your pride just this once, and think seriously about what it would be like to leave the sunshine and servants of Africa and return to South Derry, pregnant with twins, with three children under school age?"

"And years of ironing stretching in front of you," said Mummy.

"It's unlikely I'd get work in South Derry," said Will.

"I'd have to work in Dublin, or England . . . I'd only see you and the children at weekends."

And there would be no Violet to cook the monotonous nutritious food the children were used to in Botswana. Instead of lamb stew with butter beans on Thursday and cottage pie with broccoli on Friday, we'd have to learn to live on a diet of E-numbers, microwaved and eaten in constipated silence on our knees in front of the television. The E-numbers would rot the children's teeth and brains, and make them hyperactive and unmanageable.

When it was wet and dark and miserable during the annual nine months of winter they'd suffer from cabin fever and begin riding their black motorbikes down the stairs and cooking each other in the Aga.

And now that it was against the law, I wouldn't even be able to resort to that staple favourite of mothers, used with such effect down through the ages, since the first days when Eve put Cain over her knee, and spank them.

I'd be forced to resort to a modern method of child control – I'd have to brainwash them with more television. I could become a member of the video shop in the village. And with no Violet in the house to help me, I'd have to take the children with me. Five children under the age of four. Five children who all needed booster seats or car seats or a Rock-a-Tot. They wouldn't fit into my BMW – I'd have to change it to something as big as a minibus, with blacked-out windows, so the curious would be unable to see just how many children were in there and report me to Social Services for neglect, when I left them unattended to race into the video shop for another video.

It was enough to make anyone reach for the Valium.

Daddy's closing service at 1st Derryrose was packed. Will and I had to pull rank and park at the manse across the road because the acres of shiny black tarmac around the church were already full when we got there.

"Auntie Fran, Auntie Fran, *I've* been to the seaside with my daddy!"

Kathryn Snotter was wearing flip-flops, sunglasses and a lime-green terry-towelling romper suit. She threw her arms around my neck and hugged me.

"And we stayed in Granny and Granddad's holiday cottage and I slept in the little bed that my mummy slept in when she was a little girl and Daddy read me stories every night!"

James was beaming. "I read you *Cinderella* every night. Sometimes six times!"

"That's Ella's favourite fairy story too."

"And I'm still wearing my new bikini that my daddy bought me. And we ate ice cream every day!"

"We've been having such *fun*," said James. "I never realised what *fun* it is being a father!"

He looked almost handsome with his bit of a suntan.

Mummy was at the front door of the church graciously receiving the congregation in a brightly coloured dress. Some people had brought her flowers and with her arms full of bouquets she was radiant.

"I told the sales woman in Marks & Spencer I was going to Africa to be a missionary and she agreed with me that dead clothes don't create the right impression. A missionary needs to radiate *joy*, not sobriety . . ."

Amazingly there were even Catholics in the pews.

"How do you know these people are Catholics?" Will whispered. "Everyone looks exactly the same to me."

"There's no mystery! These people are our neighbours!"

Mrs Murphy, Aunt Grace's old housekeeper, was sitting at the back.

"I'll sit with Mrs Murphy," I said.

"You should be at the front," said James pompously, "with the family. Nobody will see you at the back."

"No, thank you, James. I'll leave you to sit with the Pharisees."

"Not all Pharisees were bad," said James and he took his daughter's hand, stuck his chest out and marched to the pew reserved for *'Simms Family Only'* where shameless Sam Dawson was already sitting.

I slid along the pew to join Mrs Murphy.

She whispered, "I've never been in a Protestant church before, and if I forget myself and try to genuflect on the way out, will you please forgive me? But it's the very least I can do, to show my gratitude and respect for Reverend Simms, to come to his farewell service. Your father is a very great man, Francesca."

"Daddy?"

Did she really mean my father who'd modelled his new missionary wardrobe for us after the shopping trip and the best that could be said for his thin white legs in shorts was that they possessed reserves of hidden strength if they could carry his enormous stomach?

"Oh, yes, dear, your father. Such kindness as he has shown me over the years. No one knows the half of it."

Derryrose Church Hall was an exhibition of the finest baking in South Derry.

"I've made him toffee shortbread," said one stout matron. "Toffee shortbread is his favourite."

"I've made him Fifteens. Fifteens are his favourites."

"I've made him Mars Bar sandwiches. Mars Bar sandwiches are his favourite."

"No wonder your father is so fat," said Will. "If our children saw this spread they'd think it was Christmas Day."

"And Violet too. Violet has a really sweet tooth." Then I had a brainwave. "Let's liberate an empty biscuit tin and fill it with wee buns and take it back to Botswana with us as a present for Violet and the children! Quick, stand guard at the door while they're all in the Big Hall giving Daddy a round of applause."

I began throwing toffee shortbread and Fifteens and Mars Bar sandwiches into a tin box.

I was back in my favourite leather trousers that I've always worn travelling, quickly throwing things into a small business-like flight bag. Clean pants, a travel pack of Wet Wipes, Vaseline, eye mask, novel, a packet of crisps, but no suitcase because Camilla's clothes that I'd brought home with me didn't belong in Botswana. Will's modest backpack lay on the kitchen table beside mine, grotesquely distorted with the tin box of wee buns. The Aga was switched off, the plugs were all pulled out, and the curtains were partially drawn. We were ready to leave.

"You've no burglar alarm," said Will.

"There's nothing to steal. No fancy televisions, or stereo systems or computers. Not even a decent kettle."

"But does it all add up to a million pounds?"

Will, with his builder's eye, could not believe that Lisglasson Lodge, with its loose slates, rotten gutters, creaking staircase, peeling wallpaper and mouse problem was worth half as much.

"It would cost thousands to rewire and thousands more to fix the roof and thousands more to lift the floorboards and put down a damp-proof course."

"It's called dilapidated grandeur."

"It's called a death-trap."

"You think I should sell to Alex Flood?"

"If I was you I'd have been up the avenue to the Big House the afternoon after you found Aunt Grace dead, banging on Alex Flood's front door, begging him to take it while he was still wearing rose-tinted glasses. If he ever gets a structural survey done . . ."

I smiled at my husband. "Patience is a virtue."

When Aunt Grace gave me Lisglasson Lodge as a wedding present she said, "I don't expect you to keep it, my darling. Alex Flood wants to buy it, and I will be very happy if you sell it to him."

"But why don't you sell it to him and live comfortably off the proceeds for the rest of your life?"

Aunt Grace rolled her eyes in despair. "Why don't you

show him who's boss just once in your life? Now you have something he wants. Charge him twice as much as the asking price. Make him chase you. Make him beg for it. Make him suffer."

"He didn't break my heart, Aunt Grace."

"Well, he broke my heart. Because of him you went away and left me."

Will and I were outside with our bags waiting for the taxi to take us to the airport when Alex and Emma pulled up in their fancy Volvo estate car.

"We missed you at church," said Emma. "Were you there? Where were you sitting?"

"With Mrs Murphy. At the back."

"I'd like to buy your house," said Alex. "Would you mind, Francesca?"

Not to be completely left out, Emma added, "Now there's a fox-hunting ban in England we want to turn it into a hunting lodge. Alex thinks we should be able to attract wealthy hunting people to come for package-holiday weekends. They can stay here at the Lodge and hire the flying armchairs and ride out with the South Derry . . ."

"Would you like a guided tour?"

I took them upstairs first.

"Naomi sometimes appears upstairs. Bouncing on beds, running along the landing."

"A real, live ghost!" Emma was delighted. "Have you seen her?"

"Yes."

"Oh, goody! Then I'm bound to see her, because I'm

303

very sensitive to ghosts, and when I do see her you'll have to believe me, Alex, because if Francesca says she's seen her . . . I'm sure there's a ghost in the Big House, in the old nursery with the barred windows. Alex swears I'm imagining things but a couple of times when I've been in the room by myself I've felt my clothes tugged from behind and once I was tapped on the shoulder."

Then into the main bedroom.

"This bedroom has a fraying carpet, but a nice view across the wild-flower meadow."

Then into my bedroom with its mouse-attracting double bed and enormous Narnia wardrobe.

"This room attracts mice."

"We're plagued with rats at Lisglasson," Emma announced indiscreetly. "About a week ago I was reading the children *Little Red Riding Hood* and each of them had a finger puppet – Catherine was Red Riding Hood, Oliver was the Wolf, Ralph was Grandma and Sebastian was the Woodcutter. We'd just got to the part where the Wolf had eaten Grandma, and the Woodcutter was cutting open the Wolf's tummy to rescue Grandma when a huge rat ran out from under my chair and sprinted across the room and disappeared. I spent the rest of the evening searching for it and when I couldn't find it I had to set traps. Have you ever seen a rat trap? They're huge. But the rat was so cunning it was actually eating slices of streaky bacon off the traps and managing not to spring them so in the end Alex had the inspired idea of *melting chocolate* on to the traps and that was how we caught it. It was as big as a shoe and –"

"Emma," said Alex quietly, "would you please go downstairs and wait for me."

His eyes were so sad.

I used to wonder, during quiet moments, why Alex walked away from me after our love affair on the Maldives. The near-death experience at the diving platform broke the ice between us and for the rest of the fortnight I really thought we were a love story with a happy ending.

There were honeymooners getting off the boat when we were leaving. The new wife was still in her wedding dress – a Cinderella creation with a full skirt. There was confetti in her hair and she was holding her husband's hand, gazing into his eyes with adoration, and laughing. I remember Alex watching her with a faraway look in his eyes.

We stayed in the Galle Face Hotel in Colombo before our flight home to reality. It was Sunday night and, on Galle Face Green men were selling balloons, windmills and burgers, and girls were standing in huddles nudging and pointing to boys standing in huddles pretending not to notice. We were approached by a man who told me I looked like a film star, and then asked for money for the blind school where he worked. Alex and I argued when I dug into my pocket to give him a handful of change.

"He's a confidence trickster," said Alex.

"Not everyone is a confidence trickster. You should trust your heart, Alex."

"Francesca," Will called to me from the bottom of the stairs. "the taxi's here."

I threw my keys at Alex. "Lock up when you've finished your inspection. Of course, I'll sell to you if you want to buy it."

I ran down the stairs and out into the sunshine to join my husband.

Chapter Twenty-five

I had the oddest dream on the London Heathrow-Jo'burg flight back to Botswana.

"Cup of rooibos, Francesca?" Camilla beamed.

The Mummy Gang was meeting at my house and Camilla was the perfect hostess in her pretty flowery summer dress and big hair. Baby Isobel slept contentedly in Violet's sturdy black arms. When she woke up and started to cry, Violet handed her to Camilla who effortlessly, without a break in the staccato of her Afrikaans, unbuttoned the front of her dress and plugged her on. When she was finished, Camilla handed the baby back to silent Violet, whose job it was to wind and settle.

I woke up feeling slightly sick. It was between services and the cabin was dark and most passengers were trying to sleep. The cabin crew were flitting through with glasses of water, firmly advising anyone sleeping on the floor to get up and get strapped in. I could see from the flight picture on the screen at the front of the cabin that we were flying past Mount Kilimanjaro. If we'd taken a day flight we'd have been able to look out of the aircraft window and admire its snowbound peak above the clouds. Beside me Will breathed softly and evenly. He was fast asleep. I blew in his ear. He slept on. I bumped up his seat from recline to upright. He slept on. Finally I pinged his eye mask and elbowed him in the ribs.

"What? Decompression? Hijack? Cup of tea? What do you want?"

I told him my dream.

"What's the Mummy Gang?"

"Remember after Ella was born Estelle de Villiers invited me to meet the Mummy Gang at church. Every week we left our babies out in the church hall with a group of trusted nannies and someone gave us a little talk about Mummy things and we did crafts like fabric painting and had a cup of tea together."

"Yes, of course, I remember. You were a big success at the start because you baked Fifteens and toffee shortbread and the rest of the Mummy Gang wanted the recipes."

"And then it all went horribly wrong," I reminded him, "because the very next week was the week that Mummy and Camilla were visiting me, and Camilla came with me to church and that was the week they were giving out prizes for any wife who regularly gave her husband a pedicure and Camilla pipes up and says, 'Can I have a prize? I regularly give my husband a blow job.' And the Mummy Gang didn't realise that I had a twin, they thought it was me . . ."

"And then you wondered why no-one spoke to you afterwards and Ella wasn't invited to any of the baby birthday parties?"

"And when I engaged in the briefest of banal conversations with any strange man sitting beside me in church his wife grabbed his arm and hustled him away . . ."

I've always known that when Camilla came to visit me in Botswana there was more to it than the simple urge for a holiday. If she'd fancied a holiday Camilla would have come with Sam's holiday gang. At most they'd have spent one night in Tlokweng before flying to the north of the country, to the luxurious, exclusive game lodges of Chobe and the Okavanga Delta.

"Do you think Camilla sent me back to Ireland in the hope that I'd tell James Snotter she's pregnant again? She hasn't told him yet. She hasn't told anybody, not even Mummy."

"If she hasn't told, it was none of your business to tell."

"But she's been having an affair with Sam Dawson. Maybe she thinks she's carrying Sam Dawson's baby?"

"Just leave well alone," my husband advised. "Jesus already has that job – worrying about the lost sheep."

But still I worried.

We landed into Botswana and the first thing I noticed was a big billboard taking centre stage in the airport – Air Botswana were recruiting pilots and cabin crew to fly their new international routes to Lusaka, Maputo and Capetown. An almost painful longing came over me, to put on a uniform, pick up a flight bag and sit down again behind the controls of an aircraft.

"Where else does Air Botswana fly?"

"Harare, Windhoek, Jo'burg. The domestic routes are to Francistown, Maun, Orapa, and Kasane."

Will watched me with amusement. Then he said one word.

"Twins."

Dorothy was waiting for us in Arrivals.

"Don't tell me. God told you we needed a lift to Tlokweng."

"Not this time. Camilla told me when she came to see me this morning."

"Is she all right?"

Dorothy shook her head. "No."

"Is there something wrong with the baby?"

"You know I'm not going to tell you," said Dorothy. "Patient confidentiality and all that. She'll tell you herself when we get home."

I hardly recognised our road in Tlokweng. The tumbledown house was painted, and the stray dog had put on weight.

"Has somebody moved in?"

"Not yet. Soon, we hope. The church has bought it for your parents. I know your father is a DIY enthusiast – fixing it up will give him something to do. We'd thought of putting them into Pastor Bruce's house, but the boys have left the place in a bit of a mess."

"Is Estelle still here?"

"Yes, but she's going to Plumtree tomorrow, to her mother."

"Poor Estelle."

Dorothy shrugged. "It's not the first marriage that horny dentist has destroyed."

Across the street the broken-down fence round our house was gone, and brand-new, very high, electrified fencing replaced it. There was a tall new gate which opened by remote control when Dorothy spoke into an intercom. Inside, parked at my front door was the latest model of Land Rover Discovery. Charles the gardener was intently polishing its petrol cap and an unknown woman in a pretty checked uniform and headscarf was scrubbing at the children's car seats with vigorous enthusiasm.

"Madam, you're back!" said Charles and he stood to attention and saluted.

Inside, the house was full of uniformed ladies. One was ironing, one was cooking and another one was scrubbing Isobel's back-carrier. The floors were polished, the walls were freshly painted, and my international shopping was tastefully rearranged around our huge living-room. For one mad moment, it crossed my mind that Camilla had hired contract cleaners.

"Where's Violet, *Mma*?"

"Violet does not work here any more."

"Where are the children?"

"They are resting. The children rest from twelve until two every day."

"Where's Camilla?"

"Madam is in bed."

311

Dorothy said, "Excuse me, I'll just go and see how madam is."

"I never thought," I said to my husband, "that I'd feel uncomfortable in my own home," and we went back outside onto the porch. What I really wanted to do was throw off my travel-stained clothes into a pile on the middle of the kitchen floor and sink into a couple of inches of tepid bathwater and have Ella industriously shampoo my hair while Hugh attentively soaped my feet. But I was dreading what I would find in our family bathroom – almost certainly the windowsill would have no dust, the towels would be fluffy and probably new, the tiles which had fallen off round the bath would be replaced and, God forbid, there might even be toilet paper.

I'd been away less than a fortnight and Camilla had managed to transform my untidy, dusty, shabby home into a house as utterly impersonal and aseptic as No 1 Bluebell Orchard . . .

"Don't you want to go and have a look at them?" asked Will.

"The children? Are you mad? You want me to wake them up when Camilla has managed to do something with them that I have dreamed of doing since they were born – she's taught them to nap together at the same time."

Dorothy reappeared. "The bleeding hasn't stopped. I'm going to take her straight to the Mission Hospital in my bakkie. Will you help her pack a bag, Francesca? I know I don't have to tell you not to panic her . . ."

Camilla was lying on top of a large thick navy-blue

towel on top of the bed in the spare room. She was as white as a sheet, her lips were blue and she was crying large ugly, snottery tears.

"Heh! It's not like you to be a cry-baby."

"I've brought this miscarriage on myself," sobbed Camilla. "It was the exciting sex I had with James Snotter on his birthday."

"Don't be silly. Lots of people have exciting sex when they're pregnant. Even me!"

"And I've been drinking and I didn't take any folic acid, and I've been lifting heavy things and every free moment I've had I've been riding a flying armchair round Lisglasson Equestrian Centre!" Camilla began to sob even more loudly. "I never looked after myself when I was pregnant with Kathryn, and I haven't looked after myself this time either. And I've been a hopeless mother to Kathryn. God is punishing me for neglecting Kathryn!"

"But you tried at the start with Kathryn. It just didn't suit you."

(Camilla's brief flirtation with full-time motherhood started and finished the morning she took brand-new baby Kathryn to the Mums and Tots group in 1st Derryrose Church Hall. Kathryn had been awake and unsettled all night so she slept exhausted in her Rock-A-Tot while Camilla gamely did her best to join in.

First she chatted to Emma Flood who was lying across two chairs breastfeeding Catherine and trying to supervise her awful twins who'd built themselves a fort from baby changing bags and were attacking the other children with well-aimed Lego bricks.

313

"I'm from a military family," Emma told her brightly. "My father's a major. He says these two will be the first into battle and the first killed . . ."

They were joined by a woman who had not yet given birth but who was so precious about her pregnancy she already had a 'Baby on Board' sticker on her car.

And all around her the endlessly predictable conversations ground on and on.

Children – was there really so little to say about them?

Pregnancy and pregnancy scans and antenatal visits to the doctor. Deliveries and stitches and Caesarean sections. Pampers or terry towelling nappies? Breastfeeding or bottle-feeding? Weaning. Tantrums.

Camilla fought back a huge urge to yawn.

When the Mums and Tots morning finally finished she wailed, "It's so boring! I'm so bored!"

Mummy said, "What did you expect it to be like?"

"I thought there was going to be more to it than 'baby talk'. Women have been having babies forever. You conceive, you deliver, you get on with it."

"Get on with what?"

"Get on with your life. Go to work, go on holiday, read a book, listen to the news . . ."

"Only if you did all those things before you had the baby. I don't want your father to hear me saying this, but the truth is there are a very great number of very dull women in the world and having a baby is the only interesting thing that ever happened them. To be frank, Camilla, I think you're being rather mean-spirited to resent their one opportunity to blow a bit."

My sister decided there and then she was never going to be satisfied with motherhood as a career choice. The day she returned from Tonga she ruthlessly swapped places with the locum doctor who had been hired for six months to replace her. The locum, a conscientious young man fresh out of medical school, spent the first six month of his medical career changing Kathryn's nappies and ironing her Babygros.

"I never once got up Kathryn at night," sobbed Camilla. "Some nights I heard her crying and crying and I just went back to sleep and let her cry until James heard her and got up with her. Now when she hurts herself she cries for James, not for me. My own daughter treats me like a stranger and it's all my fault!"

"A miscarriage isn't a punishment. No one is punishing you."

But she was inconsolable.

"I've been a bad, bad girl . . ."

Will and I helped her to the front door and into Dorothy's bakkie.

"Do you want me to come with you?" I asked her though it was almost two o'clock and I ached to lift my darling children from their organised rest and bury my face in their fluffy red hair and kiss their tiny sticky hands, and hear them say, "Mama, Mama, Mama".

Camilla said, "Yes, please, Francesca. I'm frightened."

Dorothy said, "Have a rest first. With your legs up."

When the bakkie had pulled out of the electric gates

Will said, "*Forsooth, the lady doth protest too much methinks* . . ."

"Don't be so uncharitable! She's having a miscarriage."

"Francesca darling, *you're* the one who always says attack is the best form of defence."

"But I think she's done a marvellous job, with the electric fence and the Land Rover Discovery –"

"*Jessus!*" said Will in exasperation. "And who is paying for all of it – heh?"

At two o'clock on the dot the uniformed lady – Kopano – who had been ironing, carefully put the iron away and announced, "It is time. Let us lift the children from the nursery," and she led the way down the hall to my bedroom where I found Ella and Hugh snuggled up together fast asleep in my double bed and Isobel sleeping in her cot which was pushed up alongside the bed.

"It was madam's idea," Kopano explained. "She says she always slept in a double bed with her twin sister when she was a child. And she was never lonely in the night and never cold in the winter."

Kopano pushed aside thick blackout curtains and let light into the bedroom. Ella woke up immediately.

When she saw me she said, "Krystal is a bully but Auntie Cam shouted at her and she ran away crying."

"Who's Krystal?"

Kopano said, "This Krystal is a child at Ella's school. She is a bully. Ella has been afraid of this child since she started the school so she does pee-pee in her clothes because she is afraid. Madam spoke to the teachers in the school and she spoke to the other mums – she found that all the children are afraid of this girl, Krystal. We pray that God will give Krystal chicken-pox, and that Krystal will poo in her pants, and that a dog will bite Krystal."

Ella held out her arms to be hugged. "And I don't love bobo any more. Auntie Cam took bobo away and gave him to Baby Isobel and I was very, very brave and Auntie Cam bought me a new Barbie and I'm a big girl now."

She showed me her new Barbie. It was naked.

"I see some things haven't changed."

There seemed to no end to Camilla's excellent interference. When Hugh woke up and got out of bed he immediately opened a cupboard door, pulled out a basket full of (new) sunhats and with Kopano's assistance put them all out in a row, chose one and put it on his head.

"Pee-pee," he said.

Kopano opened the French windows and he ran outside, dropped his shorts and peed copiously into the bougainvillea growing at the edge of the porch. Then he pulled up his shorts and came back indoors.

"Smartie," he said, and Kopano produced a small box of them from her apron pocket and handed him a blue one.

"Blue Smartie," said Hugh shaking his head solemnly. "Bad Smartie."

"Estelle says the blue Smarties make her sons hyper," I explained to Will as Kopano popped the blue one in her own mouth and handed Hugh a yellow one and Hugh didn't get to eat it until he'd told her what colour it was.

"Red, Kopano."

"No."

"Black, Kopano."

"No."

"Green, Kopano."

"No."

"Yellow, Kopano."

"Hurrah!!"

And finally Isobel. It was the first time I'd held her and not felt milk stirring. Maybe she wouldn't remember me when there was no smell of milk. Gently I picked her up and held her. Ella had clamped herself around my knees and Hugh had climbed like a spider onto my back.

"I'm sure you have a very excellent routine for all of them, Kopano. An afternoon of intelligent stimulation, physical activity and nutritious feeding. But please, may I just hold them for a little while? It feels like something broke off me when I went away and now I'm back it's stuck back on again."

I sank down onto the bed and the children scrambled over me. Kopano watched Isobel anxiously for a moment, then clapped her hands.

"Truly, you are this child's mother."

"Why's that?"

"This is the first time she has let go of her comforter." Kopano held up my Mile High T-shirt. "We have not dared to separate her from this T-shirt since you went away. Welcome home, mama!"

Chapter Twenty-six

I stopped off at Estelle de Villiers' house on my way to the Mission Hospital.

"*Howzit*," I said into the intercom on her gate. "It's Francesca – can I come in and say goodbye?" and was more than a little surprised to hear her say a word which when translated from the Afrikaans means 'Fuck'.

Finally the gate swung open and I went in.

"I'm not wearing any make-up," Estelle said through the fly-screen door, "and my hair's a mess. And I'm dressed in an ugly old tracksuit. I can't let you see me."

"Estelle, I was in the delivery room beside you when you delivered Peter. We have no secrets."

Reluctantly my friend came outside. This was the first time I'd ever seen her minus the make-up, the big hair and the sequins.

"You're really, really pretty! What beautiful eyes you

have! The false eyelashes have always hidden them. And your figure is perfect. You're like a little doll! And what a waterfall of naturally blonde hair! Why on earth do you tease it up?"

Estelle sighed. "Bruce likes it."

"Stupid man. He's got the rhyme wrong. No wonder he left you."

"Rhyme?"

"In Ireland they say a man is happily married when he has a whore in the bedroom, a lady in the living room and a cook in the kitchen."

Estelle looked a bit confused. "English is not my first language."

"Probably just as well."

"Madam, you're back!"

Suddenly Violet shot out of the fly-screen door and hugged me.

"Violet! What are you doing here?"

"Mrs Camilla had a big row with me, madam. She told me I must pack my bags and go back to Gweta. But I came here, to my very good friend, Mrs Estelle, and asked her for a job."

"But I thought you and Mrs Estelle were mortal enemies."

Estelle and Violet looked at each other and laughed.

"I don't know if you have this saying in English – 'better the devil you know'?"

We went through the empty house and out onto the porch. Everything had been packed up and sent on to Plumtree. Even the boys.

"Quiet, isn't it?" said Estelle. "Ma says they've settled down really well: they've started back at their old school; they're catching up with their friends; it's almost as if they've never been away."

"I thought you lived in Bloemfontein before you came to Botswana."

"Oh, I'm often in Plumtree with the children. Every few years. For a few months. This is the longest time we've ever spent in one place, Bruce and I, since we got married . . ."

She looked sadly around the enormous garden with its swimming-pool and sandpit and tree-house and curious, brightly coloured metal climbing frame – a very African thing that would never pass British Health and Safety standards but had claimed only the top of one finger and a couple of scalps in four years.

"I'm going to miss it here. This is the nicest house I've ever lived in. We've never had grass before."

"Can't you stay?"

Estelle shook her head and tears sprang into her beautiful blue eyes. "I am nobody in Botswana, only my husband's wife. The children and I travelled here on Bruce's visa and without Bruce the children and I have to leave . . ."

I changed the subject. "Camilla has just bought us electrified fencing like yours."

"Camilla asked me about my security arrangements when I went to tell you about Bruce and Shirley Smith. I wanted to cry on your shoulder, Francesca. You're the only friend I have who never says 'I told you so' about anything."

"I'm sorry I wasn't there. I've been away in Ireland. My aunt was very ill. I wanted to see her before she died . . ."

"This was before you left. You were at the dentist. Did Camilla forget to tell you? She offered to employ some of my nannies if I was leaving Gaborone. She took four of the Batswana. I'm taking the Ndebele girls back to Zim with me . . ."

By the time I finally got to the Mission Hospital Camilla had come out of theatre. She was hooked up to a drip and her face, unguarded with anaesthetic, was very sad. Dorothy, still in scrubs, was wearing her funeral face.

"What's the matter? It was just a miscarriage, wasn't it? She can try again for another baby if she wants?"

"It's not as simple as that."

"Why not?"

I waited for Dorothy to struggle with her absolute belief in patient confidentiality and her need to tell Camilla's next of kin – me – some bad news.

"Your sister's miscarriage was not a natural miscarriage. I've only ever seen one like this before, in South Africa when I was finishing my training, but once you've seen one you don't forget. She must have gone to the witchdoctor . . ."

"To terminate the pregnancy?"

"Yes. The stuff the witchdoctor gives usually causes a spontaneous abortion within twelve hours. It works all right in the very early stages of pregnancy but Camilla was at least sixteen weeks pregnant and the foetus didn't spontaneously abort and by the time she'd started to bleed – this morning – the poison had already spread through her."

A chill, the like of which I have never experienced before in my life, not even when I first saw my cousin's ghost, not even when I realised that the landing gear was stuck, rippled over the top of my skull. The hairs rose on the back of my neck and fear gripped my stomach. I thought I was going to be sick.

"Are you trying to tell me Camilla is going to die?"

"I don't know yet. We're pumping her full of antibiotics. I don't know how far it has spread. The next twenty-four hours will be critical."

"Is there *anything*?"

"Pray," said Dorothy solemnly, "for a miracle."

When Aunt Grace predicted that my life would change utterly when I was forty, I always selfishly assumed the change would happen to me. A lottery win. A spiritual epiphany. A jail sentence. Leading lady in a Hollywood blockbuster. Me. Me. Me.

It never crossed my mind that my life might change utterly because of something that happened to somebody else. All my life Camilla has always been more than just my sister. We shared a womb, a twin pram, a double bed. When we were at school we shared our exams. She was better at languages; she did my oral French 'O' Level for me as well as her own. I was better at Physics; I did her Physics 'A' Level practical exam as well as my own. Not even our mother has ever been able to tell us apart. Mummy always said individuality was overrated.

"If Camilla dies, a part of me will also die."

"Calm down, for God's sake," said Will. "It's not like you to lose your nerve."

"You didn't see me after I landed that 767 in Abu Dhabi. Before you got there."

"Aunt Grace said you were cool."

"Aunt Grace was full of gin."

I hadn't panicked during the four-and-a-half hour flight. I hadn't panicked when we were circling the airport for landing and I could see the fire engines and ambulances. I hadn't panicked because I was doing my job and there wasn't any other space in my head for panic.

It was afterwards, after we'd disembarked and been debriefed, when I was in the hotel room, and Aunt Grace was snoring on top of the bed. And all the panic and fear that I'd suppressed for four and a half hours propelled itself out of me with inhuman retching and I vomited and vomited and vomited.

"How did you expect to feel?" said Commander Cunningham afterwards. "I'd have peed my pants."

It was time to bath the children.

"Where have the battalion of housemaids and nannies gone?"

"They all downed tools and left at four o'clock," said Will. "Even Kopano."

"That's not much use to anybody. Maybe I can persuade Violet to come back to me. Violet was always willing to help with bath-time even if she wasn't overly particular about housework"

I helped him undress the children and put them into the bath.

"Now I'm going back to the hospital to sit with Camilla. Until she dies or wakes up."

Will was dismayed.

"But you're pregnant with twins. You've just come off an eleven-hour flight. Your legs are swollen up like bananas. Your children haven't seen you for a fortnight."

"She's my *sister.*"

"Go and get Violet first," Will pleaded frantically. "Tell her I need her to help me with the children. Beg her to come back. Double her wages. Tell her we'll buy her a television!"

The last thing I heard, as I ran outside and jumped into the Land Rover Discovery was a lot of splashing as Ella and Hugh attacked each other with weapons of mass destruction, a gleeful chorus of 'Stupid Daddy! Stupid Daddy!' and Will howling "Don't leave me alone with them, Francesca! I'm afraid of them!"

So I stopped again at Estelle's house on the way back to the Mission Hospital

"Violet, why did Camilla sack you?"

"After you went away she wanted me to take her to the witchdoctor and I said, 'No, madam, the witchdoctor's magic is not for white people' and she said if I would not take her to the witchdoctor I must pack my bags and go back to Gweta."

Back at the hospital my sister was in a small private room.

Dorothy said, "The anaesthetic has worn off but she hasn't opened her eyes. Her breathing is regular, but she's not responding."

"Do you think she can hear me?"

"Only if she's listening."

I sat on the edge of the bed and took Camilla's hand. I

thought of the tiny tattoo of a flower – a camellia – on her left breast, hidden under her hospital gown.

"Why did you send me away? Why did you not tell me what you were planning? I could have helped you. I could have found you a proper doctor. You could have gone somewhere safe in South Africa – no one would ever have known . . ."

Clear as a bell I could hear Camilla's voice in my head.

"Some smart clean, clinical place where I'm wheeled in on a trolley, the 'procedure' is performed and I'm wheeled out again. With about as much emotional attachment as a tooth extraction! I want to be made to suffer for what I've done."

"What have you done?"

But she wouldn't answer me.

Dorothy was watching from the door. "You were talking to her! And she was answering!"

I rubbed my eyes. Suddenly I was very tired. And I could feel a headache starting, like a band of pressure tightening round my skull.

"We haven't done it for years. We used to do it all the time when we were children. Mummy was really freaked when she realised we were talking to each other without speaking. She thought we did it to spite her."

Poor Mummy. Women's magazines are full of feature-length advice on how to get noticed and I'm told there are ambitious parents who dream of and aspire to having freakish, interesting daughters to shine through the crowds of insipid humanity. But not my mother. All our lives Mummy has rubbed away at Camilla and me, at our personalities and our individuality and our choices, in the awful and thankless effort of bending us into a shape we weren't made for.

"You've made a cheap tart of yourself with Alex Flood. I don't care what Aunt Grace says about fish. He'll never marry you now."

And when it turned out that she was right, and I decided to run away to Ex-Pat Air, she said, "Why do you want to want to become a pilot? I've never heard of a female pilot. Why can't you just become an air stewardess?"

And when I resigned from Ex-Pat Air to marry Will she was vicious.

"Why do you have to give up your good job and follow him to Africa? You're earning more than him. Why can't he be your designated spouse and live with you in Bahrain?"

"What would he do all day?"

"Sunbathe. Buy gold in the Suq. Gossip. What do all the other pilots' spouses do?"

I even remember her humming the Marianne Faithful song about the desperate woman of thirty-seven who dreamed of driving through Paris in a sports car with the wind blowing in her hair.

"It's going to be very liberating for your mother to come here, isn't it?" Dorothy interrupted me quietly. "To a life without Chinese Whispers."

"I suppose. But I don't really understand because I can't hear them."

"Can Camilla hear them?"

"Camilla is *plagued* with them!"

It has always been my private opinion that it was

Chinese Whispers that drove Camilla to marry James Snotter. They'd been romantically linked since the Sam Dawson divorce but no one ever thought Camilla was serious about him. Especially Mummy.

"It's quite obvious you're seeing that ugly, boring little man on the rebound. I don't suppose you'll ever get over Sam Dawson."

And certainly, when Camilla went to Barbados with Sam's holiday gang and James wasn't invited it seemed that the romance had run its course.

Until Camilla discovered she was pregnant. And announced that she was going to marry James Snotter.

"Why, why, why?" Mummy asked.

"I can hear the Chinese Whispers. No one even knows I'm pregnant but I hear the words '*unmarried mother*' every Sunday when I'm in church."

"You don't really expect me to believe that Dr Snotter is the father of your unborn child? *I've* been hearing Chinese Whispers since you came home from Barbados."

"You think Sam Dawson is Kathryn's father, don't you, Camilla? You think Kathryn was conceived on the holiday in Barbados. And you think the poor little dead baby was Sam Dawson's baby too . . ."

Beyond the click of the fan and the gentle flutter of the mosquito netting, and the faint drip of the drip in the silent white hospital room, I could hear the faintest sound.

It was Camilla's voice but this time it wasn't strident or angry or hysterical. It was as soft as a whisper.

"James is a good husband. He's easy to live with. Kind.

Helpful round the house. An excellent father. Comfortable. Useful. I've always been a lady in his living room and he's been a cook in my kitchen . . . but it all went horribly wrong on his birthday. He was so disappointed with me. He said, 'I know we don't set the world on fire when we're in bed together, but I've always thought of it as 'making love'. Tonight you're just a whore in our bedroom.' It was on the tip of my tongue to say 'Sam Dawson likes it,' but instead I took a long hard look at myself. At my selfish, cold, empty life. And I just couldn't brazen it out a second time with another baby that wasn't his . . ."

"But Sam Dawson is not the father of your children, Camilla. He can't be. Sam Dawson is sterile. Sam Dawson had a vasectomy when he was a medical student, because he hates wearing condoms."

All her life, Camilla has had charm, charisma and confidence. She has laughed loudly when she's happy, screamed loudly when she's angry and tramped over anybody in her way when she's wanted something.

When we were seven, Aunt Grace bought me a snow-scene shaker in a glass dome for Christmas. She bought Camilla a book about ponies.

"Big mistake. You should've bought them the same thing," said Mummy pessimistically when we opened our gifts on Christmas Eve.

"Rubbish," said Aunt Grace, "It's time you realised that your daughters are individuals."

"That's a nice snow-shaker," said Camilla and within an hour it had disappeared.

Camilla was angry.

"Where's your snow-shaker, Francesca? Have you lost it already? Sometimes you're really stupid, Francesca, losing something as pretty as that!"

The following morning Camilla insisted that Santy had left her a snow-shaker in a glass dome at the bottom of her Christmas stocking.

"Are you sure this isn't Francesca's shaker that she lost yesterday? Perhaps it fell into your stocking by mistake," said Mummy.

Camilla began to scream. "I woke up in the middle of the night, and Santy was at the bottom of the bed and I watched him putting it into my stocking. He brought Rudolf down the chimney too and I patted him on the nose. Rudolf has a *really* red nose!"

Camilla's conscience pricked and pricked. She grew more and more angry with herself and with everybody around her. She refused to eat her Christmas dinner, she refused to sing carols round the Christmas tree, and she wouldn't play draughts with me.

"Tiresome child," said Aunt Grace. This was Aunt Grace's first Christmas without Naomi. The wound left by her death was still open and raw.

But Camilla didn't care. She could think only about the snow-shaker

Finally Daddy took her away to the manse office and said, "We know you stole Francesca's Christmas present. We know you hid it in your stocking."

Confronted by my sainted father Camilla had the grace to look shamefaced.

"How did you know? Was it the story I made up about Rudolf?"

"Your conscience has been screaming all day."

"I'm just amazed she has a conscience," sniffed Aunt Grace

When Camilla opened her eyes the first thing she said was, "Why did you never tell me about Sam Dawson?"

"Why did he not tell you before he married you?"

"But I've *always* thought Kathryn was his daughter . . . I was *sure* she was conceived in Barbados ! That randy old fake has been shooting blanks all along!"

I laughed. Which brought Dorothy running.

"You're awake!"

Tears welled in my sister's eyes. "You can thank Francesca the Puritan. She's just given me a reason to live."

331

Chapter Twenty-seven

The day Camilla came home from the hospital was a red-letter day. The children and Violet and I had been preparing for it for a week.

"Let's buy her a Barbie," said Ella.

"Smarties," said Hugh.

"Poo," said Isobel.

"This came for you," said Will and he threw me a plain brown envelope covered in British stamps but I barely acknowledged it because I was so busy fussing.

"Let's bake a cake for her. A Welcome Home cake. I know, Ella. We'll bake her a cake that looks like Barbie's frock and we'll stick a naked Barbie into the middle of the cake so it looks like she's wearing the cake-frock and we'll decorate the cake-frock with Hugh's Smarties . . ."

"Why don't you lie down and have a rest before she arrives, Francesca?"

My husband ran a practised and proprietary hand over my bump. "Your legs are swollen up like bananas again."

I kissed him. "Change the record, Will. You've been nagging me to rest more since I was pregnant with Ella. Most husbands forget after the first baby –"

"Most women don't need to be told after the first baby . . ."

"When I lie down my legs feel more tired. I've got to keep moving. I've got my medical for Air Botswana next week . . ."

Will made a strangled noise in the back of his throat but said nothing. Will is not a worrier and he has not so far confided in Dorothy but it is his private opinion that too many pregnancy hormones have gone to my head.

When I told him I'd applied for a flight-deck job with Air Botswana he thought I was joking.

"And will you be taking the twins with you? I suppose they could be strapped into One and Two Alpha at the front of the aircraft in rear-facing Rock-A-Tots and once you reach cruising altitude you'll be able to pop into the cabin and breastfeed them. And if you're busy with a landing or a take-off or turbulence maybe the air stewardess could lean over from her jump seat and give them a bottle each of expressed breast milk?"

I refused to be teased.

"It is not a question of how I'm going to feed them, but *who* is going to feed them. Lots of women with small children work. In fact, *some* people would say that I am wasting my life, my education, my talents and my potential by staying at home with a rabble of infants. It's worse than a jail sentence. At least in jail you get time off for good behaviour!"

"And *some* people would say that motherhood is a happy sacrifice, because a job can't love you back again."

"And some people would say that parenthood is a partnership. *I've* spent three full years at home with the children. Now it's your turn."

"You're turning into your mother," said Will in desperation because it's family legend that Mummy with two-faced, barefaced cheek had criticised Camilla's decision to go back to work and leave the rearing of Kathryn to others. Then when Ella was born the following year she criticised my decision to give up my excellent career and stay at home with my baby.

"But you used to go away for ten days at a time with Ex-Pat Air. I couldn't possibly spend ten days and ten nights on my own with five small children!"

I smirked sadistically at his panic-stricken face. Maybe the pregnancy hormones really had gone to my head. "Better start praying that I fail my height-weight check."

"You're not going to fail," said Will miserably. "You've never failed anything in your life, and you're not going to start failing now. With your experience I bet Air Botswana can't wait to welcome you on board. They'll probably give you any route you ask for."

"I promise I won't ask for ten-day blocks."

What Will does not know, and what I'm not planning to tell him is that the height-weight check with Air Botswana is a formality. Air Botswana accepted me as a pilot on the strength of my CV with Ex-Pat Air and although I intend to do the training and learn to fly prop planes and get my wings before the twins are born we've already agreed that I won't start work until they are three months old. And we've already agreed that I will initially restrict my routes to the Jo'burg hop, three times a day, two days a week. In effect I have applied for and been accepted to be a glorified bus driver with Air Botswana just as Alex Flood once predicted.

Something rather odd has been happening to me since Camilla's brush with death. Maybe it is too many pregnancy hormones, but the bubble I've been living in since I married Will has been punctured and I've suddenly woken up to the reality of having a husband with cancer and five small children. If Will refuses to tell me the results of his trips to the skin clinic in the National Hospital in Jo'burg, I'm not going to tell him the finer details of my contingency plan. But I've told everybody else. Dorothy was thrilled for me. "How nice for you to be 'Commander Simms' again. The leading lady on the aircraft. After three long years of being 'Mummy'!"

Camilla was still very frail. And faded. And slightly fey.

"You'll soon get better," I reassured her. "Winter is almost over and the warm spring air over Africa is so rich that you only have to stick a broken branch into the ground and it'll take root and grow."

We carried Camilla's bed out onto the porch and she lay down on it, and breathed in the rich strong air while Ella plagued her for stories and Hugh ate all the Smarties off her

336

Welcome Home cake and Isobel took her daily nap cuddled up beside her.

"My children love you. You really have a way with them. I think you've read *Cinderella* a hundred times since you came home. Are you exhausted?"

Camilla shook her head. "I'm hoarse. I need a cup of tea. Is there still Foot and Mouth disease in the Transvaal? Am I going to have to brace myself for long-life milk?"

"So you're feeling better already?"

"It's hard to feel sorry for yourself when you're surrounded by children who won't take no for an answer."

"And a husband who is, as we speak, flying halfway across the world to be with you."

Once Camilla had started to recover from her brush with death, she'd phoned James from her sick bed. I don't know exactly what she told him but he has phoned her every day since and sometimes they've talked together for an hour at a time.

Will was amazed. "They've been married for years. What on earth do they have to talk about?"

"She says they've years of catching up to do. They've never had a conversation until now."

"Your husband has been on the phone twice already since landing into Jo'burg. The first time to ask me if I knew a captain called Mike, because he'd managed to get into the flight deck and the captain was called Mike and Mike started his career working for Ex-Pat Air and maybe I knew him ...."

Camilla said, "Such innocence! James is a farmer's s

on – he never got on holiday when he was a child. Only sometimes to Portstewart Strand on a Sunday. Probably we were parked beside him when Aunt Grace took us to the seaside. And when we were students together at Queen's I invited him to join Sam's holiday gang but he couldn't come with us – he had to work on the farm all summer."

"So he was drawing silage and baling hay while we were tripping around continental Europe?"

"He didn't have a passport when I married him. He hadn't even been to the Republic. Not even to Dublin for the day on the train to watch a rugby international!"

"Why not?"

"He was afraid the Irish people would try to kill him if they found out he was a Presbyterian from Northern Ireland."

"How were they going to know?"

Camilla started to giggle. "Apart from the fact that he travels everywhere with a bowler hat and an Orange sash, whistling 'The Green Grassy Slopes of the Boyne'?"

"Well, that explains why he phoned a second time and said, 'There are a lot of black people here, aren't there?'"

Camilla's eyes shone out of her frail yellow face. "I *knew* he would say that!! Oh, I can't believe how much I'm looking forward to seeing him. He's such a fascinating person. You know they always say you should never judge a book by its cover, but in James' case, what you see is exactly what you get!"

"Oh, dear."

"Oh, but it's lovely," said Camilla happily. "It's

relaxing. I know who I am when I'm with James. We speak the same language. I've never understood why you're attracted to men who don't speak your language. A rock star's son, a Zimbabwean builder . . ."

"But they do speak my language."

"And Sam Dawson?"

I smiled. "Sam Dawson has always been in a special league all of his own."

Camilla's eyes flashed. "The All Mouth and No Trousers League. I just can't understand why I wasted so much time and effort on that phoney when I'm already married to the most wonderful man in the world."

"Love is blind."

Will was getting ready to leave for the airport to pick up James Snotter and Kathryn.

He put the potty into the Disco, and sunhats, drinking cups, a thermos of boiled cooled water, nappies, Wet Wipes, Hugh's Blankie, and couple of naked Barbies.

"There's not going to be any room left for James and Kathryn," Camilla whispered.

"He's practising," I whispered back, "for when I'm a pilot again and I'm flying into Botswana, bug-eyed with exhaustion and eyeliner, stinking of airline food and Duty Free perfume and he's picking me up at the airport any time of the day or night wearing short shorts and a wide smile. And five small children."

Will says I should have been a great deal tougher with Camilla. A great deal less forgiving of the clever way she manipulated me and convinced me that he was having an affair.

"But you were partially to blame. You went to Jo'burg under false pretences. Camilla was quite right to sow the seeds of doubt in my mind about your intentions. If you'd been a bit less secretive I'd have known you were in Jo'burg for cancer treatment. "

"And if she'd been a bit less secretive she'd have told you, no offence, that she wanted you out of the way, preferably at the far side of the world when she was trying to kill the baby and herself."

Finally Will had the Disco loaded. As he was leaving he shouted, "Have you opened your letter?"

"What letter?"

"The one with the British stamps on it. It looked important."

I found the letter and opened it to please him. Inside was the old photograph of Alex Flood and me kissing at an airport before our Maldives misadventure. And a dry letter from Alex's solicitor informing Mrs William Dallas – me – that Mr Alex Flood would be happy to pay two million sterling for Lisglasson Lodge. And should I ever wish to visit South Derry Mr Flood would be delighted to make my family and me welcome.

"Two million pounds! It's a lottery win. Lisglasson Lodge isn't worth two million pounds!"

Camilla said, "Oh, don't be so feeble, Francesca. It's worth as much as someone is prepared to pay for it. Don't you dare write back and tell Alex Flood you think he's offered you too much. *I* think you've done very well for yourself. Alex Flood is the meanest man who ever lived."

"Who told you that?"

"His wife. It's so sad really when you think that she only married him for his money and he's too miserable and too mean-spirited to share it with her."

"I don't believe you!"

"How would you like me to convince you? Where would you like me to start? Maybe you'd like to hear about the two-door Vauxhall Nova she drove when the twins were small babies and she was pregnant with Catherine. And how getting Ralph and Oliver into their car seats in the back seat when she was eight months pregnant was like gold-medal gymnastics. And how she had to get a part-time cleaning job at our doctor's surgery in the evenings to earn enough money to supplement her housekeeping money to change the Vauxhall Nova to a four-door car after Catherine was born –"

"But what about the Equestrian Centre?"

"She doesn't make any money from that."

"It's still too much money for the house. Alex doesn't owe me anything."

Camilla's eyes flashed again. "Who paid for his trip to the Maldives with you?"

"I did. Don't look at me like that. I invited him so I paid."

"But you had no money, Francesca. You'd just finished university. Mummy and Daddy were paying for your wedding and Sam was paying for the honeymoon. Where

341

did you get the money to take your lover to the Maldives?"

There was an unpleasant silence between us, broken only by the gentle snoring of Isobel and the slap of Violet's disenchanted mop. Camilla was horribly, pointedly accurate about the state of my finances that miserable autumn I swept Alex Flood to the Maldives to have my wicked way with him. Quite literally, I hadn't a penny. I had a swanky BMW car, and a pretty ring set with a large, valuable ruby but they were gifts from Sam and didn't actually belong to me. I had no credit cards so it wasn't as if I could pay off my impulse buy at my leisure. After I wrote the cheque for the two-week all-inclusive holiday I sat in the BMW with my head spinning and my pulse racing wondering how I was going to pay for it.

Finally, I sold the only valuable thing I owned – Aunt Grace's antique Cartier Tank watch that she'd given me when I graduated. And, God forgive me, I told her I'd lost it in the Maldives, off the diving platform the day of the tropical storm when I almost drowned.

"I'm not proud of what I did."

"You risked absolutely everything for Alex Flood and he walked away from you after it. And you still think he owes you nothing."

The Disco pulled in through the electric gates. The children – Ella, Hugh and Kathryn Snotter – bundled out of the back.

"Why did the house cross the road, Mummy?"

"Because it had a bum-bum."

"Why did the lamp cross the road?"

"Because it has a face and no bum-bum."

"How does a television walk across the road?"

"Because it has nothing on it."

And they ran off, screeching with laughter, into the garden.

James Snotter looked faint. "What's the matter, James?"

Will looked bewildered. "He says there's a smell. What smell? I can't smell anything."

"I thought I was prepared," said James as I led him gently by the hand into the house. "I've read the guidebook from cover to cover. I could win *Mastermind* with 'The History of Botswana' as my specialist subject. And I've watched *Zulu* on video and *Out of Africa* and *George of the Jungle* –"

"*George of the Jungle?*"

Later that evening when the children were finally in bed – with Ella and Hugh and Kathryn Snotter all curled up and sleeping together like a litter of pups – and we'd pulled Camilla's sick bed into the sitting-room and the Welcome Home cake was demolished, and James had bored us rigid describing in exhaustive detail his flight ("I had the scrambled eggs for breakfast, and Kathryn had the pancakes and we shared . . .") Will said, "What was in the letter with the British stamps, Francesca?"

I showed him the letter. He read it a couple of times. Then he showed it to James Snotter who read it a couple of times.

Finally Will said, "Why does he think he owes you?"

"I've no idea. He owes me nothing."

343

Camilla spoke up.

"It's my fault. I wanted to see if I could take him away from Francesca when we were seventeen. They were so happy together and I was so jealous. So I persuaded her to let me play 'Confusion'. You were innocent, Francesca, and so trusting. I felt bad about it, but not bad enough to stop. So I dressed up like you and went out with him that evening. But he knew it was me from the very beginning . . . And because of me he never trusted Francesca again."

"Oh, well," I said, smiling at Will, "plenty more fish in the sea!"

Chapter Twenty-eight

It was Christmas Eve. I was sitting up in bed, drinking a cup of tepid tea and biting on a piece of exceedingly brittle toast when my tooth broke. Again.

"Ouch!"

Will raced in from the bathroom, abandoning Ella and Hugh and Isobel who were standing in an untidy row getting their faces brushed and teeth combed and hair wiped with a face cloth.

"Is it time?"

"Will, I'm not due for another fortnight."

"But Dorothy said. At the first twinge. Get straight to the hospital. Because she won't get her fee if you deliver on the kitchen floor. Again."

"I thought you didn't like Dorothy. Now you're quoting her."

"Of course, I like Dorothy. I'm just a bit afraid of her."

"What is there to be afraid of?"

"Men are always afraid of women who are smarter than them," said Will with a rare burst of honesty.

The suffocating heat was doing nothing for my temper.

"I beg your pardon. Am I not smarter than you?"

"That's different."

"Well, this is my fourth pregnancy and I'm pretty sure that a broken tooth is not a sign of impending labour."

"Stay in bed!" he commanded. "I'll phone the dentist when I've finished cleaning the children."

"Please let me get out of bed and phone the dentist myself. Please don't make me lie here any longer."

"Please try to remember your Bible, Francesca. The man is the head of the woman. I speak as the head of this household. Your blood pressure is sky high and on Dorothy's advice I must insist that you stay in bed."

I have now been in bed for three days. Three days ago I was a newly qualified Air Botswana pilot, passing out with the rest of my class, the centre of attention since I was the only eight-months-pregnant female in our group. The President congratulated me personally and my photograph graced the front of the national newspaper. I was described by the reporter as an 'inspiration' to women and quoted as saying that if the babies were a boy and a girl I planned to call them Mary and Joseph. Then I went and spoiled my inspirational image at the Wings Party by fainting dead away on the dance floor during 'Leaving on a Jet Plane'.

It is my understanding that Will and the President carried

me between them to the Presidential Mercedes and I was whisked to the Mission Hospital – with an outrider, a police escort and the reporter from the national newspaper who was hoping for a Mary and Joseph scoop. (Unfortunately I was in a dead faint and missed this bit of excitement.) Dorothy was not on duty and had to be bleeped to come and rescue me – when she finally arrived in the examination room I was being prepped for theatre and, semi-conscious, was screaming, "Please don't section me. Please don't section me!"

"Your blood pressure is sky high. There's protein in your urine. Do you know what pre-eclampsia is?"

"I promise I'll lie in bed with my feet up for the rest of the confinement. I won't even get up to pee. I'll use the potty. Please don't section me, Dorothy!"

So now I am reduced to a semi-invalid status waiting for the fullness of time when the twins will be born, and my alpha-male husband is embracing the domestic responsibilities of our household. It has taken less than three days for him to abandon the nutritious menus Violet took such pains to learn – lamb stew with butter beans on Thursday, cottage pie with broccoli on Friday – and when we are lucky we dine on tinned soup; when we are less lucky we are free to help ourselves to cornflakes with long-life milk. Yesterday he boil-washed some red socks with the rest of our clothes and left the pink results on the washing line for so long they are crispy. He has not boiled the drinking water and the children have diarrhoea. And his remarkable method for keeping the house cool – the doors and windows stay shut and the curtains remain drawn – has made our home smell like school changing-rooms after a hockey match.

"I can't understand why you sent Violet to Gweta for the holidays . . ."

"You don't need Violet when you've got me."

Is this really the same husband who stood up to my mother and refused pre-marriage instruction the night before our wedding, choosing instead to go whoring and touring with my mad military cousins and the following day to take me as his lawful wedded wife with an eyebrow missing and an unaccounted-for love bite on his neck?

How I now wish my husband had spent his stag night with Reverend Adam Robinson learning that a woman's place is in the home. How I now wish he would brutally insist that I get out of bed and chain myself, pregnant and barefoot, to the kitchen sink.

"I wish you'd go back to work."

"I'm sorry, Francesca. The site is locked up for Christmas. I'm here whether you like it or not."

The most frustrating part of the revenge of the alpha male is my mother who will not hear a bad word said against Will and who insists on praising his every effort, however mediocre.

"What a good idea to dye everything pink! *So* much easier to find clothes that match."

There is only one advantage to my bedridden status: I'm missing the preparations for the Dallas Family Christmas. Until now this has been an inauspicious event. Low-key. Informal. Tlokweng deserted, our children too small to understand, Church very early in the morning before the worst of the heat and the feast a haphazard burnt offering from the barbeque.

I lost touch with the traditional Irish Christmas when I was a pilot. Even when I was 33,000 feet up I was never nostalgic for cremated turkey, non-alcoholic trifle and my mother's vicious criticisms of those who attend 1st Derryrose only on Christmas morning and only then to show off their festive finery.

But it has come back to haunt me.

Emma Flood has sent me a large parcel with a thoughtful, handwritten note. *"I know you're not going to have a 'White Christmas' so I'm sending a white Christmas to you."* (A spray can of snow for the window, paper hats and a potato peeler.)

And for the past three days I've been driven almost mad by the discordant transmission of taped carols blaring across the street from my parents' bungalow and the discordant hysteria of the Sunday School as they practise their infant version of the Nativity to be performed in Church on Christmas morning. After yesterday's rehearsal Mummy came slippy-tit into my bedroom to mention her grave concern for Ella's method acting – as the heavily pregnant Mary, Ella insists on shuffling slowly round the makeshift stage muttering, "Pregnancy isn't an illness." Meanwhile Hugh, who is a shepherd and wears a tea towel over his head, won't stop shouting out "Jesus!"

"Perhaps," I suggested hopefully, "you could sack both of them. I'm sure Ella has an understudy and nobody will miss a foul-mouthed shepherd."

Mummy laughed loudly and humorously. "I'm starting to think that Will may be right. Too many pregnancy hormones *have* gone to your head!"

It was the icing on the top of the (Christmas) cake

when Will produced a bag of Brussels sprouts and said, "Your mother says they're an essential part of the traditional Christmas feast, but I'm not altogether sure what to do with them. Are they used to stuff the turkey?"

The most magical Christmas I ever had was the year I managed to organise my roster, and I flew into Seeb Airport like Santa Claus, on Christmas Eve night, bearing Duty Free Christmas presents for Will and mince pies smuggled off the aircraft. I was on the ground just long enough to kiss him under a piece of plastic mistletoe supplied by Marian the chief stewardess when he told me the Sultan's palace was built, his contract was finished and he was leaving Oman.

"I'm going to Botswana to build a hospital," he'd said, and my eyes, under a ton of eyeliner and mascara had brimmed with sudden tears. I didn't fly the African routes. I was never going to see him again.

Marian was also in the Arrivals Coffee Shop, having a quick cigarette before we started boarding passengers for the London flight. She stood up to leave. I stood up too. I had to go with her – the airport transport bus wouldn't take one air stewardess out to an aircraft without an argument. But no one would argue with a captain. I was thirty-seven. I was at the peak of my sterling career.

"Will you miss me?" Will asked.

"OK, I've managed to get you an emergency appointment for two o'clock. They couldn't have been more helpful once I explained who you were. That photograph on the front of the national newspaper has made you the most famous white woman in Botswana this week."

"Listen. I've been thinking. Barbara is going to Khutse this evening. Why don't we pack the Disco and go with her? Khutse's not that far away. It's quite primitive though. I think we have to bring our own water."

Will raised an eyebrow. "Khutse is where the loco lions are. Do you remember what happened to the British Council teachers? The pride was so close they could feel the lions' breath through the tent material. Do you want us to get eaten by lions?"

"Of course, we won't get eaten. Isn't Barbara a game ranger? She knows what to do with lions. She says first you don't sleep on the ground. You get a roof tent on your bakkie and you sleep in that. And if a lion does get too close you shine a torch in its eyes and it'll run away."

Will sighed. "I never thought I'd say this, but I think your mother is right. I think pregnancy hormones have gone to your head."

I lay in a tepid bath, with sweat trickling unpleasantly over the curve of my engorged belly and forming a puddle in the crevice of my cleavage. This was my second bath of the day, probably I'd have to bath again when I got home from the dentist, and probably again before bed. And maybe once in the middle of the night. And the rest of the time I'd be lying in bed with a damp facecloth over my face . . .

Suddenly I realised that the only acceptable way to avoid the excruciating awfulness of the imminent new improved Dallas Family Christmas was to be in hospital with two brand- new babies and to miss it.

As if she was reading my mind, Camilla phoned.

"Are they born yet?"

"Nobody yet."

"Oh, what a bore. I hoped they might have come before we boarded."

"Any medical thoughts on how I can coax them out? If they're not born before lunch-time tomorrow I'm going to have to eat Brussels sprouts in a paper hat, and it's so hot here you could fry Brussels sprouts, with a little bit of bacon and some chestnuts, on the pavement. If we had a pavement."

"Have you tried a hot bath, hot curry and hot sex? Not necessarily in that order. Listen, darling, I'm going to have to switch my cellphone off and I don't know if it'll work in Morocco, but keep trying, will you? And I'll call the minute we get home again."

"How did you manage to persuade James to try Northern Africa?"

"Well, once we got home from Southern Africa, and his mosquito bites healed and everyone admired his suntan he sort of forgot about the heat and dust. And the mysterious smell, of course! And then Kathryn stopped saying '*Dumela*' and '*Howzit*' and '*Izzit*' and all those charming things Ella says and I stopped saying 'robots' instead of traffic lights and 'circle' instead of 'roundabout'. And I think he rather missed it. You know, we'll probably come back out at Easter to see you. When it gets a bit cooler . . ."

"Have you broken away from Sam's holiday gang?"

"I certainly have. Sam's holiday gang has become such a middle-aged affair. One five-star hotel after another.

Sometimes it was hard to remember what country we were in. And we never went to Africa because Sam and the gang thought Africa was too dangerous and disease-ridden. I've started a new gang. The Snotter family holiday gang. We're going to visit Africa every year, maybe twice a year . . . I thought we'd try Kenya during the summer holidays . . ."

"So, a hot bath, hot curry and hot sex," I said, just to be sure.

"I've also heard that massaging your nipples can bring on labour."

"Do I have to do that, or can I get help?" but her phone had gone dead.

"Will," I called, "Will, darling, can you spare me a moment, please?"

At two o'clock I struggled into the dentist's surgery. Shirley Smith looked up from her notes and smiled.

"Same tooth again, Mrs Dallas? You really are going to have to get it fixed properly. How long has it been since your last visit?"

I flopped carefully down onto the dentist's chair and left my mouth hanging open. Of all the horny little dentists!

"Ah yes," said Shirley, "the start of July. I remember now. Just after my last check-up at the skin clinic at the National Hospital in Jo'burg. That's right! Your husband was there too. Getting his melanoma blasted. Wasn't it lucky it was found so soon? Once they spread . . ."

And on she chatted, about how amazing it was that Will had had a melanoma on the top of his head when she was certain he'd been wearing a hat outdoors for the past forty years. Her own father's melanoma was on his ankle which

353

was just as curious when you realised that her father had always worn boots inside and outside the house, and even in bed, his entire life in Africa.

"It somewhat contradicts the medical opinion that skin cancer is caused by sunburn, doesn't it?" said Shirley.

On and on she chatted and never once did she mention Bruce de Villiers.

"You never told me Shirley Smith was back in Botswana!"

"I thought you already knew. Her romance with Bruce de Villiers burnt out very quickly once Bruce started to miss his family. Did I forget to show you Estelle's Christmas card? It came this morning. From Lilongwe."

"In Malawi?"

"It's not as nice as Botswana, but wonderful Bruce has started a church and I'm expecting another baby."

On Christmas Day we had no running water and the electricity was off.

"Oh, what a pity! I was hoping, while the children were busy with their presents, for another hot bath and some more nipple massage. And maybe a little bit of hot sex as a Christmas present."

Will kissed me. "And I was hoping you wouldn't ask. Let's go to church first and pray for some divine intervention. If that doesn't work I'll throw some curry powder on the top of the barbequed turkey."

I was finally mobile again. Before church I popped into pharmacy end of the supermarket to get some painkillers to help with the after-pains when I was breastfeeding the twins. I approached the young, beautiful (probably childless) pharmacist who said, "I've never heard of Solpadeine. Do you think it's necessary to take painkillers with you to the Mission Hospital? Don't you think you should be grateful for the after-pains as it means your womb is contracting?"

"How many babies do you have?"

"None."

"Then you don't know what you're talking about."

When we got back out to the Range Rover Ella said, "Mummy shouted at that nice lady and she ran away crying!"

And Will said, "Temper, temper! Do you think the babies will come before the turkey or after?"

At church we took Ella and Hugh and Isobel to the soundproof, glass-fronted room at the back where children are free to play and the Mummy Gang to supervise, yet everyone can still see my father preaching through the big glass windows and hear his disembodied voice transmitted to them through a loudspeaker.

"It's the biggest we've ever seen," said the Mummy Gang in admiration when they saw my enormous bump. "Can we touch?"

Who says God does not answer prayer? After a vigorous half hour waving my arms and singing Christmas carols, my waters burst to a chorus of 'Hallelujah, praise the Lord!'.

"What do we do now?" Will whispered.

"Take me home," I whispered back. "I need a clean pair of pants."

THE END

Direct to your home!

If you enjoyed this book why not
visit our website:

www.poolbeg.com

and get another book delivered straight to
your home or to a friend's home!

www.poolbeg.com

All orders are despatched within 24 hours.